CALL YOUR BOYFRIEND

CALL YOUR BOYFRIEND

*Olivia A. Cole &
Ashley Woodfolk*

SIMON & SCHUSTER BFYR
NEW YORK AMSTERDAM/ANTWERP LONDON
TORONTO SYDNEY/MELBOURNE NEW DELHI

SIMON & SCHUSTER BFYR

An imprint of Simon & Schuster Children's Publishing Division
1230 Avenue of the Americas, New York, New York 10020

For more than 100 years, Simon & Schuster has championed authors and the stories they create. By respecting the copyright of an author's intellectual property, you enable Simon & Schuster and the author to continue publishing exceptional books for years to come. We thank you for supporting the author's copyright by purchasing an authorized edition of this book. No amount of this book may be reproduced or stored in any format, nor may it be uploaded to any website, database, language-learning model, or other repository, retrieval, or artificial intelligence system without express permission. All rights reserved. Inquiries may be directed to Simon & Schuster, 1230 Avenue of the Americas, New York, NY 10020 or permissions@simonandschuster.com.

This book is a work of fiction. Any references to historical events, real people, or real places are used fictitiously. Other names, characters, places, and events are products of the author's imagination, and any resemblance to actual events or places or persons, living or dead, is entirely coincidental.

Text © 2025 by Ashley Woodfolk and Olivia A. Cole

Jacket illustration © 2025 by Sarah Long

Jacket design by Sarah Creech

All rights reserved, including the right of reproduction in whole or in part in any form.

SIMON & SCHUSTER BOOKS FOR YOUNG READERS
and related marks are trademarks of Simon & Schuster, LLC.

For information about special discounts for bulk purchases, please contact Simon & Schuster Special Sales at 1-866-506-1949 or business@simonandschuster.com.

Simon & Schuster strongly believes in freedom of expression and stands against censorship in all its forms. For more information, visit BooksBelong.com.

The Simon & Schuster Speakers Bureau can bring authors to your live event. For more information or to book an event, contact the Simon & Schuster Speakers Bureau at 1-866-248-3049 or visit our website at www.simonspeakers.com.

Interior design by Hilary Zarycky

The text for this book was set in Garamond.

Manufactured in the United States of America

First Edition

2 4 6 8 10 9 7 5 3 1

CIP data for this book is available from the Library of Congress.

ISBN 9781665967143

ISBN 9781665967167 (ebook)

For Josie
—O. A. C.

For the baby queers. You're so beautiful.
—A. W.

PART ONE
Late April

1
Beau

How do you give a girl her panties back?

Probably not at the party where she's going to be with her boyfriend. But I'm going to do it anyway.

"Will you get out already?" Celine says. "Daniel is waiting for me."

"For a supposedly doting big sister, you're not very supportive."

"Shut up, Beau. You should be happy I brought you at all. You could have driven yourself if you hadn't fucked up. Stealing the car like a delinquent."

"Taking without permission is not always the same as stealing. And I was going to see a girl. Not like I was joyriding or baseball-batting mailboxes. Plus, you're overlooking the critical fact that I *brought it back*."

"Like you're going to do with that girl's underwear?"

"Excuse me," I say. "They were *given* to me. I didn't *take* them. That would be a weird, perverted crime."

Celine makes a face that communicates not judgment but a universal skepticism about all my choices. She's never approved of any girlfriend I've ever had—but maybe that's because none of the girls who have been in the back seat of this very car have ever been *actual* girlfriends.

"When I want to give someone something, I give them, like, candy," she adds.

"Yeah, well, it's complicated."

"So is everything."

"Yeah," I sigh. "So is everything."

The underwear is folded neatly in my pocket. I didn't want them to be all wrinkled when I gave them back. I gaze at the house, every window already filled with people from school.

What the hell am I doing here?

"I'm not going to ask why she gave them to you," Celine says. "But why are you giving them back?"

"Because I think it's over. She got back together with her boyfriend." I pause. "Again."

"Pardon me, her *what*? Is she bi?"

"No. I mean, maybe. I don't know. I don't think she does either."

A moment of silence sits between us. I don't know what Celine is thinking, but I'm thinking two things: (1) I never should've thought Maia would stay broken up with Tatum, and (2) I never should've told Celine anything about this to begin with. Too often I think I'm talking to my big sister, and then it's like she does an internal calculation of how many daylight hours our mom has been home this week (like, seven) and decides to fill in.

When Celine finally speaks, though, she decides to stay in big-sister territory (for now).

"So she gave you her panties while she was on a break with her boyfriend?"

"Something like that," I say, deciding not to share the part where a good percentage of the times we made out were while she was still with Tate.

"But she's not bi? What's she doing giving you her panties then?"

4

One thing I've noticed about myself is that if I have too many feelings at once, they start to feel like missiles. I feel the defense shield creeping up.

"What so-called straight girls always do when they're feeling experimental," I say. "Anyway, it doesn't matter. I'm over it."

"That's what you always say when you're not."

"Shut up."

"You said you were over it about drumming, too. Now look. You're in my band. And you write ninety percent of our song lyrics."

"*Our* band. And I have writer's block."

"Surely not for lack of a muse?"

"Oh, shut *up*."

"Is this girl's boyfriend going to be here too?" Celine asks, ignoring me.

"Yup."

"Jesus. Godspeed, little sis." She leans forward, peering toward Andi's behemoth house, as if she can already see the mess of my life splattered all over the sidewalk in front of the classy bay windows.

That's my cue to get out of the car, so I do, but even after Celine has driven off, I stand there by the street for a minute, watching people stream into the house, which is already vibrating with music. Everyone shows up to these things with a plan. Dance with that guy; get that girl's attention; convince everyone there you're not the loser they thought you were for the past four years. I have a plan too, though Celine's comments are making me doubt it even more than I already was. I remind myself of the speech I rehearsed:

This has been fun, but I think it's run its course. You say I'm not just a hookup, but I only ever see you at the bowling alley. We never

5

talk in public. You break up with Tate and say you're done and then turn around and get back together. Remember the last time you came to my job? We made out in the back room, and when you left, you put your underwear in my pocket and told me to keep them for you. That was months ago. This is going nowhere, so what am I keeping them for?*

The speech is too long, now that I think about it. Declarations are supposed to be short and punchy. I could just say, *Here's your panties back, we're done.* But that implies I actually thought there was a "we" to begin with, and there's no way I'm giving her that satisfaction, let alone admitting it to myself. Ugh. This is ridiculous. I've hooked up with a dozen so-called straight girls and never planned a speech for any of them. Not catching feelings was an easy rule—until now. I'm not in love or anything like that, but something about the way she smiles after she sucks on my bottom lip has been haunting me. And her ghost has a switchblade that flicks out and stabs me whenever I see her with Tatum Westbrook.

Speaking of the crew-cut devil, the door to Andi's garage opens and there he stands, wearing one of those tank tops with the sides cut out so there's just a thin piece of material between his pecs. Slut-o-rama. And there's Gary "I Can Drink a Beer Before a Game and Still Win" Bevin backing his car into the garage, Tate directing him, shouting, "LEFT. No, cut LEFT." The trunk, I assume, is full of supplemental booze. The party has been going on for a while, so supplies must be running low. But what's important here is that this means Tate will be occupied for at least the next ten minutes. I'm doing this. Now.

I walk purposefully up the golf-course-sized lawn to the house, plotting this out. I'll get her alone, give her my too-long speech before I take her underwear out of my pocket and . . . then what? I haven't planned my exit, because it depends on what she says back. I can hear my sister's voice: *What do you* want *her to say?*

I hate that kind of question, and it's the kind Celine loves asking. But what I *want* the girl to say doesn't matter—there's only what she will or won't say. There's only what she will or won't *do*. And if the past five months are any indication, she'll do the same thing at this party that she does in the back room of the bowling alley when I'm on my break: run her tongue along my teeth and avoid answering questions directly. She's good at that. She knows she can get away with it. That I'll let her. Because what are you supposed to say when the smell of her is all over your clothes, taking up so much space in your brain there's no room for rational thought? She floats in my nose for hours after I've been close to her. Brown sugar and a smoky smell, like she's always on the edge of burning.

But that's *not* going to happen tonight. I'm focused. And also fed the fuck up.

Luckily (kind of) for me: another smell hits me when I step in through the front door of the party. The stinging scent of alcohol and . . . people.

That's the thing about parties—there are so many people. I haven't been to one since Kay left in December—RIP. (She's not dead—just moved to Toledo. Which she says is the same thing.) She enjoyed shit like this. Everyone in outfits chosen with usually one person in mind. Music like the first few notes of an earthquake. The music, at least, I don't usually mind. The louder the better. It's just never loud enough to drown out the sound of . . . well, people. And the thing about parties at Andi's house is that there are a certain *kind* of people. The kind who have the power that comes from popularity and get a little George R. R. Martin-y from where they sit on their thrones.

I muscle past two guys on the football team who are trying to out-bro each other: half fighting, half joking in the entranceway. One starts to tell me off but then sees it's me and just nudges the other guy, grinning. Their bro-off is postponed for the sake of a little casual homophobia.

"Hey, Kitty, looking for fish?"

I know humans' brains don't finish developing until we're twenty-five or whatever, but I don't have much hope for these guys.

"Were you addressing me?" I ask. "Because my name is Beau."

"Are. You. Looking. For. Fish?" he enunciates.

"Ohh." I stop now, turning back to face them fully. "Are you talking about . . . pussy? Is this a joke about vaginas? Sorry, I didn't get it, because I actually know what they smell like. Unlike you."

He's already drunk, and I can tell he doesn't take in much of what I say, but he gets that it's an insult, so he reddens in the face and neck and fires off some sloppy-mouthed slurs before his friend tells me I'm a bitch, etc., etc. Finally they drag their knuckles toward the kitchen to bond over more beer. Healthy masculinity on display.

Jesus, why isn't the music louder?

And why isn't the music *better*?

When Andi and Maia were still actual friends, she would let Maia have the aux, but this current selection has Andi written all over it. I wasn't surprised when they drifted apart. You could see it coming if you saw the way they each DJed a party: Andi choosing all the songs that she liked, regardless of the crowd. Maia, playing stuff she knew people would enjoy, whether she liked it or not. Maybe that's why everyone seems extra drunk—to cope with the playlist.

Regardless, people are dancing. I, for one, do not dance in public. The great thing about being in a band is (1) girls love it and (2) you can enjoy the music without having to dance. But drumming is not an option at a party, so I post myself on the wall and scan the room for the owner of the panties, who, conversely, loves to dance. She's not one of those girls who just flips her hair around when she's feeling the song. Her body finds all the rhythms: her legs and hips on beat, her hands finding the melody. It's bullshit how beautiful she is when she dances, honestly.

And bullshit that I'm at this party looking for her, when there's no way she's looking for me. What am I doing? If Kay were here, she'd smack me in the back of the head. But she's not. It's just me, lurking on the edge of the party like a raccoon waiting for the lights to go off.

"Hey, Beau," someone says near my ear. My skin prickles, and for a half second I think it's her. But I know it isn't. She wouldn't get this close in public, which is the problem. I turn slowly and find myself eye to eye with Trina Perry instead.

"Hey, Trina," I say.

"*Hey,*" she says, with fake attitude. She's one of those girls who thinks flirting means pretending to be mad at you.

"You okay?"

"Oh, sure," she says, arching one of her perfect black eyebrows. "I don't mind at all that you ghosted me."

I sigh.

"It's not ghosting if we talked about it. I told you I was going to be really busy practicing with my band."

"It's not your band. It's your sister's band."

I roll my eyes. "It's *our* band."

"Not too busy to come to Andi's party," she says. She drops the tough-girl act and fake pouts. "But too busy to text me back?"

Trina does this thing where she picks up conversations from weeks ago, as if you're still right in the middle of them. I haven't touched her in months. We'd been messing around after she and her boyfriend had a fight—I remember Trina's exact words: *we are so done.* But "so done," as it turned out, meant "so done for twelve days," and then I saw Trina sitting on his lap at lunch. Now she just pops up every so often wanting attention or hinting about making out. Not wanting *me*, necessarily, but wanting to know if I still want her. I always just say I'm busy—it's a lot simpler than preparing a damn speech.

"I won't be here long," I say, breaking away. "Besides, I'm sure Jeremy is keeping you company. You've been dating, what, five months now?"

She frowns playfully. "Come on, Beau."

I swear, the only things that love me more than mosquitoes are straight girls. But I'm not talking about love. I just have underwear to return and a situationship to end.

I cruise more of the downstairs, but I don't really expect to see Maia anywhere else. She doesn't usually do the pool, even if it is heated. She wouldn't be playing foosball because people smoke down there. *If it's just a hookup, why do I know all this shit about her?* When I give her the panties back, I wish I could also plop the part of my brain she's been occupying into her hand along with the red satin.

I focus back on the dance floor, watching other faces I vaguely recognize sway and grind to the music. I see Ezra King from English—the only person who was out of the closet before me, so we have a mutual gay respect. He's dancing with the girl I see him with all the time. Her eyes are closed behind her glasses, and even though she's not the girl I'm looking for, she too is dancing like it's going to save her life.

I'm just noticing the girl's smile—floating on her face like she's having a beautiful dream—when a flash of yellow in the background catches my eye.

Maia.

Distracted by the girl dancing, I almost missed her. She's by the speakers, switching the music to a pop song like a million other pop songs. It's not special, but she is. Even now, through my anger, I can smell her.

"Get your shit together, Beau," I whisper.

But by the time I do, she's melted into the crowd.

2
Charm

I love the way dancing makes my body feel.

When I'm just walking or sitting or standing, I feel lost inside myself, awash in my always overflowing feelings. My aunt Miki says I'm all heart, and I think that's true, because I'm always worrying about how other people are feeling, what other people might be thinking, what I need to do to make sure everyone around me is all right. But when I'm dancing, my heart is only doing what it was meant to do—beat. My worries fall away and my body just keeps time with the music. I feel grounded, solidly inside myself, completely and irrevocably *here*.

Unfortunately, my current "here" happens to be a popular-kid party. And even when I'm in my body like this, I can't ignore that fact, because popular kids have a scent.

It's cloying and inescapable whenever they're clumped together in large numbers. A mix of expensive perfume and new clothes, car air freshener (because they all drive) and something . . . else. I'm used to smelling it in the hallways at school, in the cafeteria, sometimes in the girls' bathroom between fifth and sixth period—though it's never been this gag-inducingly strong. But I guess I've also never been around so much syrupy, popular blood at once, because I'm never invited to these things anymore.

The song ends and the noise rises, filling the beat of silence before the next one begins. Voices mix into a din of static like an ocean wave, and I'm reminded of the beach—of the place where my heart was broken the last time I was around so many of these kinds of kids at once. The bodies are hot and close despite the expansiveness of Andi Patterson's colonial, its wide white rooms full of wasted white kids. I yank on Ezra's sleeve, because now that I've stopped dancing, I can see (not just smell) that we've made a mistake. I feel suddenly desperate to leave.

"This was a bad idea," I tell my best and only friend as I glance around, taking in how ours are two of the very few faces in the room that have any melanin; how our bodies are the only ones I see that seem to be able to feel and catch the music's rhythm. A travesty, really, when you consider the bassy song that starts a few seconds later, making the floor vibrate like a giant heartbeat. "This was maybe the worst idea I've ever had. We don't even *smell* like them."

Ezra can't hear me. I can tell by the blank expression on his face: the way his thick eyebrows furrow and lift a second later, wrinkling his freckled forehead. "What?" he screams back, directly into my face. And before I can repeat myself, he's shouting again. "Let's find Maia!" He hooks his finger into my back pocket and yanks.

Maia Moon is why we're here. Maia Moon, with her moon-colored eyes—so gray they're almost silver. Maia Moon, with her shimmering, light-brown skin and night-black curls that fluff around her face, big as my aunt Miki's bundles. Maia Moon: makeup influencer with 23K followers, captain of the debate team, the first girl drum major at Brookville High in years, and the girl I've been tutoring in trig for the last eight weeks. I was almost certain she was straight, until she started flirting with me (*me!*) last month. I haven't been able to stop thinking about her since she plucked a pencil from my fingers, tucked it behind my ear, and smirked.

I grab Ezra's wrist to stop him from tugging me along. "Maybe we should just go?" I shout directly in his ear this time. "What if I was reading into things? What if I'm wrong and she doesn't like me like that? I mean, let's be real. Why would *she* like *me* like *that*?"

Ezra pulls a face. "Oh god, Charm. Do I really need to make you list your plethora of virtues in a room where I can barely hear myself think?"

He takes my hand and starts weaving through the crowd, fast and furious, like a river slicing its way down a mountainside. The beads in my hair clack against each other with every step I take, and that mixed with the music and the rich-kid smell is too much sensory input to process. My head is starting to ache.

To make matters worse, in walks Tatum Westbrook, captain of the rugby team, with a herd of his cronies. His arms are lifted and flexing, fist pumping the air like he's just won a game. The rugby boys are all prominent brows and heavy shoulders, snorting noses and crooked teeth. The missing link personified; Neanderthals, quite literally. Pretty quickly Tate and company start choking down beer through a funnel, and it seems like it's only a matter of time before they start knocking shit (and people) over. I shudder, hoping against hope that Ezra is leading us to an exit.

Because I'm a ball of anxiety at all times, I've already clocked that the back door is through the kitchen. So, when my feet land on the sticky marble floor, I grin. After dodging Parker Beck doing a keg stand beside the island and Wyatt Chan feeling up Shoshanna Stein against the fridge, I see Enzo Espinosa, Ezra's crush, being talked up by two different people who both seem to be vying for his attention. I glance up, trying to catch Ezra's attention to see if he's spotted Enzo too, and yup, I see his eyes going wide, his cheeks turning red as a fresh bruise. But just as I see the back door's shiny knob and reach for it, Ezra makes a sudden left, swerving away from Enzo and into a dim hallway packed with kids. He hip-checks two guys making out against a door—one of whom has the freshest lineup and cornrow combo I've seen in a while—and after they toss a few sassy remarks in our direction, they slide to the left and Ezra opens it, leading us into a powder room that's bigger than the bathroom I share with Aunt Miki.

He slams the door, cutting the noise of the party in half. I can still hear the bass line of the song, but the voices are muffled and the smell is gone.

"Okay," he says. He sits on a green velvet chaise (*a chaise!*) and pats the cushion beside him. "Come here."

I sigh and take the several steps necessary to cross the huge bathroom. I sit down so close to him our thighs touch. "Now," he says, cracking his knuckles like he does when he's standing at the free-throw line during his games. "Tell me something true."

I take off my glasses and clean smudges off the lenses just to avoid looking at him. Ezra always takes me through this dumb exercise when I say something he considers to be self-deprecating. "You and Enzo are meant to be. But you have to talk to him first," I say instead of giving him what he wants.

He rolls his eyes. "He's too busy with everyone else. And anyway, you know we're not talking about me right now."

I huff out a sigh. "Fiiiine. I have great hair," I whisper, shaking my rainbow-beaded braids out of my face. Coming up with elaborate styles is one of my favorite pastimes.

"Yup," he agrees.

"I'm nice, I guess," I say.

"No. You're kind. That's way better. Realer."

I nod, conceding. "I'm a good listener?" I ask.

"You are. One more," he instructs.

"I'm smart as hell," I say.

"Correct. Maybe too smart for your own good."

At that moment the door bursts open and the same two guys who were making out stumble inside, backward. The one with the cornrows falls onto the floor in front of us, and just as the other loses his balance, I grab Ezra's hand and pull him out of the way. The guy falls over the arm of the chaise and lands on the pillows, right where we'd been a second earlier. His head bangs into the back wall.

Ezra looks at me. "Add 'reflexes of a big cat' to your list, please," he says. "In conclusion," he continues, as if the drunk, dazed boys aren't cracking up and groaning behind us, "you, Charm Montgomery, are a catch. The issue isn't why this girl would like you. It's that she better realize she's lucky as fuck to be liked *by* you."

I bite my bottom lip, feeling a tiny bit of my insecurity melt away as the tangy taste of my mango-flavored gloss coats my tongue.

But back in the fray, we can't find Maia. We hold hands and push our way across the length and width of each of the three floors of Andi's massive house, and then through the half-mile-long backyard. We even look in and around the pool.

We never see her. And I start to wonder if she's here yet, or if she's even coming at all.

• • •

A half hour later, a song I actually like bangs its way out of the speakers, and Ezra wants to dance again. I'm sick of scanning the crowd for Maia, and I haven't been able to convince him to talk to Enzo, so I can't think of a reason why he shouldn't hit the dance floor. Why *we* shouldn't. The only things left to do while we wait to spot Maia are get drunk or get out there, and since he doesn't drink, and my tolerance is dismal, it's probably best if we try to enjoy the music.

We're scream-singing in each other's faces with our eyes closed to the third song in a row when I feel a tap on my shoulder. I'm still shouting lyrics at the top of my lungs, mouth full of joy and music, when I turn around and see celestial gray eyes staring back at me.

"Hey, Charmy," the elusive Maia Moon says, grinning in a way that makes my whole body feel lit up from the inside. I become a jack-o'-lantern as soon as she looks my way, empty of everything but light.

"Hi," I say back, and her long black lashes flutter as she leans into me. Her makeup is perfect, the way it always is, eyelids shimmering with something that makes her pale eyes look like stars. Her top is a blinding shade of yellow, so she almost glows like something else pulled out of the sky.

"Can I show you something?" she asks. I lock my hand around Ezra's wrist and squeeze until his eyes pop open. He looks at her, looks at me, then grins and shoos me away without slowing his body, without lowering the sound of his loud, happy voice.

When Maia laces her fingers through mine, her touch quiets every doubt I've ever had about her. When she leads me into an empty guest room at the back of the house, my heart beats like a bass drum against my ribs. When she licks her lips and says, "Me

17

and Andi aren't really friends anymore, but when we were, this is where I'd stay when I slept over," I run my fingers over the floral duvet and look through the wall-width window. I imagine what the room would look like if it was earlier—how Maia's pretty face and everything else would be tinged orangey pink by the sunset.

"I've been trying to figure out how to thank you for the help with trig. I'm so hopeless, but you keep trying and I think I'm actually starting to get it," Maia says next, before I can ask why she and Andi aren't friends anymore.

"It's nothing," I say, but my whole body is blushing. She tucks one of my braids behind my ear and lets her fingers linger on my jawline. "You're so cute that you make me nervous," she says. "It makes it kinda hard to focus when we're studying. Do people ever tell you you're cute?"

I blink too quickly, thinking about Jada, my first and only girlfriend, and the things she said when she dumped me last summer—the way her rejection ripped me wide open. I look down at the floor, but Maia tilts my head back up, gently, by the chin. I push thoughts of Jada to the back of my mind because I'm different than I was then. I'm smarter and better and I'm here with someone else. And the way Maia sounds, like she's flirting, but also genuinely curious, makes me want to answer her.

"Ezra does," I say. "But with anyone else, I find it kinda hard to believe."

Maia's hand brushes my cheek then, and that's when I realize that she doesn't smell like the other popular girls. She smells . . . simpler. Like the burnt-sugar top of a crème brûlée. She looks at me like she's trying to understand something, like I'm a complicated painting or an abstract sculpture that's making her feel things she's never felt before. And now I don't look away.

"Charm," she says, "you really *are* cute. And I like you so much, but not just because of your face. You're so sweet and so smart that you make me . . . I don't know," she says, and her cheeks actually get the tiniest bit pink. "I'm not usually like this, but something about you feels different."

"Maia," I say, but before I can tell her she's the first girl I've wanted to take a chance on since my ex crushed my hopeless, helpless heart, she says more.

"These last few weeks, your tutoring sessions have been one of the few things I look forward to. And whenever my friends let me down, or school stressed me out, or I got some gross comment on one of my pics or videos, I just thought about the next time I'd be seeing you."

I search her face as if I'm looking for a punch line, but there's no part of her that seems to be joking. The intense sexual tension is making me stress-sweat, so I say, "You should never read the comments. Don't they teach you that in, like, influencer school?" She cracks a small grin but then steps even closer to me, leaving only a few inches between our lips.

I lick mine. I take a deep breath. And I say her name again as I wait for her to bridge the last bit of space between us.

3
Beau

"Has anyone seen Todd?!"

A girl whose name I always forget—Whitney? Britney?—flings herself through the doors beside me, which lead in from the pool. She's completely soaked, hair and clothes dripping. She is also completely wasted.

"I only looked away for a second and he's gone!" she wails.

"Did you look in the pool?" JD shouts, and everyone in earshot laughs.

"It's not funny!" she says. "He could *die*!"

"Todd is a unicorn balloon, Whitney," someone calls.

(Whitney. Right the first time.)

"He's not a balloon, he's an *inflatable*! And I *love* him!"

"Found him!"

Tatum Westbrook appears beside Whitney in the doorway, holding what I presume is Todd's deflated purple corpse. At the sight of Tate, both my fists ball up, and not just because of Maia. I've been nursing a grudge since freshman year, when he called Tasha Greenmill a carpet muncher. Now it's just more personal.

"Tatum, you murdered him!" Whitney wails.

I don't hear the rest of the tirade—at the sight of Tatum, I'm redirected to my purpose in coming to this stupid party. I've already been here for an hour, roaming the edges and taking a lap every now and then with no luck, so until now I had actually started to think that maybe Maia left. But if he's still here, then she must be. At least in theory. Star couple. Shoo-in for prom king and queen. Joined at the hip. That's what everybody thinks.

But if that's the truth, why have me and his girlfriend been making out a few times a week since February?

In any case, the ghost with the switchblade is stabbing me again at the sight of him, and I refuse to let it win. One last idea comes to me. Maia is always the friend holding someone's hair back when they puke, so I'll check the bathrooms. Fingers crossed that whoever she's with will be unconscious, so I can actually have a minute alone with her to get this over with.

I cruise through the upstairs, but the bathrooms are surprisingly empty. From the window of one I can see the whole backyard: people making out in the grass, guys cannonballing into the pool and making those on the sidelines shriek. And there's Tatum again, back outside, holding court with the other rugby guys, captain on and off the field. He hasn't found her out there, though, which means I've still got a shot. I go back downstairs, skirting two girls crying into each other's arms, and end up in the hallway by the kitchen, searching for the last bathroom.

When I find it, the door is open. But the only people inside are two guys giggling on the floor, wrapped up in each other, oblivious. I back into the hall, ready to admit defeat, when suddenly . . . I smell her.

Just a passing scent—so faint I think I'm imagining it at first. But no, that *is* her perfume. It's been clogging my nose almost every Saturday in the back room of the bowling alley. It catches me now the way blood might catch a hound, that burnt-sugar smell, and leads me to a door at the end of the hall. It fills my nose the closer I get to it. When I arrive, I see the door's not fully closed, but cracked, and it feels like an invitation. I clutch the panties in my pocket and slide in.

4
Charm

"Maia," I whisper.

But she doesn't answer. At least not with her mouth.

She backs me against the wall, her palms on my shoulders, her nails gripping my back so that I don't fall. I pull her hips against mine by the belt loops in her jeans, which I'm surprised my unpracticed fingers find so quickly. One of her hands snakes up the front of my shirt, and I slip my own into her thick curls. She's looking at me like she wants to consume me, wants to swallow me whole. I want her just as badly.

Maia will be only the second girl I've ever kissed. But before I lean in, Jada's in my head again, whispering things that make me slow down and move more deliberately, the way she taught me. *Don't rush,* my head says, in her voice. *Move like butter melting in a pan.* The wall is cool against my back, and as I ease forward, there's a noise at the door, like someone has stumbled against it. It opens and Maia pulls away, quickly pressing the back of her hand against her lips. Lips that had been millimeters from touching mine. She looks over at the door, at the girl standing there, and her posture tightens, changes, shifts in a way that can only be described as *away*. She's walking toward the other girl and then past her, while looking back at me with something like sadness in her translucent eyes.

All at once, me and the other girl are alone. Beau Carl crosses her arms and leans against the doorframe, like she can't be bothered with standing upright. She's in shredded-up, all-black clothes, though I don't think I've ever seen her wear another color. She looks like a rock star in the ripped tight jeans and a T-shirt that's torn in an on-purpose way I could never pull off. And though she doesn't say anything, her expression is as dark as her outfit. I can tell she wants to kick my ass.

5
Beau

There's a movie whose title I can't remember, but at one point the main character is in a dream and he opens a door. Just before he takes a step through, he teeters at the edge and realizes that there isn't a floor on the other side, just empty space.

That's how it feels, watching Maia Moon back away from another girl. Another girl I could swear she was about to kiss. It's how it feels, watching her eyes go big and blank when she sees me standing in the doorway. Watching her do the thing where she transforms back into Maia Shooting Star and streams out of the room, taking all the light with her.

It's not the other girl's fault, but it feels like it. I almost wish I had the energy to cuss her out—even if it would be pointless—but Maia took that with her too. So I just do the only thing you can do when the girl you were sort of falling for pushes you into deep space.

I go get waffles.

6
Charm

Jada wanted to be a writer. She loved metaphors and similes—creative comparisons that sounded like something you'd read in a book. Whenever she was explaining something to me, she'd say it simply, then describe it in a clever way that made it stick in my head. Like going slow being like butter. Or that my feelings reminded her of eggshells.

Metaphors feel like all I can process in the wake of what just happened. Maia's lips being so close to mine—and then not—has left a hairline fracture in the shell of my heart. Beau's face falling like I'd just kicked her puppy has done a number on me too. I'm cracking, or splintering, or a fragile place inside me has a new, devastating fissure. Beau disappears just after Maia does and I feel left in the lurch, teetering just on the edge of something. Tears, probably.

I exit the room, looking for Maia. Jada always used to say some girls like to be chased. That you'd know you had a runner if they spooked as easily as cats: get too close and they get gone. Jada was like that, so I'm used to the chase. Good at it even. And as I push through the close crowd at Andi's party, searching for the yellow shirt I just had crushed between my fingers, I'm thinking Maia must be like that too.

But I find her too quickly. She isn't hiding the way cats cower under sofas or burrow under sheets. She's right out in the open, dancing . . . with Tatum Westbrook. He's pumping his fists again like he's beating up the air above and below him. I hate when dudes "dance" like that. Then, before I can blink, Tate grabs her by the hips and kisses her, hard.

Jada was wrong about my feelings being like eggshells. When I see the girl I'm falling for, the girl I nearly kissed only a moment ago, kissing someone else, something inside me blows the fuck up. My feelings are a bomb exploding in blinding light, sending debris flying. My heart breaks into fragments sharp enough to slice. I inhale and it hurts.

And then Jada's in my head again, telling me all the ways I fall short. I need to silence her, need to soothe all the points of pain stabbing at so much of me, so I do what everyone else at this party is already doing: I grab a cup.

I only go to Oscar's Diner after the party because I know Aunt Miki is working. And because I know most of the popular kids at Andi's would never be caught dead on this side of town. After the night I've had, I need to get far, far away from each and every one of them.

I was a little tipsy when I leaned against Ezra on the dance floor, red cup nearly empty for the first and final time, and whispered, "SSTC, ASAP," my bottom lip already quivering. He took the cup, threw an arm over my shoulder, and beelined for the exit without another word.

SSTC is one of our many bestie codes. It stands for Safe Space to Cry, and Oscar's is at the top of the list. The cry-teria, if you will, for these spaces include being mostly empty of anyone I know, being mostly dark and/or having dark corners, and having at least one or more of my favorite comfort foods on offer. And after Andi's party, where I was nearly kissed by my crush only to witness her run away from me and make out with Tatum, who is apparently still her boyfriend (*boyfriend!*) even after their very public breakup last month, I definitely require darkness and pie.

I didn't get to tell Ezra any of this until we'd already made it to the diner and were tucked into our favorite corner booth—the one that's nearly been swallowed by half a dozen pothos plants. Their sprawling vines remind me so much of my own emotions—endlessly trimmed, hoping to be tamed, but remaining impossibly wild.

"I just don't understand," I sob, tears staining the flawless, flaky crust of the peach cobbler Aunt Miki deposited on the table the second I walked in already misty-eyed. Ezra is sitting on the same side of the booth as me, his warm hand rubbing small circles on my back. Miki eases herself down on the opposite side of the table, ties back the indigo box braids that I just finished for her last night, and spoon-feeds me some cobbler even as the owner yells at her to get up.

"Ozzy, please take a breath," my aunt says, and even though she's in her waitressing uniform, she uses her yoga-instructor voice. (She has a lot of jobs, which requires having a lot of voices.) "My niece is in crisis, and this diner is basically empty."

Ozzy, the "Oscar" of Oscar's Diner, is a cranky old Iranian man whose real name is Osama. ("But I couldn't exactly call it Osama's in your racist country, could I?" he has said to me more than once.)

Now he says, "She want pie. You give her pie. I need you giving other customers pie." He walks over to our table and shoves a vanilla milkshake at my face. "Sorry you sad, Charmy girl, but I don't pay Miki to hug you. Shake's on the house, but you pay for pie, yes?"

"Yes," I agree, weeping openly now, touched as I always am by Ozzy's gruff kindness. I look at the shake in my hands and take a calming sip, as the greenery curls around me like all my spiraling thoughts. To Ezra and Miki I moan, "Why would she flirt with me if she has a boyfriend? Almost kiss me, if she has a boyfriend? How did I *not know* she had a boyfriend?"

"You *can* be a little oblivious, my love," Aunt Miki says, to which I nod and gulp down another swallow of milkshake so large that the icy fingers of brain freeze instantly begin creeping their way up from the base of my skull.

Ezra leans forward. "But in Charmy's defense, Maia and Tate are more on-again, off-again than a light switch." He turns to me. "Just let me know if you want me to kick her ass."

"Just because Zeke's solution to homophobia is violence," Miki replies, referring to Ezra's older brother Ezekiel, whose reaction to Ezra's coming out in middle school was to teach him to throw a punch, "doesn't mean you need to go beating up people who may just have some unanswered questions about themselves."

"Well, *I* wouldn't beat her up," he backtracks. "I'm trying to make varsity captain this year—can you imagine the optics? I'd get my little cousin Paige to do it, though."

"Ezra J. King, please," I say, massaging my temples. I don't know if it's the booze, the situation, or the milkshake making my head ache now. But he ignores me, still looking right at Aunt Miki.

"I'll be damned if I let some straight girl use Charmy as her experiment," Ezra says.

"You really think she's straight?" I ask him, stroking a leaf of the plant closest to me. It's veined through with white and shaped almost exactly like a heart.

"I do," says a low but feminine voice, and I frown at her words, which land heavy as a warning. The sound is like the color of the sky before a storm—all dark blues and hazy grays.

When I look up, the person standing there is Beau Carl, with her broody eyes, brows sharp as daggers above them. She doesn't look like she wants to beat me up anymore, but I am wondering what the hell she's doing here.

"Crying over Maia Moon won't get you far, Monty," she says.

"Monty?"

"Charm Montgomery, right? Can I call you Monty? I don't think I can call anyone over the age of four who isn't a fairy-tale character 'Charm' with a straight face."

I scrub at my eyes with my sleeve, then frown at Beau through my mostly dried tears.

"If I say no, will you call me by my actual name?"

"Probably not. But we can try other options. Char? Charmander? Cha-Cha?"

"Oh god," Ezra says. "Please stop."

"I'm not a Pokémon. Or a dance," I say. I tuck my hair behind my ears and push my glasses back up my nose. "I guess Monty is fine."

Aunt Miki looks Beau up and down with something like hesitant approval. "I've seen you in here before," she says, this time using her substitute teacher voice, "but remind me: Exactly who in the midnight munchies are you?"

"Beau," Beau says, and nothing else. Aunt Miki raises her eyebrows and smirks.

"If I were you, Charmy, I'd listen to what your friend Beau here has to say. The vibes"—my aunt moves her hands around in front of Beau's black clothes, her neatly tattooed forearms, and furrowed brow—"are simply immaculate."

Beau shrugs in a smug way.

"This girl knows things," Miki says before standing and walking back to the counter. She grabs the coffeepot and makes the rounds, filling empty mugs for the few customers inside, but I can feel her keeping one eye on the three of us.

"So, you were saying?" I ask Beau, despite kind of wanting to hide from her. She's hot in a scary way, and she's everything I'm afraid I will never be: edgy and confident, at ease in her own skin. She licks her lips, making them shine, and then that stormy voice of hers is filling the air again.

"Maia's trouble. Like most straight girls. They just want to see what it's like, no matter what it does to your heart. They are always 'just drunk' or 'just kidding' or 'omg, who hasn't kissed a girl at least once, like at a party or whatever.'" Her voice goes high and whiny at the end of her sentence, like she's impersonating a particular kind of person, namely girls like Andi or Trina or Whitney. "And popular girls like Maia are the worst ones, out to get what they want by any means necessary. The same way she puts that makeup on for her followers, she puts on a different face depending on who she's around."

Every word she says cuts like a knife. Mostly because of Jada. She got what she wanted out of me, and then dumped me like it was nothing.

But I must be a masochist, because even as I remember how that all went down, I ask Beau for more. "So what are you saying? That Maia's using me?"

Beau looks frustrated for a fraction of a second before the

expression clears. "Yes, Monty. I'm saying don't be an idiot. Maia sucks. Don't let her suck the life out of you."

Ezra gets between us as my throat tightens, the threat of tears returning full force. "You sound like you speak from experience," he says pointedly. "So maybe you need to take your own advice."

Something in Beau's face shifts. The mask she's been wearing falls away and something softer appears, making her look vulnerable or even a little scared. But before I can be sure I saw it, it's gone.

Beau shakes her head and lifts her hands, taking a step back from our table.

"I was just trying to help," she says. "Maia doesn't care about you. She doesn't care about anyone but herself. But do what you want."

I watch as Beau tosses a few bills on her table (my second choice, the dark one in the opposite corner, partially hidden behind a big potted elephant ear) and abandons what's left of her waffles.

Something about that fleeting, pain-filled look on Beau's face settles in the pit of my stomach like a rock, though. And even as Ezra changes the subject and scarfs down his plate of pancakes, I can't touch what remains of my cobbler.

7
Beau

All of that, and I still have Maia's underwear.

When I got home last night, I stuffed them back where they'd been for the past three months—in my nightstand drawer. They were wrapped around a pair of drumsticks before, but now they just rest crumpled on top, no longer folded neatly as they were in my pocket.

Then I went to bed with my clothes on, on top of the comforter. I'm still there at noon when Celine comes in.

"Don't you knock?" I say, face still in the pillow.

I know it's her. The only other person it could be is Mom, and she won't be home until tomorrow. Back-to-back shifts in the ER. At least I know where to find her if I break my leg instead of whatever part of me feels like it's in pieces after seeing Maia with Charm Montgomery.

"I'm guessing last night did not go well," Celine says.

"Stop looking at my stuff," I tell her. I can feel her scanning the room, looking for . . . whatever.

"I'm just admiring the chaos."

"What do you want?" I groan.

"Daniel will be here in ten minutes. He's bringing donuts. Let's play."

I'm silent for a minute, weighing the benefits of staying in bed until I have to work versus donuts, drumming, and an almost certain interrogation from Celine about my life choices. Before Kay moved to Toledo, we would meet up on a day like today. Get tacos and sit in her car and talk about anything but college. For the last year and a half, that's all people have seemed to talk about, but not Kay. She's going to take a year off like me. I can still barely talk to Celine about it—she gets real mommish at the idea of me not going.

With no Kay—and no Maia—I do the math. Hibernation vs. donuts. Donuts vs. hibernation.

I sigh and turn over.

"Jesus!" I cry, jolting backward.

Celine is directly next to my bed, at eye level, wearing a frog mask.

I shove her, and she falls over, laughing.

"What the hell is wrong with you?" I demand, swinging my legs to the floor.

"What the hell is wrong with *you*?" she counters. "Why do you have a frog mask?"

"Why do you always have to touch my stuff?"

"Again, why do you have a frog mask?"

I roll my eyes. "It was for school. I was going to do the play for extra credit, but Mr. Hoagland was going to make me be the frog prince, and fuck that."

"Why? I love a good gender-bent fairy tale."

"No, no, I was still gonna have to play a dude," I say.

"Boooo. A frog lesbian would heal society's ills."

"Yeah, exactly."

"But you kept the mask?"

I nod, laughing finally. "Yeah, it's cool."

"Maybe we'll wear frog masks for the show next weekend," she said. "All three of us."

"How are you going to sing with a frog mask? Also, Favorite Daughter doesn't evoke frog imagery."

"You're always shitting on my ideas," she says brightly. "Now change clothes and come out to the garage."

"Sure thing, Mother Dearest," I say. It may be noon, but it's still too early to have already rolled my eyes this much.

I refuse to improve my appearance, so five minutes later my teeth are brushed and I'm entering the garage, where Daniel is on a stool tuning his guitar, donut held between his teeth. He grins when he sees me, almost dropping the donut.

"Good morning, sunshine," he says when he has a handle on everything. "Nice bedhead. Heard you were restoring underwear to their rightful owner last night."

I turn and glare at Celine, who shrugs.

"He's my safe place," she says. "You should know that whatever you tell me, I tell Daniel."

"I'm her safe place," he echoes, beaming.

I pantomime vomiting, but I don't *actually* mind. Daniel is like my brother. He and Celine have been dating since they were fourteen—one of those one-in-a-million middle school relationships that beat the odds. They just turned twenty-one, and everyone who has ever met them knows they'll turn a hundred together too. Literally. They even have the same birthday.

"The underwear was not actually returned," I say, picking up a donut. Daniel's parents have run a bakery since they got here from South Korea like forty years ago. Best donuts in the city, hands down.

"She told you to keep them?" Celine says.

"We didn't really have a conversation."

"Boyfriend?" Celine sounds grim.

"Worse."

"What's worse than her having a boyfriend?"

"Let's rehearse," I say, loping over to my drum kit. I didn't drink at the party, but I feel like actually puking now. The memory of last night is crawling up my throat again. I want to play loud music. I want to fill the garage with so much noise that there's no room for Maia Moon.

"Present first," Daniel says. He goes to his bag where it sits on the floor. He pulls out a folder from which he withdraws something thin and shiny. He shields it with his body while he walks over to where I sit. "Ta-da!"

He holds it up. A decal, with FAVORITE DAUGHTER in awesome lettering.

"Holy shit," I say, smiling. "Is that for the bass?"

"Yup," he says with a nod. He holds it up and makes a noble face. "May I?"

"Go for it."

He peels off the backing, and a moment later the name of our band is emblazoned on the front of my bass drum.

"Wanted to do it in time for the show next weekend," he says, standing back to admire it. "It looks sick."

I peer over the top of my kit. It's perfect. This is the first set that's actually mine. As a kid I would go down the street to this guy Jacob's house. He used to play in middle school and kept an old set in his garage. I'd hang around and beg him to let me play until I got to middle school myself and joined the school band. It wasn't until my job before the bowling alley, working at Chai-kovsky, a music- and tea-shop fusion that closed last year (a great personal tragedy, as the employee discount was extremely sweet), that I was able to buy this very kit. And now it really feels like mine.

"Good timing, too," Celine says. "We're playing at Pack of Eight next month, and I have it on good authority that a music reviewer for *Elicktric* will be there."

On any other day that would perk me up. We're always looking for ways to get press for Favorite Daughter, and *Elicktric* being the magazine that launched more than one band's career could mean exciting things for us. Plus, I know it would especially mean a lot to Celine. I love this band—I quit school band for this band—but really, it's her baby. And yet she's two kinds of moms when it comes to the band: (1) doting, and (2) reluctant. Sometimes I think she's afraid of the life she would have if she went all in.

"That's really cool," I say, trying not to sound like a parade-pisser. "Good timing, yeah."

"Maybe you can polish up some of those songs you've been working on," Daniel says encouragingly.

"Sure, yeah, I'll work on them."

Celine positions herself at the mic stand. I can see her hesitating. She brings her mouth to the mic, but then turns to me.

"Before we start," she says, "you *sure* you don't wanna tell us what happened last night?"

I do. But I don't. "Let's just play," I say, and Celine gives me that look that's too soft, the one that makes my heart bend in ways I can't handle right now.

I'm not a big crier, but I have a feeling that if I talk about Maia, this band rehearsal will turn into a sob session. I think back over the last few months: Maia stopping by my job more and more often, hanging out a little longer each time. Her breaking up with Tate (for the third time in six months), and some stupid part of me wondering if maybe I was starting to matter to her beyond the back-room orgasms I gave her at the bowling alley. After the last time she and Tate broke things off (on the rugby field, after a championship game, in the rain), I asked her, "So, do you think you and Tate will get back together after that shit-show?" And she looked at me all sparkly-eyed and said, "Maybe I'm moving on to something else."

But then she got back with him.

Rinse.

Repeat.

So of all the things I expected to happen at that stupid party, seeing Maia Moon almost kissing some other girl was not on my fucking bingo card. I had spent months thinking maybe she just wasn't ready to fully break up with Tate, which, okay, I at least kind of understood. Being strung along had started to suck. But even with my panties-returning plan, that stupid part of me thought that when she *was* finally ready, she would turn to me. Instead she turned to some random girl. One-way ticket from righteous anger to *holy shit I'm pathetic*.

Uber-ing to the diner was the only thing I could do. That and immediately scrolling through Ezra's followers until I found the face and name of the girl Maia had nearly had her lips against.

Charm Montgomery. Like back in that bedroom, I wanted to hate her, of course. I still kind of do. But when I saw her crying over her cobbler at the restaurant, the hate leaked out of me. It wasn't her fault she got spun up in Maia's web. If I was going to hate her for that, I had to hate myself, too.

I don't say any of this, though. Crying seems like a waste of time. So I shake my head again. Daniel nods. Celine gives in. And we play, until the only thing in my heart is music.

8
Charm

I'm sitting in the kitchen Monday morning, holding the backs of two big cold spoons to the puffy pillows that used to be my eyes, when Ezra pulls up in front of our town house. I'm embarrassed to say I spent most of the weekend curled up in bed crying, my back to the door just in case Aunt Miki checked on me. I didn't want her to see. It's always been just me and Miki, so we're super close, and while I'm normally very open with her, the situation with Maia still feels raw even after we talked about it at the diner. Since she works so much, it was easy enough to avoid her most of Saturday and Sunday, even if I couldn't avoid my own messy thoughts. But this morning, just as Ezra rings the doorbell, Aunt Miki sweeps into the kitchen in her yoga pants, looks up from her phone, and notices me. It's the first time I've looked directly at her in a while, and she looks like she has a lot on her mind too.

"Hey, hey, hey," she says in her softest voice. "What is going on with you this morning?" Ezra rings the bell again, so she holds up one finger and heads down the hall to open the door for him. They walk back into the kitchen together arm in arm, and when Aunt Miki sits down across from me, I try to smile, but she sees right through it.

"Do you need help with anything? You look tired," I say to her. I'm always a little bit worried about Miki, because she'll go until she can't go anymore. Even with Maia on the brain, I can see the darkness under her eyes.

"And you look like you've been crying," Miki says, ignoring my question. I look at Ezra so I don't have to look at her. "Did your . . . mom call you?" she asks after a long pause. "Dammit. I told her I wanted to talk to you first."

"My *mom*?" I say, feeling more confused than I have all weekend—which is impressive considering the complete headfuck that was everything that happened at the party with Maia. "Why would I have heard from *Brianna*?"

"Shit," Miki says under her breath. "They're . . . in town. Bree and your dad." I give her a look. "Sorry. Bree and Chauncey. And Dallas. They . . . want to see you."

I laugh. It's the dark cackle I reserve for times like these, when I need to laugh so I don't do something more embarrassing. Like sob. Again.

"It's that time of year already?" I ask, my voice dripping poison. "When they remember I exist?"

"Now, Charm," Aunt Miki starts. "We said we wouldn't do this."

Ezra pokes my side. It's his way of letting me know he's here even if he isn't saying anything. He tries his best to stay out of my messy family crap.

"No. *You* said I *shouldn't* do this."

"She really doesn't need this today, Mick," Ezra says, unable to stay completely out of it.

"I mean, neither do I! But I can't exactly tell my sister she can't see her own daughter, can I?"

Miki starts aggressively taking things out of the pantry and fridge: oat milk, strawberries, blueberries, flax seeds, kale, and peanut butter. Then she pulls down the blender so hard, the cord unravels and knocks over the milk. (I must not have screwed the top on all the way the last time I poured a glass. Oops.)

Ezra jumps up and grabs the kitchen towel. He starts mopping up the mess.

"What do they want anyway?" he asks. "To swoop in and pay for Charm's prom tickets?"

I laugh the dark laugh.

Miki leans on the counter and hangs her head. "I wanted to talk to you about this later, Charm." My aunt looks at the floor before meeting my eyes. "Bree says they're moving back."

"Back where?"

"Here. They already put in an offer on a house."

My parents—high school sweethearts who conceived me the night of their junior prom and were homecoming king and queen, for god's sake—show up every now and then wanting to pretend we have a relationship. My nana Coley had just gotten married to a rich guy and was making plans to move to his beach house in Miami when my mom found out she was pregnant, and let's just say the pregnancy didn't change Nana's mind about moving in with her new husband. So Miki, who was only twenty-three at the time, took in my mom (and eventually me) so my parents could go off to college and not "ruin" their future. But the plan had always been that eventually I'd live with them. After I turned six and then seven and then eight, and they never made good on their promise, I started feeling more resentful of their visits. I was anxious about not knowing when they'd come, or worse, how long they'd stay and when they would leave. And when they finally said they were ready to have me, it was couched next to the reveal that they were pregnant again.

I moved in with them (to a town a hundred miles away where I knew no one) for one disastrous year when I was ten, but they were so busy with the new baby that it felt like there was no room for me. So I moved back in with Aunt Miki. Even though my brother Dallas has always been with them—their pride and joy, do-over kid—he's so cute and sweet that I try my best not to hold any of this shit against him.

"Why the hell are they moving here *now*? I graduate in, like, a month!"

Miki throws everything in the blender and doesn't reply—she probably can't even guess anyway. Instead she asks, "So wait, if you weren't upset about your parents being in town . . . what else would it be?" then searches my face as if the answer is hidden there while the mechanical grind of the blender fills our kitchen. Ezra bites his lip like he's fighting the urge to tell her. He looks at me, asking for permission, but I shake my head.

"Not about Maia, right?" Miki asks. "You wouldn't still be upset about her." When she glances at Ezra for confirmation, he looks up and over at the paintings that have been on the wall since his first after-school visit when we were in fifth grade as if they're new. I kick him under the counter.

"Charmy. Boo-boo. Honey. Why are you so hung up on this Maia girl?"

The memory that has been on an endless loop in my head all weekend resurfaces in that moment and my eyes fill again, against my will.

I'm standing in Jada's bedroom in just my underwear. I'm covering my chest with my hands, moments after going farther with her than I've ever gone with anyone, and she's saying she's tired of having to teach me everything. She's pulling on her shirt while saying that she'll be going away to college in a couple of months and that I'll still be here. She'd rather be free, she said, to find someone who isn't so predictable. Someone who might surprise her.

The next day was the Fourth of July and Ezra dragged me, still moping and heartbroken, to the beach to watch fireworks. And there Jada was, illuminated by colorful explosions, already kissing someone else.

"It's not just Maia," I say through the tears I can no longer hold back. And Ezra, bless him, finishes the thought for me. "It's bitches like Maia *and* Jada. And Brianna, to be honest. Bitches who play with hearts like they're not beating, bleeding things." He walks around the counter and puts his hands on my shoulders. "Don't worry, boo. I'm gonna get Paige to kick her ass."

"Which her?" Miki asks.

As I half laugh, half sob, Calypso, my calico cat, curls around my legs, her orange-and-black face turned up like she's worried about me. I scoop her up, nuzzle my face into her fur, and look at Aunt Miki, who I can tell is gearing up for a pep talk.

"Listen," she says, "Jada didn't deserve you. Maia is missing out if she doesn't appreciate you. And even my sister isn't worth your tears. The one constant in life is that you can't control anyone's actions but your own. So if and when people let you down, you have to decide where your boundaries are, and what exactly you'll allow to happen next."

It's a typical morning in the Montgomery house, Aunt Miki spouting off deep-as-a-river wisdom like it's nothing, but the idea of having to see Maia today for the first time since the party is making it all much harder than usual to stomach. Without another word I clean Calypso's litter box, wash my hands, shove an untoasted s'mores Pop-Tart in my mouth, and head toward the door. Ezra grabs my bag and runs after me.

Once we're safely in his car, I turn the radio up as loud as I can stand, and Ezra allows me to, which means he can tell I'm in deep distress. We don't speak the whole ride to school, and after he parks and cuts the engine, he reaches for my hand. His gentleness makes my heart ache.

"You ready?" he asks. I shake my head.

"You're right. You're not," he says. I'm surprised because I was expecting another pep talk. Instead Ezra flips down the mirror and tilts my head up so I can look at myself. "There's Pop-Tart chocolate all over your face."

And instead of crying again, like I thought I might only a minute ago, I crack up laughing.

At my locker, with my head buried deep inside it, I repeat the desperate prayer I've been muttering since midday Sunday. *Please help me avoid Maia until our (unavoidable) tutoring session. Please help the hallways to be too full, the cafeteria too crowded. And please, if I do run into her, I pray to the gods of high school and humiliation, do not let Maia speak to me.*

As I whisper *amen*, Ezra nudges me in the ribs.

"Heartbreak ho at three o'clock," he says through his teeth.

I turn in what feels like slow motion to see Maia easing her way down the long hall. She's looking down at her phone, barely registering the fact that the other students seem to part around her like they're a rushing river and she's a deeply rooted stone.

I want to hate her. It would make this all so much easier. But as soon as she pockets her phone and tunes back in to the world around her, she's stopping to pick up a pen someone dropped and waving hello to Mr. Ellington, the janitor, and telling Mx. Anderson, the freshman bio teacher, that she'll feed their tarantula while they're on vacation. She's being the Maia I've gotten to know over the last eight weeks, which means she's mostly being kind, and it's easy to see in this moment why so many people love her. She's the kind of pretty that almost feels imaginary; the kind of sweet that makes teachers and parents smile. She could be mean—could use her power to decimate or dominate. But she doesn't. If she were like the other popular girls, like Andi Patterson or Whitney Taylor, who are also worshipped but cruel, it would be so much easier to write her off. But Maia is more complicated than that. I can't square this girl with one who would toy with my barely healed heart, and for some messed-up reason I feel even more drawn to her because of that duplicity. I stand there, unable to look away from her, and then she raises her eyes and sees me.

"Fuck," I whisper, spinning back to face my locker. As if the beads in my hair aren't clattering like applause; as if those gray eyes didn't just lock with mine. Ezra steps behind me, like if he blocks my body with enough of his, I'll vanish. But a second later he whispers, "Incoming," and I know my prayers haven't worked. The nightmare will soon be my reality.

"Is it too late to run?" I ask Ezra, as I yank roughly at the zipper on my bag and throw it over my shoulder. "Do I have time to just, like, sprint down the hallway?"

"'Fraid not, dude," he says. "She's still looking this way and she's like, max, a minute from impact."

What could she possibly have to say to me? If she says she didn't mean any of it, I'll cry. If she acts like our almost-kiss didn't even happen, I'll shatter. If she pretends she was drunk, I'll need to murder her. None of these outcomes are things I want. So I squeeze my eyes shut.

I wait.

And wait.

And wait.

"Oh," Ezra says. "Plot twist."

I open my eyes and cast a sidelong glance in his direction. "What?" I whisper. He smirks.

"Look," he says.

When I turn around, less than ten feet in front of me is Beau Carl. And she's just intercepted Maia Moon.

I can't hear what they're saying, but Beau is frowning and moving her hands a lot, and Maia looks like she's in pain. "I guess Beau *was* speaking from experience at the diner," Ezra says. "Shit. Now I feel like an ass."

As I watch them talk, the constellations of expressions that cross their faces make me wonder what exactly that experience is. But before I can run away or try to silently shift myself into a better position so I can read their lips, I hear the quick snaps and clicks of a . . . snare drum? And then, seconds later, the unmistakable blast of a trumpet.

Everyone turns to look down the long hallway toward the school's double-door entrance, and there, spilling through with a gust of warm spring wind, is what looks like the entire marching band.

"What the . . . ?" Ezra whispers.

"Ayyyyy!" shouts Enzo, sidling up to us.

"Hey, Ezra," he says, yanking on one of Ezra's hoodie strings. Ezra looks like he's seen a ghost.

"Hi?" he says, which is the only word I think I've heard him say to Enzo since he saw him star as Puck in our school's fall production of *Goodfellow*, a musical reimagining of *A Midsummer Night's Dream*. Ezra's part of the stage crew (in addition to track and field, moving heavy props is a great way to stay in shape in the basketball off-season, apparently) and was half in love with Enzo *before* he performed for two hours as a fairy wearing nothing but a green felt loincloth, his glittering bronze chest on display for all to see. He's been complete trash for Enzo ever since.

"Charm City," Enzo adds, nodding at me. We're in the same bio section, and he saved me from having to dissect a foul-smelling earthworm back in October, so I too am an Enzo-lover. "What do you think this is all about?"

I shrug, then look back over at Beau, who is still frowning. (She frowns a lot, it seems.) Maia just looks confused.

The band continues down the hall, sounding like the ones that parade through the streets of New Orleans whenever we go visit my uncle Theo there. Kids sandwich themselves against the walls and each other to make room, and a second later the band parts to let a guy walk through their ranks as they continue to play. I can't quite make out who it is until he gets to the very front of the line, and then I see his tousled brown hair and cheeky grin; his sleek designer jeans and douchey polo. Tatum Westbrook is wearing his rugby letterman jacket and holding a big poster board with lettering that matches our school's blue and gold colors. And he's looking at Maia, who is, awkwardly, still standing right beside Beau. It's not until that moment that it all clicks into place.

"He's promposing," I say, more to myself than anyone else.

"Awwww!" Enzo says, clueless.

"Beau," Ezra mutters. *"Run."*

9
Beau

I almost talked myself out of it on the way to school.

At the bowling alley over the weekend, I had spent my shift going back and forth about whether I would say something to Maia. I wasn't even thinking about her panties in my drawer anymore—things had changed. This was about the girl she had almost kissed. I realized now that confronting her at the party had been about more than returning underwear and ending things. I wanted an explanation. When I saw she'd gotten back together with Tate, I'd mainly had one question, really: Were we just an experimental hookup or were there feelings involved? Now I had about fifty, the biggest ones being: Do you give a shit about Charm Montgomery? Or are you using her, too?

This morning, though, I almost decided it didn't matter. Maia wasn't my girlfriend. It was a secret hookup. So what if she had other secret hookups? So what if those secret hookups were girls, and in public she dated Tate and told people she was straight? She was cheating on *Tate*, not me. But then I saw her walking down the hall looking like a fucking angel, and it made me want to kiss her and yell at her at the same time. So suddenly it mattered again.

And now, before I can stop myself, I'm intercepting her in the hallway.

"So. Charm Montgomery?" I say.

Maia's eyes say so much . . . until she decides she doesn't want them to. She has this way of putting a veil in front of them, and she's doing it right now.

". . . goes to our school," she says innocently, as if finishing a sentence.

"No, that was a *question*," I say. "Which you know."

It's subtle, but I see her cheeks flush.

"Can we talk later?" she asks quickly. Her eyes dart around the hallway.

"Oh, right. We're in *public*. Sorry."

The sarcasm cuts her exactly as I hoped it would. The flush deepens and she narrows her eyes.

"I don't care about that," she says quietly. And the quietness cuts me back, because it means her words are a lie. I'm used to being a secret. Back seat, back room, empty rehearsal hall, dark movie theater. It's just the way things are. But it feels different now. Maia and I have been at the same party before, and she'd sparkle her eyes at me across the room but never, ever let our paths cross. Kept her Heterosexual Reputation bulletproof. Wildly public Instagram Makeup Girlie, whose secrets were so secret, they existed only in the vacuum of the bowling alley. And yet she took the risk with Charm Montgomery.

"So what *do* you care about?" I demand. Maybe I also mean *who*.

"Beau, can we just—"

We cannot. I interrupt her.

"No, I would really appreciate an answer. What *do* you care about?"

Her mouth opens, but the brassy sound of a horn answers.

For a moment, the tension between us is replaced with confusion.

"What is that?" she asks.

"How the hell should I know?"

The answer is coming toward us, a wall of noise barreling down the hall. The school band. At first it's just my ear that cringes—whoever plays the snare always hits off-center. I've never mentioned it to Maia, but there's no way in hell she doesn't notice.

But as bad as the snare is, nothing makes me cringe as much as who's leading the band down the hallway.

Fucking Tate.

I think if Gaston from *Beauty and the Beast* wore a polo shirt, he still wouldn't look as douchey as Tate Westbrook looks right now. If Joffrey Baratheon gained thirty pounds and took up rugby, I might still want to punch Tate more.

And by the look on his face, he wants to punch me, too.

"Hey, Carl, can you move?" he says. "You're kind of ruining the moment."

I've been so fixated on the absolute absurdity of his entire being that my brain completely pivoted from the presence of the band. But now all the pieces crawl slowly together. Band. Hallway. Tatum Westbrook. And the big poster in his hands.

I lower my eyes to read it.

THIS IS MAJER. GO TO PROM WITH ME?

His girlfriend is the drum major . . . and he can't spell "major." Oh my god.

"*Carl,*" Tate emphasizes again. "Get fucking lost."

He looks at me like he can't believe I still exist, then looks at Maia, then slowly back at me. A grin cracks his face.

"Wait, I'm not interrupting *your* promposal, am I?" His laugh is like Styrofoam. "If this is yours, it's looking preeeetty weak, bruh!"

He says it loud enough so that the people around us hear, and they laugh. I don't know what hurts worse: standing like a deer with a death wish in the middle of the hallway while the boyfriend of the girl you were falling for asks her to prom, or the fact that the girl in question says nothing when her boyfriend is a flaming dick.

It doesn't matter. Either way I feel like I could cry, and I'd rather be that aforementioned deer on I-65 than cry in front of Tatum, so I turn on a dime, walk as quickly down the hallway as possible, and dive into the nearest bathroom.

I lean against the door inside a stall with my fists against my eyes. I shouldn't have done it. I shouldn't have said anything to her. I could have just gone about my life like I'd never met Maia Moon, the same way she surely would've done with me if I'd had the chance to tell her things were over. And fuck that, why stop there with the "I shouldn't have done it"? I have to go farther back, really. Never should have kissed her. Never should have let her touch me. Never should have fallen for her bullshit when she showed up at the bowling alley and started toying with the keys on my belt.

"God," I whisper, and press my fists even tighter.

Not one single tear. I swear to god, Beau Carl, you better not shed one single tear over this girl.

"You okay?"

A soft girly voice comes in through the crack of the stall's door. I jump. I didn't hear anyone come in.

"I'm fine, what do you mean?" I say. Whoever they are, they can't see me, so I keep my hands pressed against my eyes.

"You just made your voice deeper," she says. "And, like, you already have a pretty deep voice. You don't have to hide that you're sad."

I recognize the voice now. From Oscar's. It's her. Charm. I passed her in the hallway as I escaped the promposal. Besides the obvious, she's literally the last person I want to be talking to right now.

"No offense," I say, "but . . . can you go away? This is really not a good time."

"I know," she says, but she doesn't leave. "That was really shitty out there."

"Yeah, well, that's life."

The sound of a text tone pierces the quiet.

"It's Ezra," she says quietly. Then through the bathroom door I hear her laugh a dry, humorless laugh.

"Breaking news," she says. "Ezra reports from the hallway that Maia has accepted Captain Douche-Canoe's promposal."

I lower my hands from my eyes just so I can roll them hard as hell.

"My only surprise is that he at least managed to spell 'prom' correctly," I say.

She scoffs. Then silence falls between us again.

"I wish we could make her feel what we feel," she says finally. Her soft voice heats up a little. I recognize that tone: bitterness. "Have somebody do to Maia what she did to us."

We. Us. It works in distracting me. I was stupid enough to begin thinking about me and Maia as a *we*. As an *us*. And now I see that the only *we* and *us* is me and Charm (and whoever else): the girls Maia played like the fucking school band. She's the drum major and we all just march to her tune—it makes me want to drown myself in this toilet.

I'm bitter too, I realize. Just like Charm. There's definitely no point in hating her. Maia screwed both of us over.

I slowly open my eyes. The tears are absolutely gone—replaced with something else.

52

"What did you say?" I ask Charm through the door. "Do to her what she did to us?"

"Yeah, so she'd know what it feels like," she answers. "So she knows she can't just play with people's hearts."

I turn and slide the latch on the stall door open. Charm looks surprised, but she doesn't speak. We just stare at each other. For the first time, I notice her eyes are round and deep brown, rimmed in thick lashes that sweep down when she blinks. Her lips curve in a delicate frown as she studies my face right back. This girl is pretty as hell, and I can still hear how she said, *You don't have to hide that you're sad.* Which, disagree, but she's clearly a sweet person. Pretty, smart, nice—Maia could have kissed this girl on Friday, but instead she turned around and accepted a promposal from the Joffrey Baratheon of Brookville High School? Dumb.

"Monty," I say. "You said I can call you Monty, right?"

She rolls her eyes. "I guess."

"Hear me out, but . . . I think I have an idea."

She drops her chin. We don't know each other—at all. But somehow she gives me the same X-ray look that Celine does when she knows I'm up to something.

"Go on . . . ," she says.

It's all unfurling in my mind. But we need to go somewhere uneavesdroppable.

"I have one question for you, Monty."

"Okay . . . ?" she says impatiently.

"What's the only thing sweeter than Maia Moon's lips?"

Her eyebrows shoot up, then furrow. I bet if I put my fingers to her cheek, it would be blazing. It's adorable, to be honest, but instead I put a hand on each of her shoulders.

"Revenge, Monty. Revenge."

PART TWO
Four Weeks till Prom

10
Charm

Oscar's Diner looks different in the daylight. Or maybe everything looks different now that I see the truth about Maia—the world less shimmering, less full of possibility. I can't stop thinking about the way her eyes went from full to empty after our moment at the party; how she looked the same way in the hall at school when she saw me and then like someone poured everything out of her when Tate appeared. I want to know what her many faces mean as much as I want to chop her in her dainty little throat.

"Earth to Monty." I glance across the table at Beau, whose voice has been rumbling in the background of my thoughts like faraway thunder. A pool of syrup is all that remains on what was her full plate of waffles the last time I looked up, and I realize she must have been talking for a while. "There you are," she says, the words coming out slow and breathy. Her dark eyes are glinting in the late afternoon light, and it's only in this moment that I notice they're a deep shade of blue. Processing that information helps me dial back my thoughts about Maia, and that's when I notice that Beau's pointing to something in her notebook. Her nails are bitten down to the quick. "I asked you to take a look at this list."

Aunt Miki isn't working right now, or rather, she isn't working in the diner. After her early morning classes at Namaste Yoga Studio, she drives for a rideshare app during daylight hours unless she gets called to a school as a sub. She doesn't clock in at Oscar's till after six most days, and I'm grateful. I wouldn't want to have to explain why I'm sitting across from Beau Carl, notebook between us on the table like we're studying. (Because we aren't studying, and I'm a terrible liar.) I absently consider if I need to ask Ozzy not to mention seeing me to my aunt.

I sip my milkshake, wondering if paying for it will keep him quiet about me stopping by. Then I look down and read what I can make out of the list written in Beau's tiny, slanting scrawl.

> Step 1: Ask Maia out.
> Step 2: Kiss her in a way she can't forget.
> Step 3: Get her to post a photo with you.
> Step 4: Convince her to dump her dumb boyfriend.
> Step 5: Ask Maia to prom.
> Step 6: Dump her.

"Wait," I say, as if I haven't been sitting here for the last five (twenty?) minutes at all. Though my mind is still tempted to linger in every place that reminds me of the emotional roller coaster I've been on for the last few days—the small, warm room in Andi's house; the crowded, noisy hallway at school; my own messy kitchen; the deep well of Maia's silvery eyes—I look right at Beau. "What is this?"

"So, were you zoning out this entire time, or . . . ?" Beau asks. She does this thing where she roughly rubs her hand through her short hair and it stands on end, making her look like a hot and bothered cockatoo. She sighs with what seems like frustration, but when she looks back up at me, she grins. "You're a little spaccy, huh?"

I look to my left, expecting to roll my eyes with Ezra, but my bestic isn't there. He had track practice, and he doesn't miss practice for anything or anyone, including me. It throws me a little, to be honest. He's been so omnipresent in my life since I was eleven that on the rare occasion he isn't with me, I forget. Which, to Beau's point, is a bit spacey.

"I can be," I admit. "Sorry."

"Not a problem. But if we're gonna do this, I kinda need you here. With me?"

There's a slight pause between the word "here" and the phrase "with me," and I know she's asking if I'm with her, as in, paying attention, but I can't help but hear it all as something else: that she needs me here, with her. I blush, more grateful than ever that my skin is such a dark shade of brown. I nod and look at the list again, but the math still ain't mathing.

"Explain this to me one more time?" I say.

Beau takes a breath, and this time when she speaks, I really focus on what she's saying.

"We want to get Maia back for fucking us over, yes?"

"Yes," I agree.

"I'm suggesting we do that by getting Maia to fall for you, for real, over the next few weeks. Play with her heart the way she's played with ours. Then, once she's all in, we drop her, the way she dropped us."

"So," I say slowly, "you want me to ask her out? Kiss her? Take her to *prom*? Even though she's dating *Tatum Westbrook*?"

Beau tenses a little, like even hearing Tatum's name pisses her off. She relaxes quickly enough, though, and shrugs.

"She already almost kissed you. And let's just say that Maia's relationship status seems . . . flexible."

I look at her. "I don't know what that means."

"Don't worry too much about it. And actually, asking her out was Ezra's idea," Beau says, pointing to the first item on the list.

"Wait. When did you talk to Ezra about this? Ezra doesn't even like you!"

She widens her eyes comically. "Wow, Monty, wow."

"My bad, it's just . . . you were kind of a dick after the party the other night, and Ezra can be . . ."

"Protective," she finishes, grinning.

I'm relieved she's not offended. I nod.

"I get it," she says. "I can be . . ."

"Dickish?"

She laughs, then looks me directly in my eyes. "Dicks aren't exactly my thing."

My mouth drops open, the invisible blush intensifying. But she moves on.

"Anyway," she says. "I talked to Ezra before he went to practice, and yes, I could tell he's not my biggest fan. But I figured he'd have some thoughts. Step three was his too. Four through six are all me, though."

I shake my head, like I can get any of this to make sense just by jostling my brain. "But why would she say yes to a date with me? Why would she"—I glance back at the notebook—"post a picture with me when her profile aesthetic is so curated and pristine? Doesn't she make money from her content? What if she signed some kind of agreement with the companies that sponsor her? Has she ever even posted a photo with Tate?"

"Well, no," Beau says. "Which is why we want her to post one with you, get it?"

"No? And, I'm sorry, does that say that we'll get her to dump her boyfriend . . . for *me*?"

"Charm," Beau says, and I think it's the first time she's called me that, which is the only reason I stop spinning out. She's doing this eye thing where it looks like she's watching me over a pair of invisible glasses, and her gaze has a kind of . . . weight to it. "Trust me. This will work. And besides, there's no way you don't know how . . . charming . . . you can be."

I smile at her dad joke, pulling off my real glasses to clean them with the hem of my shirt. But when I put them back on, Beau is still watching me. She doesn't look away or laugh. I feel goose bumps of embarrassment creeping up the back of my neck and I look away. She can't be serious.

"No, I don't. I mean, I'm *not*."

She's quiet for long enough that I hazard a glance back in her direction. She's smirking. "Well, you are," she says. "But don't stress. That's where I come in."

Over the next hour, Beau explains that she will teach me everything I need to know in order to woo Maia Moon.

"I know her," Beau insists. "I know what she likes. I can show you how to get under her skin. And I have no doubt we can have her head over heels for you before prom night."

"If it's that simple," I say, after Beau has listed a few foods Maia loves, ways to touch her that will make her weak, particular things to say and precisely when to say them, "why haven't you done this already? Why won't *you* do it now instead of me?"

Beau's face, which was open, confident, and a little bit playful, shuts like a slammed door. "Because," she says. But she doesn't explain. "Just believe me. You're the best girl for the job."

I want to ask how she knows Maia so well; what their history is; why Maia would be with Tate if she really wants to be with a girl. I want to ask Beau why her face changed like that—

closed itself off the same way Maia's did, like a flower reversing its bloom. I want to ask if her reaction has anything to do with how she feels about the gray-eyed girl who has crushed us both. And if it does, I need to know she won't hate me if, by some miracle, this plan works and Maia starts to like me back.

"I'm down," I tell her, trying to ignore the level of detail with which she's describing the way Maia reacts to everything from fried pickles to secrets. "But we need to establish some ground rules."

Beau crinkles her nose. "Ground rules? Like what?"

"Like, for one: I need to know how you feel about Maia. For real. Because if you like her as much as it seems like you like her, I don't know how comfortable I am with trying to get her to like *me*."

"Why?" Beau asks, like she genuinely can't figure it out.

I shift in my seat, then flick away one of the pothos leaves tickling my ear. "Girl code," I say.

She makes an incredulous face, and for a second she's all eyebrows. "Girl code?"

"Yes, Beau. The unwritten rules of female friendship. I know you think you're tough shit or whatever, but you still have feelings. And I don't want to hurt them."

Beau looks at me like I'm speaking another language, and then something in her stormy-blue eyes, her stormy-blue voice, calms.

"Look. Yes, I liked Maia. And yes, there was a time when I thought she liked me, too. But at this point she's done too much messy shit for me to still want her the way I used to."

"And you're sure that you won't be upset, with me or with yourself, if this somehow works and Maia really starts to like me back?"

The smallest smile I've ever clocked as an actual smile twists Beau's lips. She shakes her head and then her face is open again, like curtains pulling back to reveal a sunny window. "How could anyone ever be mad at you?" she asks. "And anyway, if the Plan works, you'll dump her before I even have a chance to be truly jealous."

I clear my throat. Look away because she's doing that eye thing again. "Whatever. Let's just write that down." I grab the notebook and a pen, and slide them over to my side of the table. I write: *Ground Rules*. And then:

1. Don't hate Charm if the Plan works.

Beau laughs. "Why do we need to write it down?"

"Because it's a rule. Rules are always written down."

She gets a mischievous look on her face. "Except the unwritten ones."

I roll my eyes. "What about the law? That's written down. People have to go to school for years to, like, read and learn all that written-down stuff."

Beau shrugs. "I guess. And I suppose the Constitution is a thing."

I slap the table. "The Constitution! This will be our constitution."

I cross out *Ground Rules* and write, *Charm & Beau's Constitution.*

I tap the end of the pen against my bottom lip. "Both of us should have the option to call the whole thing off, too. Like, if at any point it's all too much for one or both of us, we can stop, kill it with fire, no questions asked."

"Right," Beau says, immediately agreeing in a way I never would have expected her stubborn, bossy ass to. "This has to be something we're both doing by choice the whole time. We're saying yes to this now, but we can always change our minds. Consent ain't permanent," she says, then presses her mouth into a hard line.

"Period," I add with a nod.

I write:

2. Don't hesitate to cancel the Plan if either of us no longer wants to do it.

As I take another sip of my milkshake, Beau's face changes again. She clears her throat and runs her hands through her hair, and if I didn't know better, I'd say she was feeling nervous. "We should probably add a rule about not . . . you know . . . having feelings for each other."

I cackle.

"I'm serious!" she says.

I gather myself as it occurs to me she could be suggesting this rule for my benefit. "Wait. Are you saying this because I'm not your type? I kinda already knew that. If you're into Maia, I know you wouldn't be into me, and you don't have to worry—"

"No, no, no. It's not that." She lowers her already low voice. "It's just that girls tend to . . . I don't know. Like me. Even when I'm not trying to get with them like that."

I lean forward and lower my voice too. "In that case, it's kind of you to . . . let me know." When I start giggling again, she covers the bottom half of her face.

"Beau Carl!" I shout, and then, when Ozzy yells, "Inside voice,

Charm!" across the whole diner, I cringe, apologize, and whisper, "Beau Carl! Are you blushing?"

"Oh my god. No! Forget it," she says.

I'm still half laughing as I say, "Don't you worry, boo. I don't plan on falling for you."

Still, I add it to our constitution as Beau stares at the wall like it's a complex painting:

3. Don't fall in love.

I look at the list she's written, the list I've written right below it. And it's then that part of me wishes I'd met Beau sooner. I wish Beau had been there the last time someone treated my heart like a doormat, to spur me into action. Or even earlier, when it became clear my parents would never be there in the ways I wanted and needed them to be. To show me, even in this vengeful way, that my feelings aren't too much. That they matter.

For a brief moment, I consider telling Beau about Jada. How we met at the inaugural meeting of the Queer Student Association last school year, only a few months after I came out. How Jada had seemed so knowledgeable about all things queer and femme, and how I was immediately attracted to her because expertise has always just done it for me. How she taught me everything I know, transitioning me from a baby gay to a bit more experienced one, only to use that fact against me in one of my most vulnerable moments. But this doesn't feel like the right time to delve into my extensive history of humiliation.

I want to show Beau what she's shown me—that her feelings are important even if she pretends she hasn't been and can't be hurt. Despite being scared, I'll do this for us both.

I'm not very brave, but I am smart. So I make a decision that may have protected me from Maia had I made it sooner: from now on, I'm trusting my head over my messy, mushy heart.

Logically, Beau's list and my rules make sense. Logically, the Plan will work if we do everything right.

So I close the notebook and rest my hands on top. I push it toward Beau.

"When do we start?" I ask.

11
Beau

No one has been allowed to smoke cigarettes indoors for as long as I've been alive, but the bowling alley still smells like my uncle Marv's house. I lean against the shoe counter, watching the big group on Lane 10 vape, little clouds of mist evaporating around them. If Mr. Ben were here, he'd go tell them to cut that shit out, but it's just Milo as the manager today, and the girls on Lane 10 are too hot, so he will of course avoid all interaction. I don't get paid enough to care, so I just handle the rest of the customers and occasionally check my phone. This time, when I do, there's a text from Charm:

Pulling up.

It feels weird to think about a girl other than Maia coming behind the counter. Maia was the only girl I ever hooked up with at work. At first she'd come with her friends. If I was working concessions, she would start meandering to my counter between turns. I'd keep the flirting to a minimum when her friends were nearby, but I remember the first time she circled back after they left, hanging out for a little while, being flirty. She started doing it regularly after that: coming before her friends, or staying after, leaning on my counter. We'd talk about music and she'd rest her hand on my arm or pull on my shirt while she rhapsodized about whatever indie band she'd gotten into that week. After about two weeks of her little pop-ups, there came a day when she said she was hungry. I asked her if she wanted a pretzel, but she answered with "Is your boss here?" When I told her no, she said, "What's back there?" Before I knew it, she'd ducked under the counter and into the supply closet. When I followed her, she flipped off the lights and I could feel her smiling while I kissed her against the shelves of popcorn kernels.

"Size six," someone says, and I snap out of it.

Charm stands staring at me with her eyes round, eyebrows arched a little sarcastically. I get the feeling that this time she's the one who's been watching me zone out for just a second too long.

"Do you actually wear a size six?" I ask, turning to the shelves of shoes. "Those are like baby feet."

"One, yes I do, and two, no they're not. But ew, do not actually give me those shoes."

"You've got something against shoes that have been worn by hundreds of people for thirty years?"

She considers this.

"That's actually romantic in a 'vastness of the human experience' way, but I hate bowling. And that's not what I'm here for."

"You sure aren't," I say, and smile at her. "I have a chair for you and everything."

"Am I allowed back there?" she asks, looking doubtful.

"Yeah, it's fine. The only person who would care isn't here. Just don't, like, empty the cash register behind my back or something."

"I'll check with you before committing any crimes. Promise."

I lift the counter section to let her in, and as she passes by me, a fruity smell follows her: it's sweet, like a freshly cut melon.

"You smell amazing," I say. "What is that?"

She pauses before sitting, and I can tell by the look on her face that I've made her shy.

"Have the lessons already started?" she says, her voice going up. "I wasn't ready."

That's why she's here—to practice for the reeling in of Maia Moon. The plan is for Charm to watch me flirt with any girls who come in, and I'll explain what works and what doesn't. Sort of a real-time, in-person handbook. It feels kind of douchey, to be honest, and Celine would literally puke if she knew I was masquerading as some kind of Lesbonova. But the truth is, girls really like me and always have: I may never have had an actual girlfriend, but I know what turns a girl's head, and more importantly, I know what turns Maia's.

But still . . .

"This feels kind of wack now that we're actually doing it," I admit.

Charm has just sat down, but at my words she instantly leans forward like she's going to get up again.

"Which part?" she says quickly. She looks like she could bolt. "You training me to be a Venus flytrap for cute girls, or all of it?"

I laugh and wave her back down before she stands. Even if I feel kind of like a fraud—a girlfriendless misfit teaching another girlfriendless misfit how to reel in the prom queen—I'm determined to see Maia take a swig of her own medicine. And hanging out with somebody as fun as Charm is just an added bonus.

"No, no," I reassure her. "The Plan is genius. Just . . . this part. Upon further consideration of the steps, I don't think you need help flirting with girls."

"Um, trust me, I do." She gets this look on her face sometimes when I can tell she's feeling insecure: it's like there's a string in what's being said that's tied directly to something else. It seems too soon to ask personal questions, so I limbo under the string.

"You're gorgeous and funny," I say. "I'm sure you do just fine."

"See! You're doing it right now!" she cries, pointing at me like I'm a girl doing math in Salem, Massachusetts.

This time I burst out laughing. She's almost a cartoon character, her face is so expressive. Not in a goofy way, just a . . . very visually fun way?

"Doing what?!"

"You say things that make girls blush, and it's like you do it without thinking. Like the same way someone digests food."

"I make you blush?" I say in my huskiest voice.

"Goddamn it, Beau!"

"Fine, fine, that one was on purpose. Wait, you think my flirting is like digesting food? That doesn't sound hot."

She sighs.

"Just an example. What I mean is you flirt without any extra mental effort. Whereas with me, if I want to even speak to a girl I think is cute, it takes like weeks of preparation and a series of intense pep talks from Ezra."

"And yet . . . Maia was ready to kiss you at the party."

It makes us both squirm. Like I've pressed on the matching bruises on our hearts.

"Well, now *I'll* be ready," Charm says. She sweeps her arm out regally, like a queen commanding the players on a stage. A queen who looks very uncertain and is putting on a brave face for the peasants. But a queen nonetheless. "Begin!"

I'm still feeling a little like an impostor, so I turn to the counter before she sees.

Except there's . . . no one there.

"I will," I say. "As soon as . . . you know. Someone comes."

"How embarrassing," Charm drawls, teasing. "Beau Carl, chick magnet, and no one to magnetize!"

"They'll come," I insist, laughing.

"Sure, lover girl."

It feels good to laugh. It feels good to be at my job and not—

Charm interrupts my thoughts, studying me. "So is this where you would hang out with Maia?"

The question surprises me. I guess I'm not used to anyone knowing my business. After those months of regular visits at work—occasional pauses when she and Tate were doing their back-and-forth bullshit—Maia faded back into the distance she came out of. (That would be a great song if I didn't have writer's block.) But either way, now I see why she stopped coming to the bowling alley. In the landscape of Maia's beautiful life, I became background; Charm became foreground.

"Yeah," I answer. "She would come flirt on the low when her friends were here, or she'd hang back after." I pause, then laugh. "You know, I don't even have her phone number? She would message me on Instagram sometimes, but usually she'd just show up. I should block her, honestly, so her damn makeup videos will stop showing up in my feed."

Charm seems to take this in, looking thoughtful, then gazes around the bowling alley.

"It must be nice to be able to worry less about that now," she says. "I feel like that would make me super anxious if I just never knew if she was going to show up. Or when she wouldn't."

Then it's like she does a double take at her own words.

"Yikes, that was so shitty of me," she says, eyes wide. "You're over here dealing with your feelings about this girl and I'm all 'must be nice she treated you like shit and disappeared.'"

I can't help it—I laugh again.

"No, no," I say. "Honestly, it's weird—I was literally thinking that just before you said it. How it's kind of a relief. Sitting here at work and not worrying about whether she's going to show up and hang over there acting like . . ."

I don't really feel like finishing the sentence. That's a lot of feelings, and I don't personally enjoy those, so I just shrug, and then we sit quietly for a minute. When I glance at her, she has her thinking face on.

Fuck it, I'm asking.

"So is Maia the only girl you've dated?"

"Me and Maia were *not* dating," she says quickly.

"Well, you might be soon," I say, and bump the side of her foot with mine. "But you know what I mean."

"There was one other girl," she says slowly. "Jada."

"Jada," I repeat.

"Wait, here come people," Charm says, nodding over the counter.

I can't help but think she conjured them, but I turn to look, and sure enough, they're real.

When it comes to girls I flirt with at work, it usually goes one of two ways. There's one in a group of girls, or—more often—there's a girl who shows up with her boyfriend who makes eye contact for just a second too long.

Today it's the latter. She has light brown skin and black eyes, and her hair falls in waves around her face. She's pretty as hell and her boyfriend is on the phone, with what sounds like friends who are meeting them there.

"What size?" I ask the girl. I can feel Charm watching. It makes me self-conscious, but I try to ignore it. The girl across the counter is giving all the signals: holding eye contact, smiling the sort of crooked smile girls do when they're interested but don't want it to be obvious.

"Eight," she says.

I get the shoes and hold her gaze. With other customers I would ask her what size for him, since he's distracted, but instead I say:

"Do you like bowling?"

"Do I like bowling?" she echoes with a laugh. "I'm here, aren't I?"

"Doesn't mean you like it." I fold my arms on the counter and lean in just a fraction of an inch.

"It's . . . okay," she says. A one-shoulder shrug.

"But it doesn't excite you."

"Who gets excited about bowling?"

A cheer from Lane 13 goes up.

"They do," I say, smiling.

She laughs.

"You have a great laugh," I tell her. "Really. What's your name?"

And there it is: she blushes.

"Mariah," she answers.

"You look like a Mariah."

I don't smile, and I maintain steady eye contact. I never really have a goal when I flirt with girls—they set the pace, and the destination is wherever they decide. For Mariah, it feels like enough to have made her blush. It spreads, and what was left of her laugh fades off her mouth.

"What's *your* name?" she says, almost a demand.

"I'm Beau."

I put out my hand, but I don't wait for her to shake it. I gently lift hers from where it rests on top of the shoes and give it one soft shake.

Her boyfriend hangs up the phone.

"Rod and everybody will be here in a minute," he tells her. Then to me: "You have a size eleven?"

I give Mariah one more smile and then retrieve her boyfriend's shoes. When they walk away, I stay watching, waiting for . . . There it is. She's about ten feet away when she looks over her shoulder. And when she sees me still watching, she gives that half smile again, like I knew she would.

I turn back to Charm and find her sitting with her mouth open. She also has a notebook open on her lap, pen in hand.

"What the fuck?" she laughs, wrinkling her nose.

"Are you taking literal notes?" I ask.

"Right under her boyfriend's radar? Holy shit." She shakes her head, and she is indeed taking literal notes because she writes something else down.

I shrug. "Not my fault she was into me."

"You're kind of a terrorist, Beau."

"Hey." I hold up my hands. "I didn't say anything terrible! I crossed no lines."

"I guess not, but damn. *How* do you do that?"

"I'm just honest," I say. "And I listen to what they say and how they say it when I ask a question. I didn't lie to her or spit game. She *did* look like a Mariah. She *did* have a great laugh."

"There's more to it than that," she insists.

I think for a second. "It's like taking what people see as typical girl interactions and . . . shifting them out of neutral? Like straight girls will say, 'You look like a Mariah,' but you can't do it in that usual friendish way. Questions are questions within a question. Statements have to make them ask *themselves* questions. Like I said she looks like a Mariah. Now she's thinking, 'What does she mean by that? Does she think Mariahs are hot? Does she think *I'm* hot? How do I feel about that?'"

"Wow, sexy psychology," Charm says in a note-taking voice. "It's not what you said, it's how you said it."

"How do I say it?"

"Like . . . like . . ." She fishes for words, tapping her pen on her bottom lip. "Like sex on toast."

I laugh hard as hell. *"What?"*

"Toast is wholesome and, like, a regular breakfast food. But you put . . . sex on it?"

"Sex on Toast should be a band name," I tell her. "But yes, it's all about tone, I guess. And I also mean that literally. Like, when straight girls give each other a compliment, they're all 'you are so *beautiful.*' You know? Like almost high-pitched. Don't do that."

"Yeah, white girls anyway. Goes up an octave."

"Right. None of that."

Charm makes a note, then raises her head.

"So what else, Yoda?"

"Oh my god." I roll my eyes. "Look, it's not like me giving you tips means I'm some master of all this. Like I said, Maia already liked you enough to be close to kissing you. She just . . ."

I pause, and I feel the bruise on my heart again. Whatever we were or weren't, I had begun to know Maia. When she would get back together with Tate, she wouldn't show up at my job for a few days, and when she did, she would be almost shy. We'd talk for much longer before she slid her hands into my pockets and whispered in my ear. We'd talk about real shit—her dad was basically the dude version of my mom, a specter she rarely saw—and I'd start to see the things that made her tick, apart from how she liked to be touched.

But saying any of this doesn't really seem helpful to the mission. Honestly, just thinking about it makes me want to hide under a rock.

"She just likes to be drawn out sometimes," I finally say. "One minute she'll be in your face, and the next minute she wants you to chase her. So if we're gonna get her back, we use what we know. That's all. I'm not the Pussy Whisperer. This is just . . . friendly advice."

"Pussy Whisperer," she says, closing her eyes and shaking her head. "I just . . . oh my god. Okay. So what's some other friendly advice then, Non-Pussy Whisperer?"

"Look her in the eye, always," I say. "Especially when you compliment her or notice something about her. So to recap: the difference between this and straight girls complimenting their friends is eye contact and tone. And, ya know, sex, obviously."

"Sex," she says. "Check." Her voice is casual, but I can tell she's flustered.

"Look at me when you say it."

Her eyes dart up. "What?"

"Say 'sex' to my face," I say.

She laughs, abruptly, almost like a sneeze.

"Why?"

"Because you're squirmy!" I say, laughing. "Maia can be shy, and you can't *both* be shy."

She looks hesitant, like something I said struck a nerve. I rein it in.

"I'm not saying you have to talk about sex with her," I say

quickly. "Like, not until you're ready. I just mean looking me in the eye and saying 'sex' is good practice for getting over shyness."

She seems to relax. I wait.

"Sex," she says, staring me in the eyes. She winces, laughs again. "Sex."

"Again," I command, laughing now too.

"Sex!" she cries. "Sex!"

We dissolve into laughter, and when she catches her breath, she dabs at her eyes with the corner of her T-shirt. It exposes her stomach, soft and curving at the waist. I don't say it out loud because I don't want to make her self-conscious again, but she's going to reel Maia in like a fish.

"So yes, eye contact," I say. "Never look away. It should feel like weight. You know? Oh, and don't call her 'girl.' That's full-on friend zone."

"Do I really need to worry about the friend zone?" she says. "I mean, like you said, we've already almost kissed."

That catches me a little off guard, hearing her say it this time, and for a moment I'm back at the party, walking in and seeing them standing close. Seeing Maia's eyes wall off when she looked at me.

"True," I say. "The parameters are a little different here, because you don't have to give 'I'm gay' cues like you would if she were a stranger. She knows you're gay. That's why all this is even happening."

Charm studies her notebook.

"So honestly, a lot of this is stuff I would do anyway? Like asking questions and actually listening to the answers."

"Yes, but . . ."

"But what?"

77

"Eye contact, Monty!" I say, clapping my hands. "Sometimes Maia is a shark, but after what happened at the party, she's probably going to need extra encouragement to get comfortable enough to let you behind the force field again. Remember what I said about drawing her out? She's gonna need that. Eye contact!"

Charm does . . . the exact opposite. She drops her eyes and her bashful energy skyrockets. I step toward her and put a finger under her chin, lifting it.

"Up here, Monty," I say. "Look at me until I say stop."

We hold each other's gaze. Her eyes are the richest shade of brown. If I were a poet, I'd know just how to describe them, but instead I just swim in them as she struggles not to look away. She bites her lip with the effort.

"That's better," I say quietly, then smile. "We'll keep practicing. Even if that means you shouting the word 'sex' in crowded places."

She stands from the chair, tucks the notebook and pen in her back pocket, then ducks under the counter.

"Who knew Lesbian Lessons were like boot camp," she says in a voice like she just ran a marathon. "Jesus. I need, like, a protein shake."

She looks like she's leaving, and I realize I'm a little disappointed she's not hanging out longer. When I saw her with Maia at the party, the instinct to hate her was like a tidal wave and a surfboard handed to me on a silver platter. But she's nice. And fun. Kay's been gone for eight months, and it's not until now that I realize it's been that long since I hung out with someone who wasn't (a) Celine and Daniel or (b) trying to get in my pants.

I push off the counter where I've been leaning.

"No pain, no gain. Isn't that what Tate and his army of orcs always say?"

She makes a gagging face.

"Anyway, I must leave you. I have an appointment," she says.

I wonder where she's going, but I don't ask. "Okay. Practice the eye-contact thing," I say, like I'm assigning homework.

"Fiiiine. What's next?"

"Are you gonna be tutoring Maia anytime soon?"

"Well," she says, looking uncertain, "we had a session scheduled for the day of the promposal, and she rescheduled. I thought she'd cancel it, but she hasn't yet, so . . ."

"Brilliant," I say. "That'll be your chance."

"To make eye contact?" she says, rolling her eyes.

"Hopefully more than that," I say. "The Plan has steps, and you're gonna climb them."

"That's very aspirational," she says in a slanted voice, but still smiles, and waves when she leaves.

After she's gone, I lean against the counter. I can still smell that sweet melon scent. It's so different from the smell Maia would leave when she left, which kind of blended into the leather. The sweetness of Charm's perfume—or lotion, or whatever it is—actually overpowers the stench of cigarettes. I glance at the chair where she was sitting and notice something by its leg on the floor.

I go to pick it up—it's a tube of lip gloss. It must have fallen out of her pocket.

I set it on the counter next to me so she'll see it if she comes back. I can't help it: when I look at it, my mind wanders. Was this the lip gloss she was wearing when Maia leaned in to kiss her at the party? After hanging out with Charm, I can absolutely see why Maia would be into her. Enough to . . .

I fish out my notebook from my bag and open it up to the

pencil tucked inside, staring down at the song I've been trying to write for two weeks.

I have two lines.

> *Button up, go invisible*
> *Disappearing girl, my god you're so predictable.*

It's not exactly Pulitzer material.

Still, sometimes the simplest songs I write feel the truest. But that's also why I haven't been able to finish it. Every time I try . . .

Jesus, feelings are like sharks. They smell a little blood, and all of a sudden the water is full of them. For once I wish the bowling alley were busy, just to crowd out some of the thoughts in my head, the main one being: *Maia likes Charm enough to risk being close to her in public. To risk being visible.*

Why not me?

12
Charm

Enzo Espinosa has a very hot older sister.

It's unfortunate (for me) that she happens to be visiting from college this weekend, because after I leave the bowling alley, I'm still a bit blushy from Beau touching my chin and staring into my soul when I ring Enzo's doorbell and *she* answers.

Noemi Espinosa is the only girl I've ever had a sex dream about. She's lived in my imagination since I was a freshman at Brookville and I saw her in the first field hockey game I ever attended. I'm not really into any sports or balls, but I was *very* into watching her run around in one of those tiny uniform skorts. Waking up grinding on your own pillow is a very humbling experience. Especially when you're not out yet—even to yourself.

I try really hard not to picture her in that uniform after she opens the door.

She grins at me and tilts her head like I'm a small, fluffy puppy. Her wild hair is in a pile of dark waterfall spirals, and I swear her big mocha eyes literally sparkle. "Hey, mamacita," she says. "Aren't you adorable. You lost?"

When I recover from the tiny stroke I have at her calling me adorable, it's clear she has absolutely no idea who I am. It's sobering to realize you were barely a flickering star to someone who was as huge as a planet in your universe, so my eyes, which went wide at the sight of her, slowly return to their normal size. I crash back down to earth.

"Umm, no," I croak, then clear my throat. "No. Definitely not lost."

"Well, the only boy here your age is fruitier than a farmers' market."

I snort. I can't help it. But then I think maybe I could practice some of what I've just learned from Beau on her. Noemi doesn't remember me, so I have nothing to lose. I lean against the doorframe. I look her up and down. "Oh yeah? Well, lucky for you, so am I." On the word "you," I shoot finger guns at her for some reason, like I'm a forty-year-old white guy.

Noemi frowns a little, but even that is cute—the tiny wrinkle creasing her forehead, the way her lashes brush her cheeks as she blinks. "Um, okay," she says in a way that lets me know I've fumbled. I stand up straight again, instantly realizing how cringe I just was. I look anywhere except at her.

Beau specifically said not to try and spit game. And I, having never attempted to spit anything but my gum after it's lost its flavor, should have known better. *Head,* I think to myself. *Use your head.* "Look," I start, about to apologize, when she turns and shouts into the space behind her. "Lorenzo, one of your cute, weird friends is here!"

By the time Enzo shows up five seconds later, my face is on fire.

"Harsh, sis," Enzo says, appearing beside her, his black curls a chaotic riot all over his head, a soft-looking towel draped around his neck. He's blowing on his nails, which seem to be freshly painted. They shimmer in a glittery shade of purple.

"Hey, you," he says to me. "Ignore her. Come on in."

I step into Enzo's warm house, the whole place smelling of something freshly fried.

"Charm City," Enzo says, "you might remember my sister, Noemi. Emi, this is Charm."

I wave like the whole exchange at the door didn't happen, hoping my face isn't screaming, *Hi, hello, yes, I had a wet dream about you once.*

Noemi somehow looks like she's never seen me before *and* like she's trying to pretend she remembers me, her eyes bright and friendly but empty. I try not to take it personally.

"So where do you want me?" I ask Enzo as we move deeper into the house. I'm here to braid his hair, a little side business I started last year after half the dance team asked me to give them beaded cornrows before homecoming. They all wanted the same *Lemonade* braids I'd done for Jada, and I realized that even though they were all friends with her (she was co-captain), I should probably make them pay, because it wasn't like any of them were friends with *me*. I got pretty good at braiding by watching videos and trying out different styles on myself and Aunt Miki so we didn't have to spend so much at salons after we both decided to go natural. And then working at a salon over the summer made me feel like a low-key pro.

Now I kind of love it. I think hair might even be something I want to do long-term. But it's hard to talk or even think about it as a real possibility when Aunt Miki won't hear a word about me doing anything after graduation that isn't college. She's the blue-collar queen, but she always says, "You're smart like Bree, so you need to use that big, beautiful brain of yours." I always tell her how smart she is, how I'd rather be more like her than my flyby mama any day. But she doesn't listen.

"We were playing video games in my room," Enzo says, bringing me back.

"Till *someone* decided we needed a manicure break," Noemi adds.

"You're so dramatic. We were at a checkpoint!" Enzo replies.

"Yeah, and I just happened to be owning your ass seconds before you decided your cuticles were of the utmost importance," she says, laughing.

I glance over my shoulder at his sister, who is trailing us down the hall.

"You like to game?" I ask her. She does that head tilt again.

"Don't sound so surprised. I mostly play with Enzo when I'm at school," she says. "It was the one way I could make sure he still talked to me once I left home."

"I'm booked and busy, what can I say?" Enzo almost sings.

"That rehearsal schedule is pretty intense," I agree as we turn into Enzo's bedroom, which is all dark walls, mirrors, and clothes piles. A Broadway musical soundtrack is blasting from his Bluetooth speaker.

"Yep. Sometimes it feels like Mr. Franklin thinks he works at a performance arts high school. I was actually hella surprised Ezra did the fall show, since it was basketball season."

I smile to myself, but I don't tell Enzo that Ezra did it for *him*. "Other than handling balls, lifting heavy things is his passion," I say. I don't hear how it sounds until it's a little too late to do anything about it.

An awkward silence passes over us (probably because I'm so awkward, *Jesus*). "Kidding," I mutter, as I busy myself with getting ready to do his hair.

I sit at the foot of Enzo's bed and pull out my wide-tooth and rattail combs, some shea butter, rosemary oil, and gel. Enzo sits on a pillow right in front of me so his head is between my legs, and I waste no time digging into his curls. I've done his hair a few times now, and he always wants the same style—cornrows straight back with zigzag parts. Noemi shakes up a bottle of shimmering green polish and starts on her own nails, and I'm surprised she's still hanging around. But they seem like the kind of siblings who enjoy each other's company. I wonder what that's like.

Since she's staying, maybe I'll have a chance to try the whole flirting thing again—and actually follow Beau's rules this time.

"You wanna listen to something different, Charm?" Enzo asks. I'm trying to figure out how to get Noemi to look at me instead of her nails. Beau's rule about eye contact is echoing through my head, so I hand him my phone and tell him to cue up one of my playlists, that he can pick whichever one looks good to him.

"Noemi," I say before I can overthink it. "You don't remember me, do you?" I time the question so that I'm finishing a braid just in time to look up. I see her squint at me, like she's trying to make my features rearrange themselves into something recognizable. I smirk when she shakes her head slowly, and I force myself not to look away.

"Well, I remember you," I say, trying to embody that *tone* Beau showed me.

She squints again, but this time it seems different. Less confused and more . . . interested. "Oh yeah?" she says.

Just then my phone starts ringing, and Ezra's name appears on the screen. "Ooh," Enzo says, because the phone is still in his hand. "Does he know you're here with me?"

"Can't remember if I told him or not, but I share my location with Ezra," I say without thinking. "So if he checked it, he does." I put my hand out, expecting Enzo to give me the phone, but he answers the call instead.

"Hey, you," Enzo says. I can see a tiny thumbnail of Enzo's face on the screen, because it's a video call and he's all fluttering eyelashes, a crooked smirk on his lips.

Ezra, who takes up the rest of the screen, stares blankly at his crush for a few long seconds. Then he blinks once and says, "Hi?"

"Charmy's in my bedroom," Enzo continues, then he flicks out his tongue and looks off-screen at his nails. "Jealous?" he asks, glancing back at the phone.

Ezra blushes so hard even his freckles seem a little darker. "Umm," he says, his voice an octave higher than normal.

Half of me feels like I should save Ezra, because I'm not used to seeing him so discombobulated, but it's also kinda funny. My confident bestie, bested by a boy he likes, despite all his bravado when he was trying to get me to talk to Maia. The other half of me wants to listen to and learn from Enzo. I knew he was a flirt, but seeing it in action is like watching another sexy breakfast food get plated. If Beau is sex on toast, Enzo is sex on *French* toast *at brunch*—everything about his moves is decadent. He's not subtle at all.

"Um, Charm, I'll call you back," Ezra says in a panic. Then my screen goes blank.

"Booooo," Enzo whines. "He's no fun."

I'm about to tell Enzo he may have just given poor Ezra a heart attack when I realize Noemi's eyes are still on me. And when she says, "Wait. What do you remember?" I'm a bit shocked that she's interested enough to circle back. Maybe these lessons will be more useful than I thought if just *looking* at Noemi has her looking right back. I return my attention to her.

"I remember seeing you for the first time," I say, and the way she smiles makes me smile. I look down at Enzo's hair, even though I know I'm not supposed to, grateful I have a legit reason to break eye contact. "You were playing field hockey. You looked"—I sweep my gaze back over to her, thinking of Beau's rule about telling the truth—"really beautiful."

Noemi rolls her eyes. "You thought I looked beautiful at a field hockey game? With no makeup on, my hair in a frizzy, sweaty ponytail, my knees probably scraped up and bleeding?"

I finish another braid and look back up in a way that I hope erases her doubt. "You did. You looked tough and badass, and all those things you mentioned? The messy hair and bloody knees? That stuff *is* beautiful. Sexy even. Because that shit is *real*. I mean, have you seen you today? I almost passed out when you opened the front door."

I think I'm being a little *too* honest, because something feels off. This doesn't feel as smooth as it did when Beau made the moves on Mariah. But instead of shutting up while I'm maybe slightly ahead, I start getting nervous, which makes me talk more.

"I mean, you know you're gorgeous, don't you? You have to know that. A baby gay like me didn't stand a chance when a girl like you was just casually walking down Brookville High's hallway in those field hockey skorts and, like, if I hadn't been sure I liked girls before I saw you in that uniform, I *definitely* knew after...."

I finish another braid and push my glasses back up from where they've slid down my nose. When I meet her eyes again, Noemi is watching me, but much less like I'm just a cute, clueless puppy.

Enzo chuckles and pipes up with, "Jesus, Charm City. Thirsty much?"

"Says the boy who mentioned his bedroom two seconds after saying hello to Ezra," I shoot back quickly.

"Oop!" Noemi says. Then she cracks up laughing. She puts down the green polish, even though she's only painted six of her nails, and cuts her eyes at me in a way that feels dangerous.

"When you finish his hair, can you braid mine?" she asks.

"Um," I say. "Sure. Just, uh, find a photo? Of what you want me to do?"

"K," she says, standing up to leave. "I'll be in my room."

She doesn't wink at me, but something about her face as she peeks over her shoulder makes it feel like she has. I pretend to be very focused on making the next part in Enzo's hair.

"Damn, Charm," Enzo says when she's gone. "That was . . . immaculate."

"What do you mean?" I almost whisper, my heart still pounding from Noemi's heavy expression as she walked away.

He chuckles again and shakes his head in a way that almost makes me lose my grip on the strands of his hair I'm holding. "My sister is tender-headed as hell. She hates getting her hair done."

I have to bite my bottom lip to keep from smiling. If after one lesson my amateur moves are working with Noemi, I might actually have a chance to make the Plan work on Maia.

13
Beau

Asking Celine to borrow the car is never a simple request—it's sort of a black market deal. I have a license, but Mom has forbidden me from driving Celine's blue Buick since the time I borrowed the car to go see Carmella Malone while her boss was on vacation. (Everything was fine until I backed into a bush and then, unbeknownst to me, drove all the way home with it dragging from the bumper.) And then there was the run-in I had with a grocery cart. To my credit, it was rolling across the street. To . . . not my credit . . . it was in a pedestrian walkway. Daniel called me Cart Killer for six months, and my mom banned me from ever being behind the wheel. But that was nine months ago. And now I mentally brake at all crosswalks, even when I'm in the passenger seat.

Celine does let me borrow the car sometimes without telling Mom, but I always have to have a good reason, and I always have to do something for her in return. So when I walk up to Wonderdough, the bakery Daniel's parents own, I'm already mentally preparing my request and brainstorming the collateral I can offer my sister to woo her.

Celine works at the bakery a few random days a week, but always Saturdays. She sits in the window and reads while Daniel works until the post-soccer-practice rush, when she goes behind the counter and helps until they sell out. Wonderdough is the best bakery in town. When they're out, they're out. It's never stayed open past one.

It's eleven a.m. and Celine is in the window, right where I knew she'd be.

I stand on the other side of the glass, staring at her. She's absorbed in her book, so she doesn't notice. I stare harder and harder, but she's really locked in. Slowly I lean closer to the window. Closer and closer, until my face is fully pressed against the glass. I smoosh my nose and cheek against it and wait.

Finally her eyebrows twitch. I'm in her light. Her eyes shift up and . . .

She jumps so hard she almost knocks over her coffee, and through the glass I see her mouth, *Jesus Christ!*

Cackling, I enter the shop.

"Goddamn it, Beau!"

She pretends to hate it, but she loves it.

"Beau Carl," Daniel's mom squawks. "You better—"

"I know, I know! Sorry!" I grab the Windex and towel from behind the counter, dash back outside, and wipe away the smudge I left. When I return the Windex, Mrs. Kim rolls her eyes, but she laughs, too. She always says I remind her of her sister.

"What are you doing here, Beau?" Celine drawls. "You still owe me ten dollars, if you're about to ask me for—"

"Nope. Don't need money. My needs are . . . more complicated than that."

She shuts her book. I can tell it's not one of the books for the online courses she takes—but this would be the wrong time to ask whether she only cares about college when it comes to me enrolling.

In any case, Celine stares at me knowingly.

"Where are you going? I'll just take you."

"Nope."

She narrows her eyes. This is when Mom says Celine looks like our dad, but I can't quite tell from the photos I've seen. I think it's something you'd have to have seen him do.

"Is this about a girl?"

"Yes. But not how you think."

"Is this the girl whose panties you have?"

I pause, thinking.

"Yes, but not how you think."

"Give that girl her underwear back!" Daniel calls around a mouthful of donut. His mom smacks him.

"If Mom finds out I've been letting you use the car, she'll pitch a fit, Beau. And she'll blame me."

"How would the Invisible Matriarch even know?" I ask.

"She's working, Beau," she says, and I realize I've dipped too close to something un-fun. I dodge away.

"Don't I always make it worth your while?" I say, waggling my eyebrows.

She crosses her arms. "What do you have to offer?"

"Well, let me see." I pull up the Notes app on my phone. "According to my records, you're sick of the third stair squeaking at the house. I can fix that."

"What the hell? How did you even know that?"

"Well, for starters, I hear you say, 'God, I'm so fucking sick of this stair squeaking' every time you pass my room."

She glares at me.

"And you, what, keep a list of things that I complain about? To barter with?"

"I mean, yes, exactly. What else would I do?"

"Oh, I don't know, just *fix* it on your own? To be *nice*?"

I laugh. "Yeah right. So, third stair. Check. Give me four hours with the car and that stair will never bother you again."

"Three hours."

"Three and a half."

"Three," she says, stone-eyed.

"Ugh, fine. Deal. Keys, please."

"The Cart Killer is released onto the streets!" Daniel hollers. "No Target parking lot is safe!"

"Can it, Kim!" I shout.

"Everyone stop yelling!" Mrs. Kim yells.

"Bye," I say, still shouting.

"At least work on some lyrics later!" Celine yells after me. "One shiny new song for the show would help us make an impression if the reviewer comes!"

"Maybe!"

I really am a careful driver. And even if I weren't, it's dumb that ever since I hit the cart nobody wants to let me drive, because how do you get better at something if you never get to practice? This is why I'm on my way to Charm's house, actually. She told me she practiced the flirting rules and felt good about it—I wonder if that means she's ready to engage with Maia. Prom inches closer, after all. It feels symbolic. Prom queen and prom king both getting dumped? Iconic.

I follow the directions on my phone screen while also keeping a close watch for carts and pedestrians. Charm gave me her address with the ominous warning, **Brace yourself.** Then didn't answer when I replied, **????** Luckily, Ezra is walking up just as I park on the street outside the cute, flower-covered town house where my directions say Charm lives.

"Beau," Ezra calls. He gives me a cool stare. He definitely still thinks I'm a dick. "You're here for the Dinner, I presume."

"Dinner? Isn't it kind of early? And wait, why did you say 'the Dinner' all weird, like you're Hannibal Lecter?"

"Today is . . . a complicated day," Ezra says.

"Complicated how? Charm told me to brace myself but didn't tell me why."

"Ohh," he says, and momentarily softens. "Well, her parents are here for a visit. They pop up on her and Aunt Miki every now and then with her brother and wanna do a little catch-up. I'm always invited for distraction."

He pauses, looking me up and down.

"And now you are too, apparently."

"Dude, she didn't say anything about dinner," I say, aghast. "I would have brought something!"

"Oh it's not that kind of dinner," he says. "It's kinda . . . tense? And mostly Charm and Aunt Miki wanna get it over with, so they have a really early dinner. The best part is her brother Dallas. He's a sweet kid."

"So why don't they . . . ?" I trail off, not wanting to be rude.

"Live with her? I'll let her tell you the long version, but the short version is they had Charm really young, so Aunt Miki stepped in to raise her. Then they got older and tried it once, for a year. It didn't work out, so she moved back in with Miki."

"Awkward," I say.

"Yup. So now they come visit every few months, but it's kind of a pain in the ass for Charm."

Ezra leads the way to the front door, and when we reach it, he opens it without knocking. He does, however, stick his head in first and shout:

"Ezra has arrived, and I'm coming in! I found a lost white girl wandering the sidewalk, so can she come too?"

Charm's head appears around the corner of the hall.

"You found what? Oh! Beau! I'm glad you're both here. I need to show you something."

Ezra yanks off his shoes inside the door, so I do too, and the next thing I know I'm walking down a hallway and emerging in the kitchen, where Charm's aunt Miki turns from the stove to wave.

"I know you!" she says. "You always order hash browns, extra crispy."

"Hi!" I say, waving back. "Nice to see you again, ma'am."

"Miki is fine."

She's wearing a frilly black apron covered in skulls with chef hats—it's clearly from some goth Etsy shop. It suits her vibe.

"Do you get tired of cooking?" I ask. "My mom says after working at the hospital all night that if I break my leg, talk to somebody else. I can help if you need it."

Aunt Miki's face breaks into a warm smile. "Charm, you hear that? Beau offered to *help me*. Not just eat everything. Imagine that!"

"I always offer! You always say no! And anyway, don't you know I'm in a crisis?" Charm says.

"When aren't you?" Miki replies. "But nah, I'm good. You hang out with your friends."

"Okay, if you're sure," I say.

I glance at Charm, and she's looking at me with a funny expression on her face.

"I'm not trying to stay for dinner," I say quickly, before she can say I'm not invited. "I was just offering to help."

She wrinkles her forehead in a frown I'm starting to learn is her *Are you serious?* face.

"Why would I ask you to come over around the time we're having dinner and not *also* be inviting you to eat with us? Do you think I'm some kind of heathen?"

"Who thinks you're a heathen?" someone calls from the next room.

Charm briefly closes her eyes, sighs, and then opens them. She gestures for Ezra and me to follow her.

In the living room sit the people I assume are Charm's parents—they're on the couch looking not uncomfortable, but not comfortable, either. Charm's dad is long-limbed and narrow-waisted, with skin the same rich shade as Charm's. Her mom is clearly where she gets her killer curves and big brown eyes. Their outfits feel too trendy for a mom and dad to wear, and that's when I remember Ezra saying they had Charm young. They're sitting close, but I can tell they feel like outsiders here, even though they're with family.

"No one thinks I'm a heathen," Charm says. I note her forced smile. Some people would take their discomfort and turn it outward, make everything awkward for everyone. Not Charm. I can tell she wants to keep things smooth, even if she'd rather not be in this room. And then I realize it might kind of suck for Charm to have to introduce her parents *as* her parents when to her they probably don't feel like parents at all. I'd feel the same way. At this point, if my mother were ever around long enough to introduce to someone, I don't think I could say, *This is my mom,* without a little bitterness.

"Hi, I'm Beau," I say, waving. I glance at Charm. "I heard you have a cool brother. Where's he?"

95

"He was sitting there playing his Switch two seconds ago," Charm's mom says. She smiles at me, and it feels the same way Charm's grins feel—filled with light. "I'm Bree, by the way. Are you a hugger? I'm a hugger." She stands and hugs me before I can answer. "Chauncey," the dad says, awkwardly reaching for my hand. He's tall but not broad, and I can imagine him as a nerdy high schooler, feeling lucky he bagged a girl like Bree. I bet he's where Charm gets her smarts. And maybe her anxiety, too.

Miki emerges from the kitchen, looking around.

"That daggone game. What's it called? *Pizza Rat*?"

"*Pizza Rat*!" I say. "Oh man, I love *Pizza Rat*!"

"You play *Pizza Rat*??" Charm says, incredulous.

"It's so good," I say. I try not to nerd out about video games, because it's not really something that girls tend to be into when you're trying to flirt. But *Pizza Rat* is for me what yoga is for other people. "There's this board where you have to roll these big cheeses down from these shelves in just the right order. . . ."

"That's the board I'm on," says a voice, and a second later a head pops out from behind a huge potted plant by the window. "How do you get the ramp to let down? I've been trying for an hour."

"Oh, I'll show you," I say, and practically fling myself across the room. "Here, go to that alley."

Dallas has Charm's focus and his eyes fly over the screen, following my instructions the same way she takes notes. He has the face of a kid becoming a not-kid—baby fat being shed, serious expression. He probably feels how tense this dinner is too.

The rat on-screen hops on the spoon that acts as a catapult for a sugar cube, knocking down the ramp.

"Yes!" Dallas cries. "Were you a rat in a previous life?"

"Never," I say. "Snitches get stitches."

He pauses, thinks, then laughs.

"Charm," he says, "why are your friends always so weird?"

"Hey!" cries Ezra.

But I feel the significance of the compliment within the insult, and it makes me smile.

Then I jump—something is curling around my ankle, soft and creepy.

"Oh, that's Calypso," Charm says.

I look down and find an enormous calico cat circling my leg, staring up with luminescent green eyes.

"This is a conspiracy!" Ezra says, outraged. "I've been coming over here for years and Calypso has never done me like that. Took her two years to even let me pet her! You got catnip in your socks?"

"Do you know people who walk around with catnip in their socks?" I ask.

"People do a lot to impress girls," he says, shrugging dramatically. "Including winning over their famously aloof, very violent cat by putting catnip in their sock—"

"Wellll," Charm interrupts, talking fast, "Beau isn't here to impress me, she's here to help me, Ezra, so let's get to it?"

I nod and lean down to give Calypso a little rub, then wave to Charm's parents and follow her out of the room. I can almost see her shoulders relaxing as we leave.

There's a room toward the back of the house that overlooks the yard, where Charm flops into a big floral chair. There are two more, so me and Ezra do the same. He wiggles down to the ottoman on his, stretching like a human Calypso.

"What did you need to show us?" Ezra says, looking at her upside down from where he lies on his back.

"This," she says, and holds up her phone.

"Can you turn it upside down?" Ezra says, unmoving.

"Oh my god, Ezra."

"Pleeease," he whines. "I am a sedentary creature!"

"You're a star basketball player!"

"Okay, but that's then. This is now."

Charm sighs and rotates the phone so he can read the screen. I lean over from my chair and twist my head around too.

It's her notification tab from Instagram—Maia has gone on a hearting spree. The whole screen is *maia_luna liked your photo*.

"Wow, she went *in*," Ezra says.

I'd be lying if I said my stomach didn't twist a little. I remember when Maia would DM me links to my own photos with a horny emoji. She'd never do it publicly. But now she has no problem liking all of Charm's pics?

"I don't know what to do!" Charm says. "What does it mean?"

"It means she's encouraging you for sure," I say. "This is good. We need to make moves."

"What kind of moves?!" Charm wails. "Doesn't that seem *sudden*? *Rushed?*"

Ezra turns his head right side up. "You went up about two octaves there."

"Oh, what do you know about octaves?" she snaps.

"Well, I know Beyoncé has an almost four-octave range. And Enzo can hit three."

He sighs and lets his head drop down to the ottoman again. If we weren't here to focus on Charm's panic, I'd ask what the deal was with Enzo. But Charm is staring at her phone like it might catch on fire and need to be thrown through the glass.

"Charm," I say. "Listen. When a girl goes and likes all your pics, that's like her waving at you from across the room and saying, 'Hey, I'm right here, let's do something!'"

"But *what*?" Charm says. "And *how*, when she clearly doesn't want to be seen in public? Plus, what if I ask her to do something she thinks is wack and it tanks the whole Plan?"

"So think about it," I say, looking her in the eye. Today she makes it easy. Some girls shy away from eye contact, and usually Charm does too—but right now her anxiety makes her lock in. She listens intently. If I weren't focused on the task at hand, it would actually be *me* struggling with eye contact—her eyes are that intense. And, to be honest, distractingly beautiful.

Not the time. I clear my throat.

"Think about it," I repeat before going on. "What has she said lately? What's she excited about?"

The fact is, I already know what Maia is into generally. I know what songs make her want to dance. Which songs make her want to straddle me in the supply closet. I know what she eats when she's on her period—I know how she *acts* when she's on her period, because she only let me touch her through her jeans. But I don't know what Maia is into *lately*. It's been a month since she last ducked under the counter, and if Maia is anything, she's changeable.

"In our last tutoring session, she was talking about the fair," Charm says, thinking. "But that's not till this summer! She really wants to visit New York, but that's obviously impossible. What else . . . she said something about a band called the Oranges, but I've never heard of them. . . ."

"The Oranges," I interrupt, beaming. "She *does* like the Oranges. I forgot about that."

Charm stares at me, her eyes slowly narrowing.

"So . . . ?"

"Sooo, this is good news because they're playing Sligo next weekend. It's only thirty minutes away. Close enough to go, but far enough she'll be comfortable being out with you."

"She did mention the show," Charm says slowly, but then shakes her head. "She said she couldn't get tickets, though. If she can't, then *I* can't. Ugh."

"You're forgetting one thing," I say.

She and Ezra look at me, waiting.

"That *I* am in a very cool band."

Ezra throws his hand up in the air and makes an *eh* gesture.

"Shut up," I say, laughing. "My band is *very* cool, and we've played Sligo like four times. I know the kid who runs the door. Bex. They'll give me tickets for sure."

"Why are you so sure?" Charm says, raising her eyebrow.

"Because I once let them use me to make another girl jealous," I say. "They owe me one. So now you've just gotta ask Maia to go."

"Upon further consideration," Charm says, "doesn't asking her out as Step One feel a little . . . rushed? Shouldn't I be flirting first? Shouldn't I be, I don't know, testing the waters?"

"Flirting is a given," Ezra says. "Make a little flirt sandwich. A little flirting, a little asking out, a little more flirting."

"Love a good sandwich!" I cry. "So how are you going to ask her, Charm?"

"How am I going to ask her?" Charm demands. "Isn't that what *you're* supposed to tell me?"

"Oh, this part is easy. You don't ask, actually. You suggest."

"Suggest?"

"Take all the stuff we talked about before—the eye contact,

the listening—show her you remember what she said, but not in an obvious way. If you're close enough and you think she's comfortable, touch her hand."

I lean forward and rest my hand lightly on top of Charm's. Then I tap her knuckle once, softly, with my middle finger, never taking my eyes off hers.

"You should go see the Oranges with me."

She goes on staring at me. Her lips part.

"With you? I thought . . . Maia?"

"She's giving you an example, nerdo!" Ezra says. "That's what *you* say to *Maia*!"

I can feel the embarrassment flood through her, and she moves her hand.

"That simple?" Charm says. "Just 'you should'?"

"If she's feeling shy, she doesn't have to give a yes or no. She'll say something like 'I should?' Or if she's feisty, she'll say, 'Oh I *should*, should I?' And you can just say, very smoothly, 'Just a suggestion.' The main thing is confidence. Everyone gets nervous asking someone out, but people get nervous being asked out too. So just be chill and kinda pose it like she's already going to the show, she should just decide to go with *you*. Does that make sense?"

She picks up her notebook and scribbles away. I wonder what she's writing, what shape my words take when they're translated into Charmish. When she glances out the window to collect her thoughts, I catch sight of the bottomless brown of her eyes again.

Maia Moon doesn't stand a chance.

The Dinner could've been much worse, in the sense that it's not a total disaster. Miki can cook her ass off, so we're eating incredible roast chicken, potatoes, collard greens with bacon, and jalapeño-and-cheddar corn bread. When we're not eating, we mostly get by on small talk or school talk, and whenever things get a little too awkward, me and Ezra intervene to compliment the food. It's a winning strategy.

Until we get to dessert.

"Peach cobbler is my favorite," Charm tells me. "And Aunt Miki's is the best."

"It's always been your favorite," Bree says, and I wince inwardly.

"Has it?" Charm asks.

Me and Ezra exchange a look.

"I meant to say, Mick," Bree goes on, "I love what you've done with the entryway. Where's that wallpaper from?"

"It's a Black-owned company called Leff. The owner is in my yoga class."

"You'll have to give me her card or something! I'm sure the new house will need wallpaper in some of the rooms."

Oh god.

"How's all that going?" Miki asks. Her sister really must not come around enough, because I barely know Miki and even I can hear the tone that would signal me to stick to the weather.

"We're still negotiating," Chauncey says. "Even though we offered over asking."

Charm puts down her fork. Oh no, oh no, oh no.

"So why are you buying a house here now, when I'm literally graduating?" she asks.

Bree, batting her Charm-eyes, says, "We thought it would be nice, you know, when you come home from college, if we're close by."

"Why would I need you to be close by *now*? And who even said I'm going to college?"

"What do you mean?" Bree asks. "You've been accepted."

"Accepted isn't going. What if I want to go to cosmetology school?"

"Well, if that's what you want, honey, I think that's great! Follow your dreams!" Bree says.

Now Miki puts down her fork. "She can follow her dreams *after* college."

"I meant to ask about the potatoes earlier," Ezra pivots. "Was that rosemary? And how did you get them like that? Crispy on the outside, pillowy on the inside?"

It goes downhill fast after that, and I watch it all happen as if watching a play from the wings.

CHAUNCEY: Now, Miki, we want our daughter to have the opportunity to explore her options! Charm, why not take a gap year and—

MIKI: You should have thought of that before I took on four jobs to make sure you could explore *your* options.

ME: I need more of that cobbler! It's just so good. Is that nutmeg?

BREE: Miki, you know we appreciate everything you did for us, and everything you still do for Charm, but don't pretend we don't contribute—

MIKI: I double-bake the potatoes. And yeah, it's rosemary and thyme.

CHARM: Who cares what you contribute?

DALLAS: The ice cream is melting.

CHARM: Let it melt.

EZRA: What brand is the ice cream? Or did you make that, too?

MIKI: I didn't make the ice cream, Ezra.

CHAUNCEY: Oh, is it from that ice cream shop that just opened?
BREE: I bet it's from Milk It. Charm, do you remember us taking you there when you were little?
CHARM: I remember *Miki* taking me there. And Wonderdough. And basically everywhere.
ME: It's really good.
BREE: We would take you there every time we visited—
CHARM: Can we just go back to eating?

Scene ends with ten minutes of eating in silence until Chauncey asks Charm about school and it starts all over again.

After we're all full of cobbler and out of small talk, Charm walks me to the door while her parents help her aunt clean up in the kitchen, where Miki is wisely blasting music too loud for further conversation. I don't get to say goodbye to Ezra—he's been in the bathroom for a while. He's lactose intolerant, Charm tells me. "But he's constantly eating stuff he knows will run him right to the toilet." We all have our flaws.

"Thanks for bearing witness to that freaking fiasco," she says now that we're alone. She leans her forehead on the doorjamb and then mimes banging her head against it. I laugh.

"It wasn't so bad."

"It wasn't so bad to you because you're so good."

"I'm what we would call slightly above average—let's not get carried away."

"A solid B+."

She smiles her warmest smile. I want to tell her that it's her parents' loss, missing out on her life, missing out on *her*, but it doesn't feel like it's my place. All I know is my place was here tonight, and I'm glad about it.

"Text me when you're home," she says, "and that's not just a suggestion."

"Sheesh, strict around here!" I huff, then give her a wave before I walk to my car.

For some reason I want to look back at her, but I don't.

14
Charm

"I hate spring," I say to Ezra as I slam my locker closed.

"Who hates spring?" he asks, tucking literal flowers behind my ear. Ezra turns into a freaking wood nymph this time of year—his mom's a florist at Roots, a combo flower shop and hair salon, and she sets out fresh bouquets in their house almost every day. On mornings when he swings by the shop to help her do arrangements for big orders (weddings or funerals or baby showers), he always shows up at school with a few flowers tucked into his hoodie pockets, or tiny bundles he hands out to teachers or students he likes. I think it's part of the reason he was so taken with Enzo after he played Puck.

Though I love Roots and actually worked there over the summer, I can't get with Ezra's spunk for a season that literally makes me ill. I yank the baby's breath from my hair, blow my nose, and take a double puff from my inhaler. Then I growl at Ezra in a way that makes him hop away from me like a bunny.

"Don't take your seasonal hatred out on me," he says. He makes his fingers into an X in front of his face. "*I'm* not the reason you're allergic to outside."

Truthfully, I'm not only cranky because of my allergies. It's because my parents are still in town waiting to hear about the house, and even though dinner with them was fairly tame, they want to do it *again* next week. It's also because I have to meet

Maia for our first tutoring session since the Almost-Kiss Incident. It will be my first time being alone with her in over a week, and my first opportunity to truly implement the Plan. I don't know how my heart (or my nose) will feel.

I sniff and pout as I pull out my phone and shoot Maia a text to let her know I'll meet her in our usual tutoring spot. **Heading to the library,** I send.

Other than her liking all my photos, our near-constant communication stopped abruptly ten days ago, right after Andi's party. But her messages from before are flirty as hell, and it's fuel to the fire of my crankiness; it renews my annoyance with her and my commitment to getting even. I have to remember that she deserves what Beau and I are planning because she flirted with me, led me on, almost kissed me—all while she was dating Tate. Not to mention whatever happened between her and Beau. If I don't regularly remind myself of Maia's treachery, my soft heart will melt like ice cream the second I see her icy-gray eyes.

Ezra is explaining how he can't wait for Enzo's next performance—he's the lead in the spring musical too: *Something Wicked*. "He plays a maniacal singing Macbeth, Charm. I'm going to lose my shit," he says, and I laugh, about to pocket my phone when it buzzes in my hand. I glance down at it to see a new message roll in from Maia: **It's so nice out! Can we study on the bleachers by the track instead?**

"Oh god." I stop walking.

"What?" Ezra stops too.

"Maia wants to do our tutoring session outside. Which means my allergies are going to be on ten. Also, is she just going to pretend what happened at the party didn't happen? Because if she does, what am I supposed to do? And like, do I bring up the fact that she liked my entire feed? Or am I expected to pretend too? And another thing! What do I do if—"

"Charm," Ezra says. He puts both his hands on my shoulders and backs me up slowly until I'm flush against the wall, out of the crowd of students streaming down the hall. "Breathe."

"I can't!" I let out a nasally shriek. "That's part of the problem!"

He presses his lips together like he's holding in a laugh. I narrow my eyes and glare at him.

"Here," he says, swinging his backpack around and reaching into one of the pockets.

He pulls out a packet of pink allergy pills and pops two out of the foil into the palm of my hand before giving me his water bottle. I swallow them while still staring at him murderously.

"Here's what's about to happen: you're going to tutor Maia. If it feels like too much to pretend you're not hurt, don't hide it. If you want to wait to ask her out, just wait. I know you and Beau have this whole elaborate Plan, but it can change. You didn't sign your free will away in blood."

I look down the hall toward the doors that lead to the track and field. I heave a sigh.

"Okay," I say. Then I hug him, because I love him. He always knows how to calm me down, and plus, he smells like flowers. Which I do love even if they're trying to kill me.

"I'll also be out there in a few. Track practice. So if you really need to be rescued, just yell 'Mayday' or something."

"How about if you see me drop my inhaler? It could be like my Bat-Signal?"

"Charm. You know I love you more than peonies, but I'm not going to be staring at you waiting to see you drop your inhaler. I literally have to run suicides."

"Ugh, fine."

He kisses my cheek. Pokes my side. "You'll be okay," he says.

I take as deep a breath as I can. Then I tuck my thumbs into my backpack's straps and head toward the double doors.

"Wait," I say, turning back. "That was non-drowsy Benadryl, right?"

"Ummmm," he says.

"Ezra! You *know* regular Benadryl makes me loopy and weird unless I can take an immediate nap!"

"I'm sorry! Try to tutor her quickly?"

I whimper and stomp away.

My eyes go watery as soon as the air outside hits my face. The pollen count today is outrageous, and I don't know why I didn't just ask Maia to meet me in the library anyway. Why didn't Ezra suggest *that* instead of poisoning me with medicine that's guaranteed to knock me on my ass within the hour?

"Pull it together, Charm," I mutter to myself as I approach the field. It is wide and unnaturally green, and half the track team is warming up on the sidelines, the coach prepping them to start running drills. I hope I didn't make Ezra late. I can see the bleachers in the distance, and there are a few small groups of kids sitting around at different levels. Some are laughing and drinking sodas. Some are studying or reading with headphones on. When I get a little closer, I see her.

Maia smiles big and waves me over. She's sitting near the very top, so she's backlit by the sun, the halo around her dark curls seeming almost golden in the late afternoon light. I sniff and start up the stairs toward her, and I can see that she already has her notes and textbook open. She's using her phone and water bottle as paperweights to stop everything from blowing away.

"Maybe this wasn't the best idea," she says as soon as I'm close enough. The wind tosses a few curls across her brow, and she daintily shakes them away. I shrug half-heartedly and let my backpack fall at my feet. I sink down beside her and dig out my own supplies, pinning my stuff down too.

"You're quiet today," she says after a long and admittedly uncomfortable silence, but I don't know how she's expecting me to respond to that, so I just blow my nose again. Then, when I can't stall any longer, I finally look over at her.

She's watching me. When our eyes meet, I hold her gaze until she looks down at her feet. It hurts a little, to look at her so intensely, because it reminds me too much of how close we were at Andi's party. Still, I don't look away, following Beau's flirting lesson as best I can, so my eyes are waiting to meet hers when she glances back up, and then away from me again.

"Look," she says, and I don't know why, but her saying that word, when she's the one who can't seem to keep her eyes still, pisses me off. "I feel like I need to apologize."

I freeze. I wasn't expecting an apology. I blink and keep watching her. Keep waiting to see what she'll say next.

She puts a hand on my knee, which is peeking out through a hole in my jeans. The skin of her palm is smooth and warm.

"What happened back at Andi's . . . the stuff I said. I wanted to clear the air, let you know that things with Tate were in a weird place. But, like, since everything with him is fine now, I wanted to make sure everything was cool with you."

I don't know what that means. I don't understand what she wants me to believe.

"I guess I just love our tutoring sessions," she continues.

"They're my favorite days of the week. And I wouldn't want to lose that just because of something dumb I did while I was drunk."

She shrugs a little, then smiles, and it's just as dazzling as her eyes.

Ah, the old "I was just drunk" excuse. If Beau were small enough to fit in my pocket, I know she'd be climbing up onto my shoulder right now and yelling, *She's full of shit!* in my ear. Even though Maia is beautiful, and my heart is tempted to fall into the universe of her eyes, I use my head to focus on what I know to be true: Maia is lying. She wasn't drunk when she almost kissed me—I could smell her breath. She wasn't drunk until she was kissing her "boyfriend," red cup still in her hand. I continue to hold her gaze, but this time she never falters. So she's used to lying. She's *good* at lying. I file this information away for the sake of the Plan, but I wonder who or what made her feel like lying would keep her safe.

I nod as if I'm accepting her apology, keeping my mouth shut because I'm not as skilled at deception as she is. But I am good at honesty, and if Beau has taught me anything, it's to lean into what I'm good at. Luckily, honesty was a big part of her flirting lesson. I know I don't have the guts to ask Maia out right now, but I can still try to move toward that objective.

What were the rules again? I wish I could check my notes.

There was something about hands, right? I put my hand on top of hers, which is still resting on my leg, and I let my face soften. I know I'm taking a chance, since we're in a semi-public place, but she doesn't pull away.

"Okay, Maia-Maia Moon," I sing, trying to channel Beau's tone when she told the girl at the bowling alley that she looked like a Mariah.

It must work, because she blushes a little and shakes her head, relief flooding her features. When she moves her hand, she does it gently, slipping it from mine to turn a page in her trig book. I take the moment as a win.

I'm grateful when we start working. I walk her through her latest trig assignment, which is full of sines and cosines, tangents and cotangents. It's complicated enough that I can lean into it and forget about all that is swirling between us. For a while, as I focus on the kinds of problems that only have one solution, I leave behind everything that's on the line.

But I feel it when it starts to descend—the haze that is the first step of the drug-induced coma Benadryl always puts me in. I'm not sneezing anymore, but everything around me feels a little less real than it did a few minutes ago, a little more like I'm floating through fog. The symbols, letters, and numbers on the page go all wavy, and without thinking I say aloud, "Uh-oh," and Maia stops furiously erasing her last mistake to look over at me.

"What?" she asks, and the sun is hitting her face at an angle that I want to write a formula to figure out, just so I can always position her this exact way. She's *so* pretty. And that's what I say, without really deciding to: "You're so damn pretty."

She blinks a few times, and it feels like it's happening in slow motion, the way her dark eyelashes flutter, the way I feel myself leaning forward just a little. "Did you know there are little flecks of blue in your eyes?" I ask her. And she blinks some more, but now she's smiling. I feel *so* sleepy all of a sudden.

But it's not only that she's pretty. She's sweet and kind sometimes, but then, days or even minutes later, she's deceptive and manipulative. I think I'm having a hard time shaking this crush because with her, I never know what to expect. Whenever I see her, I don't know which Maia she'll be.

"I think I've done all the math I can handle today," I tell her, talking about trig but also about the Maia Moon Math I can't seem to stop calculating, the way my brain won't stop trying to figure her out. I close my book and lean back against the level of seats behind us. I tilt my face up toward the sun and close my eyes.

"Are you . . . good?" she asks, and I nod without opening my eyes, but my whole body feels suddenly heavy, like someone's tossed a weighted blanket over my limbs. It's almost like I'm already half-asleep, because I can suddenly hear Beau in my head like I'm dreaming about her, the words in her deep and resonant voice: *You should go see the Oranges with me.* And I want to. I mean, I would want to go see the Oranges with her, if she asked me like that.

"You like the Oranges?" Maia asks, and I slowly open my eyes.

"Huh?" I say.

She laughs. "The Oranges. You like them?"

And as my consciousness attempts to hold on to the light, I realize I must have said it out loud—channeled Beau without even realizing it—as I was slipping under.

Oh shit. I just asked Maia out.

"Oh," I say, and, worried I haven't done enough to convince her to say yes, I backtrack. My Benadryl-hazy mind produces this gem: "Well . . . I mean . . . who doesn't like oranges?"

Maia just looks at me.

"Oh shit, you don't hate oranges, do you?" I ask her.

Maia laughs. "Charm, what are you talking about?"

"I guess I'm more of a tangerine girlie myself, but there's also clementines, mandarins . . . the, uh, farmers' market has it all!"

"Oh. I thought you meant the band, the Oranges. I thought you were . . . never mind."

Maia looks frazzled, and she's clearly embarrassed, but I can't tell if it's on my behalf or her own. I blink at her, trying to catch up to this conversation, which feels like it's gone off the rails. I'm all over the place, and I know I'm being heady and strange. "You thought I was what?" I ask softly.

"I thought you were asking me to go to a concert. The Oranges is the name of my favorite band." She clears her throat. "Sorry, I clearly didn't hear what I thought I heard."

"Yo, Maia," some guy yells from the track. He has sandy hair and a gap between his two front teeth, and I vaguely recognize him as one of Tate's flunkies. He has one of those single-syllable white-boy names. Craig, maybe? Or Cal?

"Hey, Cole," Maia replies, and her whole energy changes. She arches her back so that she's suddenly very boob-forward. She tosses her hair in a theatrical way that makes me question if what I'm seeing is really happening.

"Tell Tate he left one of his shin guards in my car. Must have fallen out of his bag after practice."

"'Kay," she says, smiling. As soon as Cole turns away from us, she folds back into herself, smile warping and then melting away like plastic. It's so fucking weird.

I realize then just how many Maias there are. There's Maia Luna, the makeup influencer who is always put-together, always picture-perfect. There's Maia Moon, the popular straight girl dating Tate Westbrook, who hides behind a plastic smile. And then there's the real Maia, the one who wants to be good at trig and who tries hard to be kind, who almost kissed me at Andi

Patterson's house and who is terrified that she likes girls as much as she clearly does. I saw her for a split second when she said, so earnestly, so self-consciously, *The Oranges is the name of my favorite band.*

"What?" she asks when she looks back over at me. I must be making a face. I'm too out of it to rearrange my features much, but I try.

"You can just be yourself, Maia," I say, because it seems so simple to me in this liminal space, this bizarre twilight-zone moment. Nothing feels real, or like it matters much. "Are there people who make you feel like you need to, I don't know, perform? Do I?"

It's too much, too honest of a question. I'm lucid enough to know that. So when Maia's face shifts into a combination of shock and—is that fear?—I go back to the Oranges. Because asking her out now feels safer, easier, than having the conversation my question might start.

I squint and lean forward with my hands on my knees.

"What if I *was* asking you out, what would you say?"

She looks at me, her eyes roaming my face like she's trying to find something.

"This is the most confusing conversation I've ever had," she says.

"Sorry. I remember you saying you liked them. The Oranges. The band, not the fruit. So I pulled some strings to get tickets because I figured you might want to go. Do you?"

Maia twirls one of her curls around her finger. When she lets it go, it legit bounces, and again I wonder if I'm fully awake. She nods.

"Do you want to go with Tate?" I ask.

Maia laughs a single loud *ha*. "Tate would never go see the Oranges."

"What about with me?" I ask. "Would you want to go to the show with me?"

I imagine the pocket-sized Beau on my shoulder dropping to her knees, fists lifted, screaming, "Nooooo!" at every word I'm saying.

"So, wait. You *are* asking me out?" she says.

When I nod, Maia's face blooms. That's the only way I can describe it. Everything about her opens wide.

"I'd love to go see the Oranges with you."

"Okay," I say. I close my eyes and sink back again. But the bleachers are hard and she looks so soft. "You mind if I . . ." I can't help but lean my head against her shoulder. "You smell good," I say. "And sorry. Full disclosure, I'm slightly high on allergy meds right now, but I still think you should go to the show with me."

Maia giggles. She pats the top of my head. "I should, huh?" she says, or maybe I dream it. By then I'm yawning, leaning a little harder against her. I look up at her sleepily over my glasses, and she's grinning down at me in a way that steals my breath. Literally.

I sit up to wake myself up, and then I look out at the track. Ezra's there, and despite what he said earlier, he seems to be watching me. I lift my inhaler to show him it's still in my hand, and he grins.

I think of Beau as I turn back to Maia and say, "It was just a suggestion."

15
Beau

"You were on *Benadryl*?!" I say when Charm tells me about the situation with Maia. I am incredulous. "I'm going to shake Ezra by his beautiful neck. What did you say? How did you ask?"

"I . . . think I took your advice?" she says sheepishly.

I rub my face. My advice was aiming for strategy, not hallucination.

"So . . . she said yes to the Oranges, but what was the vibe? Did she seem flirty? Or is it all a haze of Benadryl?"

"I mean . . . it was fine?"

At that point she makes the Charm-face version of the *yikes* emoji, so *I* make an executive decision.

"Okay, this calls for a practice concert," I tell her. "Favorite Daughter plays at the Tortoise tonight. Bring Ezra and we'll run some lines after the show. You need a dress rehearsal before you go see the Oranges with Maia. And no Benadryl."

But a few hours later, standing backstage with Daniel and Celine, I'm second-guessing the brilliance of this plan. I've never gotten nervous before shows, not even when we first started performing. I love drumming. I don't have to smile, I just do my thing while Celine does hers and Daniel does his. And people I know have definitely been in the audience before—even Maia—so why does this feel different? Just the *idea* of Charm being here distracts me, even if I can't see her right now. It's like trying to pat my head and rub my stomach at the same time, even though girls say I am—*ahem*—great at multitasking. This whole Lesbian Lesson shit must be doing something to my brain, making me forget I'm not the one trying to win over the girl. Instead of thinking about the music, I'm thinking about how I'm going to *look* playing the music. If I'll look good, if I'll look charismatic, if I'll look like the kind of girl who can teach you how to make a girl fall in love with you. It all makes me want to gnaw on my drumstick.

But then I have an idea: I can't exactly ask Charm to leave, but if I can look out at the audience and not run the risk of seeing her face, I can focus on my songs.

Next to me, one of the stage managers, Nadir, is standing by the curtains, looking at a clipboard with a schedule on it. He goes to the other high school, so I don't know what his reputation is, but if there's a gay overlord over there, I'd bet it's Nadir. I call to him.

"Nadir, do you see a girl out there? She's really pretty and she's with a guy."

Nadir peeks through the curtains out at the audience.

"A girl. With a guy. You're going to have to be a lot more specific, Beau."

"Okay, okay, she has glasses and big brown eyes and a nose like a bunny? If she's smiling, her mouth, like, goes up on one side a little. She's probably wearing purple."

"Umm . . . that's *very* specific."

"Okay, well, you asked! Do you see her? She might be with a guy, like I said . . ."

"What's the guy look like?" Nadir says, scanning the crowd.

"I don't know, he's like . . . perfect-looking? Kind of looks like he's carved out of gold with freckles and curls?"

Nadir nods immediately.

"Gilded prince. Clocked. So what about them? Bunny nose and gilded prince? We don't have to kick them out, do we?"

"What? No!"

"Oh, good. Is he single?"

I laugh. "Yes, but his heart belongs to a fairy."

Nadir side-eyes me. "Look, I know you're a lesbian and part of the family, but I don't think you can just throw 'fairy' around like that."

"Huh? Wait, no! I mean that he played a *fairy*, like an actual elf-fairy thing in a play. Ugh, never mind. Can you bring them backstage? Both of them."

Nadir brightens. "Oh, say less. You said he fell in love with a fairy? Wait till he meets this one."

He throws his shoulders back and then disappears through the curtains. The next thing I know, Charm and Ezra are backstage and being ushered to the wings. I sit down at my kit, and I only have time to wave before the other stage manager cues us, and the curtain goes up.

We're not famous or anything, but we do have what you could call fans. Five thousand followers on Instagram. People who comment, *Hey, are you playing Friday?* and then say, *Great, I'll be there!* when we say yes. They're here now: you can tell the sound of applause of people who know your music from those who are polite but enthusiastic. Without having to worry about accidentally catching Charm's eye and getting distracted, I feel the usual rush of first excitement and then calm. When Daniel starts our song "Garage Story" with the first notes on his guitar, everything that isn't on this stage melts away. No college plan? Who cares. Bruised heart? Whatever. The rhythm finds me and I let it carry me to a place that's smooth and warm and comfortable.

We're halfway through the song when I realize I'm looking over at Charm in the wings.

She's smiling with her hand over her mouth like she's surprised, or frozen mid-laugh. But she's not frozen, because she rocks to the beat. Exactly on beat, like she's perched on my drumstick, along for the ride. My anxiety about her deciding I was not only not a Lesbonova but a Lesbonobody was apparently unfounded—her face looks like sunshine. I jerk my eyes back at the audience and almost laugh at myself—*What the fuck, Beau? You brought her backstage so you wouldn't be distracted and then you do it to yourself.*

Celine is transitioning into the next song—one I wrote: "Rock, Paper"—a little early, so I get my head right and coast on the beat. I do this one song after another all the way to the end of our set.

The Tortoise is small, so after the show, people are allowed to come onstage and talk. There are *always* people who want to talk: people just being nice, or who are starting their own band and want advice, or people who want to know if they can stream our music on Apple Music (they can) and if we sell merch (we do). These are the times when the idea of taking a year off and playing music actually feels possible. I know Celine feels it too, even if she doesn't say it. At least not to me. With me, she's hell-bent on being responsible. But when people make comments on social media like, *When are you coming to Seattle?*, it makes me want to say, *Soon.*

But then there's what Celine calls "the groupies."

They're not *really* groupies. Groupies have . . . very specific goals. And that's not usually the case for the girls who come hang around the drums after the show. A lot of the time they don't say anything, they just kind of stand nearby and wait to see if I'll say something to *them*. If I went to their school they wouldn't dare, but because I'm on a stage, they want to see if I'll notice them. Sometimes I play along, but sometimes it makes me mad that these girls don't actually want to have sex with other girls—they just want to feel cool that gay girls want to have sex with *them*. I should write a song about that, I think. I'll get over this writer's block eventually.

Charm and Ezra have been standing off to the side chatting while I do band things, the groupie crowd standing just far enough away to avoid conversation, but inching closer.

But tonight I have a groupie shield.

I catch Charm's eye and motion her over. She says a few words to Ezra—who is suddenly beset by Nadir—then winds her way through the crowd to where I sit at the drums. I curl my finger to bring her closer, and when she bends, I extend my neck to whisper in her ear.

"Tonight's lesson is PDA," I say.

She immediately reaches for her purse.

"Hold on, let me get my notebook out . . . ," she says.

"This is more of a lab portion of class," I say. "Tonight is practice for Step Two, when you're out with Maia. You'll be outside town, so she won't be as guarded as she would around here. But the goal is to get her to relax. Get her so focused on you that she forgets who's watching. So. How do you think you'd do that?"

She's locked in on my eyes. At first I thought this was a usual Charm quality, but I've noticed she definitely only does it when she's anxious. Otherwise her eyes are like butterflies—they only land on you for soft little moments. Then off they flutter.

"I . . . have no idea," she says.

I keep my voice low so none of the people standing around can hear.

"Contact," I say. "Attention. Intention."

I stand up, press my hand against her shoulder, and guide her to the seat. I give more pressure, until she's sitting. Then I lean over her shoulder and guide the drumsticks into her hands.

"Um . . . you are making a very large mistake," Charm says as she attempts to open her fingers to refuse them, but I close my hands around hers.

"Just a simple beat," I say, laughing. I can feel the so-called groupies watching. I don't care, but I can tell Charm does. Charm is gorgeous, but I've noticed that unless she's dancing, she's self-conscious about people looking at her.

But if this plan is going to work, she needs to get used to the eyes.

"Eight notes on the high hat," I say. "Then two and four on the snare. And remember, it's not even about the beat—it's about focusing on the contact. I'm not touching you by accident. I'm touching you on purpose."

Her breath catches a little.

"Then just a little bit of kick drum," I tell her.

"Not computing a kick drum," she says.

"Well, I can't exactly put my feet on your feet from here, so we'll pretend."

With my hands covering hers, we play a sloppy beat. She laughs, close to my ear.

"Were you this bad when you started?" she says, a little breathlessly. "Tell me you were this bad when you started."

"Of course I wasn't," I say. "I was perfect."

She shoves me with her shoulder, her laugh rising.

"You're doing so well," I say quietly. "Contact. Attention. Intention. It won't be drums at the Oranges show, obviously. But you'll dance, right? You just gotta figure out a way to apply it."

She stiffens, then nods. I can almost hear the little pencil in her brain scratching notes.

"Don't overthink it," I say.

"Says the overthinker," she says quickly.

Surprised, I still the drumsticks, my hands remaining over hers. "Me?"

"Yes, you," she says, laughing. "When is the last time you didn't plan every version of something out before you said it?"

"It's called preparedness!"

"It's called anxiety," she says. "Have you ever messed up onstage before? Drumming, I mean."

"Not really. I try not to do things until I know I'm a hundred percent capable of doing them."

"Why?"

"So I won't be bad at them, obviously!"

"What's wrong with being bad at things?"

I laugh. "Is that a real question?"

"Everybody has to suck at something for a while," she says. "It builds character."

"Beau, hurry up and put your shit away!" Celine calls from the other side of the stage. "I'm starving!"

Charm stands, forcing me to stand too.

"Don't let Lesbian Lessons hold up the after-party," she says, smiling.

I take the sticks from her and toss them, catching them before they fall. I practiced that a million times in my garage for like a year to look cool for girls, but it turned into more of a nervous habit than anything. Why am I nervous? I sit back down on the stool and pull out the little velvet pouch where I keep my sticks.

Then I freeze. Charm's hand is suddenly behind my ear, curling a few strands of my hair around her finger. I've seen her do it to her braids. A little twirling tic. I stare down at the drumsticks in my grip until her hand falls away a second later. When I look up at her, I can't read her face.

"Contact. Attention. Intention. Right?" she says. "How'd I do?"

I can feel more than a few pairs of eyes on us. She was practicing, I remind myself. That was the point of all this. I clear my throat and orchestrate a smile.

"A+."

PART THREE
Three Weeks till Prom

16
Charm

Beau is in the library.

I'm here too . . . and so is Maia.

I see them both when I walk in—Maia at our usual table in the corner, Beau in the stacks, running her finger along a row of dark spines—but they haven't seen each other or me (yet).

I don't know how or why this happened, but we must have gotten our wires crossed. I panic-text Ezra. **SOS. Beau AND me AND Maia are in the library. I can't have Beau, like, witnessing me trying to get my mack on.**

Because (1) being perceived is embarrassing enough when I'm just trying to exist, and (2) Beau is my how-to-get-a-girl tutor. It would be like me accompanying Maia to her trigonometry class and watching her take a test. Plus, the thought of Beau seeing me and Maia together takes me back to her walking into that room at Andi's party. In all the time we've spent together since, I haven't ever seen her face look that . . . broken? And I don't want to again. Just remembering *that* makes my skin feel like it's covered in fire ants, every part of me all hot and hurting.

Ezra texts a freaking paragraph back: **First of all, if you ever say the word mack to me again and you're not referring to the signature sandwich from McDonald's, we're no longer friends. And B, what do you expect ME to do about this? I'm changing for practice and trying to get tickets for Bey's** tour this summer—something YOU are supposed to be helping me with in exactly three minutes, btw. Get it together woman.

Granted, I forgot about the concert tickets, but at that very moment a calendar invite lights up my phone with the pre-sale link. I open it so I'll be ready to refresh the page and keep my eyes on Beau at the same time. She's now crouched by a low shelf in the biography section. I look back at my phone and shoot her a text while I still have time: **WHAT ARE YOU DOING HERE???**

I've been feeling a little weird since the Favorite Daughter show, and I haven't been texting her as much. Mostly because I can't stop thinking about the way Beau's skin smelled like rainwater instead of sweat after the show, and how her hands felt like warm sand when we played the drums together, and how her hair was soft as corn silk in my fingers. The way she said, *Contact, attention, intention*, in a near whisper, and the bass in her voice even when it was quiet made goose bumps explode across my scalp.

She's . . . good at what she does. And I thought that maybe some distance would help me digest her lessons, figure out how to use her moves my way. Because even though my head knows Beau is only flirting to show me how it's done, I want to make sure I don't take any of it to heart.

At that moment Beau looks up, and instead of her usual scowl, she actually smiles. At *me*. Her hair is all tousled, and her destroyed jeans are tight enough that I can see her curves, and she is pretty, um, *blessed* in the ass department (especially for a white girl). I clear my throat as she shout-whispers, "Monty! Long time no see."

"Shhhhhh!" I shush her, rushing over to the aisle she's in. I press my hand to her chest, forcing her deeper into the stacks and out of Maia's line of sight. "What are you doing here?"

Her smile falls the tiniest bit, and those dark blue eyes rove around my face like she's a lighthouse and I'm the sea. "I wanted to see if our crappy school library had *Little Girl Blue*."

I make a face. "That's a band name," I say, and Beau's smile gains some wattage again.

"It does sound like one, now that you mention it. It was also a song by Janis Joplin." She bites her lip, and I look at her teeth like a freak. "And an album by Nina Simone," she adds. "But I'm talking about Karen Carpenter's biography."

I have no idea who that is, but I'm assuming it's a musician . . . maybe a drummer? Beau clocks my confusion. "She was a drummer, and a singer. And even though I know this book will probably be a bummer, I still wanna read it."

"Do you really like her or something?"

"For sure. But also I just . . ." She pauses and looks shy.

"Oh come on," I groan. "Say it."

"I've just been thinking a lot about next year—I'm taking a gap year. Thinking about what I'm gonna fill it with. Karen Carpenter built a career as a drummer, and it seems far-fetched, but maybe I could do that too."

I could listen to Beau talk about music forever, and it makes me wonder if I should be looking into cosmetology school, even though I've already been accepted at all three of the colleges Aunt Miki and I agreed I'd apply to.

"Did you know 'far-fetched' means 'brought from afar'?" I ask her. "Aunt Miki always knows random facts like that."

"Interesting." She pauses, thinking, and I can almost hear the drumbeat of her heart. "So maybe it's not so far-fetched if I go get it myself."

Her smile grows, and I feel mine matching it. I'm about to

ask her more about this Carpenter lady, or tease her about the fantasy novels she's holding and conspicuously left out of our conversation, when my phone lights up in my hand again. It's a message from Maia. And I remember that as much as I want to keep talking to Beau, I actually need her to go.

"Maia's here for the tutoring session." I throw a thumb over my shoulder. "You gotta get out of here."

Beau peers through a gap in the books, presumably looking for Maia. She puts a hand in her hair and her forearm flexes—elegant drummer's muscles I feel tempted to squeeze—and then, when her arm falls and her hair flops over one eye, I take a step back, overwhelmed by the sudden urge to touch her. Maybe the lessons are doing more of a number on me than I thought.

"You . . . don't want her to see me with you?" she asks, and something in her voice sounds thinner than normal. Not as solid and sure.

I blink at her. "Beau, I don't want *you* to see *me* flailing. I'm not exactly . . . good at this. But I'm working on it. However, you watching my attempts would make it much worse."

Beau presses her lips together and snorts. Snorts! "I guess you have a point. Don't worry, grasshopper. I'll clear out. Go do your thing."

I sigh with relief, but as I turn to walk away from her, she slaps me on the ass. I let out a little yelp, but I'm instantly hot all over and imagining what it would be like to whirl around and push her against one of these shelves; to slap (or grab) her ample ass back. When I look over my shoulder at her, though, the expression on her face isn't one of easy confidence like I expect. She seems a bit surprised at herself.

"My bad," she says. "Was that weird? I'm sorry. I do that shit to my sister all the time and it just happened—force of habit, but—"

I clear my throat, say, "You're good, boo," real cool. But inside, whatever candle had been burning low and warm with want is snuffed out by the word *sister*.

Beau sees me as a sister, I think as I walk away from her, something in my chest feeling like it's collapsing. *She did that because she does it to her* sister. *Any flirting she's done with me has only been about the lessons,* I remind myself, *has only been about getting revenge.* These thoughts play on a loop until I reach the table and sit down across from Maia: *sister, lessons, revenge.*

"Hey, stranger," Maia says. She immediately leans across the table and picks a piece of lint out of my hair. I stare at the piece of fuzz between her fingers. I need to snap out of it. I remember the list I wrote in Beau's notebook. Our constitution. The last rule on it is burned into my brain, because at the time, I thought it was so ridiculous: *Don't fall in love.* And while I know I'm not in love with Beau, the last five minutes have me worried that I may be a little in like with her. I can't even be upset. She warned me this might happen.

I look at my phone. Refresh the Beyoncé page. The seats are already all gone, and something about losing out on the tickets feels prophetic: even if the Plan works, I'll end up empty-handed. No matter what happens, at the end of this, I'm alone.

I glance over at Maia, realizing with unexpected clarity that I'm *deep* in my feelings. That I've already broken the promise I made to myself, and let my heart take charge. As I unpack my books, I do the opposite with my feelings—I bury them, push them out of harm's way. I rearrange my thoughts logically: Beau is important to me. We want revenge. If the Plan works, maybe I'll at least get to keep her as a friend. And maybe her lessons and my practicing will help me land some other girl for real. A girl who won't toy with my heart like Maia Moon.

I gotta give this all I've got.

I stand and go around the table to sit *beside* Maia instead.

"This is really nice," I say, looking right at her and taking the collar of her cardigan in my fingers. It's soft and embroidered with silver stars. "It brings out your eyes."

"It does?" she says, looking down at herself. I let my eyes linger. Keep them on her till I feel the weight Beau described. "Yeah," I tell her. "Your eyes are nice too."

Her cheeks go pink, and I realize she's not wearing as much makeup as she usually does. I wonder why, and it gives me an idea. I pick up her phone.

"Can I take a picture of you? Just so you can see what I mean?" She seems shy as she nods, which surprises me. Her online accounts are littered with selfies. Maia Luna posts videos of herself almost daily. But I guess the real Maia feels exposed without her usual mask. I lean back to line up the shot, then snap it, and I guess our little corner of the library is darker than I realized. The flash goes off and I'm only about a foot away from her. *Real smooth, Charm.* Christ.

Maia blinks, dazed by the light, and I say, "Shit, sorry!" But a second later she's laughing.

In the photo, she looks more frightened than cute, and because the flash went off, her eyes are a startling orangey red instead of gray. "Well, that's not exactly what I had in mind," I say, turning the phone to face her.

She cracks up. "I look possessed," she says.

"Well, you're a DILF if I've ever seen one," I say without thinking.

"Did you say DILF?" Maia asks.

Jesus, I think, before I explain myself, thanking the universe Beau isn't witnessing me crashing and burning.

"Yeah. Um. Demon I'd like to—"

"Oh my god," Maia whisper-screams. She shoves my shoulder so hard, I almost fall out of the chair, which only makes us both laugh harder.

I open my notes and pull out some pencils to get started on today's assignment. We solve for a few unknowns, write a few ratios, and then I realize something. "I don't think I've ever asked you," I say. "Why do you care about trigonometry so much? You could totally just do a lower-level math. It's senior year. Why risk your GPA on a subject you don't need if it gives you such a hard time?"

Maia doesn't take her eyes off her notebook at first. She's erasing something and pretending it's taking all her concentration. I gently slip the pencil out of her hand. When she finally looks up at me, I raise my eyebrows. "Just curious," I say. "And look, you don't have to tell me. I'm just glad I get to do this with you." I motion to the table full of books.

"I . . . want to work for NASA," Maia almost whispers.

I lean closer, sure I misunderstood. "You want to work for . . . ?"

"NASA," she says again, and something about her face turns hard. "And no, I don't want to run their social media, or walk on the moon. I'm not an idiot, and I'm not five."

I look more closely at the expression on her face. I study the way all the softness left it so quickly. Maia is definitely moody, but this is something different. It's pain. The last person she shared this with must have made a joke. The last person she told about NASA must have made her feel like she wasn't good enough.

And even though that's how she's made me feel, I say, "So you want to be, what, some kind of engineer? I can totally see that. The way you don't give up. The way you do it all."

She blinks a few times. "Wait. Really?"

I nod. "You're internet famous, which I'm sure comes with sponsorships and constant content creation. You're on the honor roll while still showing up at all the wildest parties. You feed that freaky tarantula no one else wants to go near." I pause and let loose a full-body cringe. "*And* you're the first girl drum major at Brookville in what? Ten years?"

"Fifteen," she says quietly. She touches my fingers gently and lets hers linger there for a moment. I look at our hands, and, remembering what Beau said about contact and intention, I don't move mine away until she takes her pencil back.

"Fifteen! So you're already comfortable in male-dominated spaces." I know I'm supposed to be trying to move the Plan forward, but maybe there will be a chance to do that at the concert. I look around, then grab Maia's hand. "Let me show you something."

I pull her up, and we snake our way through the stacks. "Have you read *Hidden Figures*? My aunt's book club picked it a few years ago, and I stole it from her on a random Saturday when I was really bored. It's amazing what those women were able to do even in the midst of—"

Maia steps directly in front of me, stopping me in my tracks. Then she takes another step forward, into my space, and she's so close, I can count the light brown freckles that dot her nose.

I move backward, but Maia follows, and then I feel a metal shelf, cold against my shoulder blades, and there's nowhere else for me to go.

"Charm," she says, "every time I think I've gotten over this thing I have for you, you go and do or say something so . . . so . . ." She licks her lips and looks at mine.

"You have a thing," I say, taking a shallow breath, "for me?"

Maia nods.

My heart pounds. Not because it looks like Maia Moon is thinking about kissing me again, but because it's working. She's just admitted that she has a thing for me, so the Plan is really, truly working even as I flub and foul. I want to tell Beau. But instead of imagining what Beau's face might look like when I tell her Maia's falling for me, my mind conjures an image of Beau here, in this dim aisle that smells of paper and dust, with me. I imagine what it would be like if Beau were standing where Maia is right now, close enough that *we* could kiss.

I didn't think this would happen after the camera flash and awful photo, the DILF comment and me nerding out about women scientists. I'm relieved it's somehow come so easily. But something about letting Maia kiss me while we're hidden away in the stacks feels wrong in my spirit. Something about the way I'm imagining (*kissing???*) Beau makes my insides twist.

Just as Maia is leaning in, and I'm unpacking why I feel so weird when this is what I wanted, I hear a squeak and then see a book cart round the corner moments before the person pushing it does.

Maia backs away from me, but her eyes never leave mine as Mr. Waldorf, the ancient school librarian, frowns at us, glides past, and pauses at the other end of the aisle to reshelve a few books.

My skin is on fire, but not from desire. No matter how hard I try, my feelings won't stay buried, and the weirdness simmering from a few seconds ago has boiled into anger. I have to bite my lip so hard it hurts just to stop myself from asking Maia if her boyfriend knows how often she tries to kiss girls.

17
Beau

I don't consider myself a liar. I try really hard not to be, honestly. I've gotten used to girls sneaking around with me, and I made a deal with myself last summer that just because *they* were sneaking didn't mean I would. If I was their secret, fine. But it was their responsibility to keep it.

With Charm, though—with the Plan—things are a little different. There's some sneaking around involved by necessity. I still should probably leave the library so Charm can have space to do her thing with Maia. I get it, I do. I don't even like writing a new song in the same room with Celine, even though she'll eventually be the one singing it. I remember this one time Celine was giving me shit about it and Daniel had come in munching a donut, a little stoned, and said, "Celine, come on. Genius thrives in solitude." And I had laughed my ass off because he was so serious and had custard on his lip. But I've repeated those words to myself more than once since then. Now I need to let Charm's genius thrive in solitude. Or at least, in solitude with Maia.

So why am I lurking around the bookshelves like a creepy possum when I'm supposed to be going to work?

It feels kind of shitty. Charm would get that little outraged wrinkle between her eyebrows if she knew I was still here. And yes, I would probably throw her entirely off her game if she caught sight of me over here prowling around in nonfiction. But instead of leaving, I make a little fence of books to give me some cover, and like the weirdest of weirdos, watch her sit down across from Maia. *Should've sat next to her,* my inner flirt says. But that thought bubble is crowded out by a . . . feeling bubble? Relief.

This is always the part where Celine's voice pops up. Not an angel or a devil on my shoulder, but a little mom-therapist clinging to the collar of my shirt and stage-whispering, *Interrogate your feelings! Follow the root!* Okay, fine. Relief—why? Oh, I don't know, maybe because Maia and I were only supposed to have access to each other's pants, and somehow she ended up with access to at least a piece of my heart. Is that it? That seeing her with another girl torches that little piece a little crispier?

It doesn't feel like that, though. It feels like something else. But when Maia leans across the table to pick something off Charm's hair, I'm definitely aware of something burning. It's my face.

They're just talking. I can't hear them—it's a library, after all, and they're sitting close. And then not sitting close—Charm is getting up. I duck down deeper behind the barrier of books I've built. (Jesus, I'm a creep.) But she's not coming anywhere near me. She's walking around the table to . . . sit next to Maia. *Way to go, champ,* I think.

So why does my heart sink a little?

"Do you have any intention of checking those books out?"

I jump. A foot away is Mr. Waldorf, library sentry. At least a million years old. Which isn't the issue: you'll never catch me being an ageist. Ms. Brewer, who teaches calc, is also a million years old, but she's cool as shit and knows what Instagram is and walked out with us when we protested for Palestine. But Waldorf thinks anyone born in a year that starts with a two is an infant, and if you ask him to recommend a book—don't ever do that—it will be *The Catcher in the Rye* as a rule.

"I'm sorry, what?" I say, to buy time. I'm trying to respond to him and stay out of sight at the same time. Charm just *had* to go sit on Maia's side of the table. Now she's facing me. Fan-fucking-tastic.

"Are you doing something with those books? It doesn't look like reading."

I duck lower. "I was, um, trying to decide which would be best to support the project I'm working on."

Mr. Waldorf leans forward and looks over his glasses.

"*Severed: A History of Heads Lost and Heads Found?*" he reads. "*Gone Tomorrow: The Hidden Life of Garbage?*"

"Um . . ."

"A project, you say?"

Why is he talking so loud?!

"I . . . uh . . ."

"*How to Mellify a Corpse: And Other Human Stories of Ancient Science and Superstition?* And are those the last two books in the Song of Ice and Fire series? I know those can't be for a class."

I can't tell for sure because I'm crouched lower and lower, but through a crack in the books, it looks like Charm and Maia are glancing in this direction. Karma is real. I should've left the library.

I have to get the hell out of here.

"I, um, just remembered I don't know how to read," I say.

And then, still crouching, I escape before Mr. Waldorf can call out *Rest in Pieces: The Curious Fates of Famous Corpses.*

I'm late to work, but I knew I would be. If I had the car, it would've been fine, but oh no, Cart-gate means I won't be given full vehicular trust and the ability to control my own arrival time until I'm like twenty-four. Hopefully by then I'll have moved out of this town and into a city that has a train. I'm not picky about which.

"You're fired," Talia, my Wednesday manager, says when I walk in.

"No, I'm not," I say, and head over to the shoe counter. I've worked here long enough to know that the only people who come to bowl on Wednesdays are the league guys—and at one point Maia, because she knew it was slow. But obviously she isn't (and won't be) here, and the league guys would laugh cigar-scented guffaws if I dared ask them if they needed a pair of shoes. They have their own, tucked inside embroidered bags with the two-hundred-dollar bowling balls they carry. I wonder what I'll spend my retirement money on when I'm their age. Therapy, at this rate.

As if on cue, just as I duck under the counter and drop my bag, I get a text from Celine.

Celine: Did they fire you for being late to work?

Beau: (1) They'll never fire me, I'm a star employee and (2) why are you looking at my location

Celine: I always check to make sure you get to work. How else will I know if you've been kidnapped? I need to know so I can buy thank you cards for whoever did it

Beau: Harr harr

Celine: So what's the word on Panty Girl?

Beau: Jesus, don't call her Panty Girl

Celine: She's Panty Girl now, sorry

Beau: I hate you

Celine: Ouch. Okay but PG?

Beau: PG?

Celine: Panty Girl

Beau: stfu Celine. There's no "word." It's over.

Celine: Then who have you been texting so much? That girl from the show? Is that why you needed the car the other day? I wanna know

Beau: Wants and needs, Celine. Wants and needs

Celine: Did he who made the lamb make thee?

Beau: What

Celine: William Blake. A writer like yourself

Beau: 🙄

Celine. She pretended she and Daniel were "just friends" for a full year before I caught them kissing in our garage once, yet she wants to know all about my situationship. She's always trying to be a mom. Then she asks things like a sister does, but doesn't tell them. It makes me want to poke her beehive a little.

Beau: Oh, meant to ask you: are you still going to do two classes next semester?

The little bubbles show that she starts to type, then stops. I kind of regret sending it now. Celine is a little sensitive about the online college courses. She says this is why she wants me to go to an actual college—the "don't make the same mistakes I made" stuff. How someone who is only twenty-one acts like a depressed father of four is beyond me. Besides, I think it's all a front—maybe even to herself. If she makes a big deal out of college, then she can pretend she doesn't wish she could do music full-time. Hell, maybe that's why she wants her drummer (me) to go to college so bad. Disassembling a dream on your own is less sad than watching it fall apart by itself.

Celine: Yes, it depends on how busy the bakery is.

Beau: They can always hire someone else to help out

Celine: Butt out, buttface

And that's exactly what I mean, right there. My problems are up for discussion—*Go to college, Beau! Step out of your comfort zone, Beau!*—but when I touch her life with a single finger, it's *Butt out, buttface.*

Beau: Maturity thou art loosed

Celine: Whatev. Remember Pack of Eight is coming up. Elicktric! Polish up those songs

Beau: 🙂

Work is slow. I go through ten pages of the notebook I use for songwriting, scratching out cliché after cliché as soon as I write them. At one point I actually do google William Blake, but all his poems feel like church, with things like "ah!" and "O!" and "sweet golden clime." If I'm going to read old-ass poems, it's going to be Sappho. At least she wrote about kissing girls.

"Hi, can we get some shoes?"

I look up, surprised. I was so lost in my own shitty metaphors and so used to the Wednesday evening lull, I didn't even notice the couple come up to the counter. It's two women, both around my height but old—not Mr. Waldorf old, but the kind of old where when people talk about the internet, they probably bring up MySpace, which I have gathered is like caveman Instagram.

"Sure, sorry, what sizes do you need?"

"Eight for me, seven for her," the woman with glasses says, squeezing the other's arm. She wears her hair cut short, even shorter than mine. Her skin is deep brown and her earrings are gauges. So, cool old people. *And lesbians,* I think, attempting to study them without looking too hard.

"Homework?" the shorter lady says, nodding at my notebook. She's South Asian and has on shiny lip gloss and a shirt that says LITTLE DRAGON.

"Don't ask that, Prya!" the one with glasses says, laughing.

"I'm a teacher, I can't help it!"

"That makes it even worse!"

I laugh too then—they're both nice, and people aren't always.

"No, it's not homework. I'm trying to write a song."

"A songwriter!" the one with glasses says. "Do you sing?"

"Oh, no," I say quickly. "I have a terrible voice. I'm in a band, though. My sister sings."

"What's the name of the band?"

"Favorite Daughter."

"Good name," the one called Prya says, nodding firmly, and for some reason I really believe she means it.

"Does Favorite Daughter play shows?" they ask as I get their shoes.

"Yeah, for sure. We're on Instagram . . . if you have Instagram."

They exchange a look.

"She thinks we're ninety years old," Prya says.

"I don't!" I protest, laughing.

"Yeah, yeah," the other says, grinning. "Back to your song."

They thank me and head off toward Lane 10, which Talia assigned them, arms around each other. I watch them go, surprised I've never seen them before. This town isn't so small that you know every single person, but it's small enough that I think I would know if there was a coolish lesbian couple. They would have at least come to the bakery or something, and Daniel's mom is always telling me every single thing she has heard about gay shit so that I'll know she's cool with me being queer. She definitely would have said, *Oh, Bobo, some women like you were in here. Holding hands. Lesbians, you know. They were very nice. They ordered fritters.*

I watch the women without meaning to. They bowl like they don't give a fuck—sometimes backward, sometimes between their legs like little kids. They kiss constantly. They don't even look in the direction of the league guys, who do some staring from Lane 2. But then again, that's what I'm doing too. It feels strange watching them. Like they're astronauts on a planet I've been eyeing through a telescope, and suddenly I don't know if the gravity of earth is enough to keep me satisfied with this one. When Prya gets a strike, her partner hugs her, grabs her ass, and lifts her up by it. It makes me feel squirmy, and I look away.

Right into the face of Maia Moon.

I manage not to jump, but the words come out dickish: "What are you doing here?"

"Oh, nice to see you, too," she says in that slanting voice.

I look at the clock—six p.m. I wonder how long it's been since she and Charm parted. I can't help but look at her mouth. Part reflex, part wondering if I'll see Charm's lip gloss there. Would I even recognize it?

"I just haven't seen you here in a while," I say.

"Well, I'm here now," she says, like nothing has changed.

It makes something in my body twinge. I'm not sure if it's my heart or my stomach, or maybe something lower. But I hold my ground.

"Yeah, well, things are different since you were here last."

She stares at me for a long moment, blinking in that unhurried way. I used to think she did it on purpose. Bait. Maia is so good with bait. Long, slow blinks that invite you to speak. But right now she looks like she's processing. Even after everything, I can't decide about her. That William Blake poem comes to mind. I'm not sure if she's lamb or tiger.

"I've been meaning to talk to you," she says. I know that voice. *Tiger*, I think. "About . . . you know, everything. I know there are some things I could've handled better."

I can't help but laugh at that.

"Yeah?" I say. I lean back on the stool and rest my elbows on the counter behind me. She's making my stomach knot up, but no way in hell I'll let her see that. Weeks ago I was hungry for this conversation, but right now I just feel pissed off. "No shit, Maia."

She looks hurt.

"I'm trying to apologize, Beau."

"Are you? For what exactly?"

She leans across the counter. My nose can't smell her, but my mind can. There have been a lot of Wednesdays where my fingers smelled like her for the rest of my shift. I can tell by the look on her face that she's thinking about my fingers too.

"I've been thinking about you," she says, dodging the question. "Haven't you been thinking about me? I know I don't always wear my heart on my sleeve, but . . ."

"No, you wear it under several layers of clothing," I say. "Coat, fleece, your *boyfriend's* shirt, bra . . ."

I shouldn't have said "bra."

She fastens her eyes on me. The lips I've been trying not to look at part.

"Beau," she says. She almost smiles.

This whole place reminds me of her. There's not a room here I haven't kissed her in. So when she moves to do what she always does—duck under the counter, come closer—it's hard for me to reach out my hand and stop her.

But I do.

On the tip of my tongue is my too-long speech. And it feels

longer than ever. Other things have worked their way in: the party; Charm, and Maia's willingness to risk being seen with her. Then other random stuff too: the lesbian couple on Lane 10; Tatum calling Tasha a carpet muncher and Maia saying nothing. Suddenly everything matters, but instead of saying it all, I boil it down to three words:

"Not today, Maia."

She freezes, her eyes wider than I've ever seen them. It's not shock, exactly. It's almost like she's making her eyes bigger to take in as much information as possible. I'm sure on some level she thinks I'm joking. Nobody rejects Maia Moon. That's not what I'm doing, though. It doesn't feel like rejection. It feels like . . . protection. From *her* rejection.

"No biggie," she says, and there's that starry, fake smile. The one she flashes for pictures, for teachers, for Tate. It almost makes me wince.

When she leaves, the bowling alley feels a little dimmer, and I can't bring myself to look in the direction of the couple in Lane 10. I make sure I'm in the bathroom when they head over to return their shoes.

At eight thirty, Talia sends me home early.

"You're eating up my clock," she says. "It's dead in here!"

But it's always dead on Wednesdays, and I think she's just taking pity on me because I must look sad.

When I head outside, I'm kind of glad for once that I don't have the car. It's colder than I thought, and it makes me walk faster, putting more space between me and the bowling alley. I wonder where the couple went after they left. Where they're from. Maybe they're here for a wedding. Maybe they grew up here and came back for an anniversary or some old-people shit. I don't know why I'm even thinking about them. Then I don't know why I'm thinking about Maia Moon and the library. Her reaching across the table to pick something off Charm's hair . . .

I don't know why I'm calling Charm.

When she answers, she sounds surprised.

"Beau?"

"Hey," I say. Then I realize I probably should have a reason to be calling her. "Just wanted to see how it went at the library."

"Well, you smacked my ass and put me in the game, Coach. I played my best. Put numbers on the board."

"Are these . . . sports words?"

She laughs. The night feels a little warmer.

"I go to enough of Ezra's games to know a thing or two."

"Teach me a thing or two," I say.

"I thought that was your job."

"The teacher becomes the student, Charm."

She laughs again and we talk the rest of my walk home. But I don't ask if she kissed Maia. I don't really want to know. Not right now.

18
Charm

"She called me *Charm*, Ezra."

Ezra keeps eating his sandwich and scrolling his phone like I haven't said anything, so I reach across the table and pluck it (the phone, not the sandwich) out of his hand. When I look at the screen, it's full of tiny squares, all photos of Enzo.

"Hey!" he says. He tries to grab it back, but I put the phone under my side of the cafeteria table, where he can't reach it.

"Sorry to interrupt your Insta-obsessing, but did you hear anything I just said?"

Enzo pops a chip into his mouth and looks guilty. "Honestly? No."

"Blinded by Enzo's golden pecs, huh?" I ask, glancing down at his feed. "I guess I get it. He is objectively beautiful. How's all that going, by the way?"

Enzo puts down his sandwich and grins as he lowers his voice. "I was backstage with him for a bit yesterday."

"And you're just telling me this *now*?"

"Well, it's kinda been the Charm and Maia show around here lately. I mean, you forgot about *Beyoncé*."

"In my defense, we had no chance of getting those tickets."

Ezra rolls his eyes.

"That said," I continue, "you're not wrong. Have I been the worst? I'm sorry if I've been the worst!"

Ezra steals one of my fries. "I forgive you, I guess."

"So . . . what the hell happened backstage?"

"You know, the usual. Him flirting, me hiding. Him shining, me pining. You would think for someone who has as much mouth as me, I'd be able to, I don't know, *speak* to him at least. But it's like his beauty literally takes my breath away."

"If you had game, I'm afraid we could no longer be friends," I tell him. "Your awkwardness in social situations is the only thing that puts weirdo me in the same league as superstar-athlete you."

"Charmy-poo," he says, "don't make me make you list your star qualities again."

"We're talking about you right now, sir. What are you going to do?"

Ezra nibbles on his bottom lip, then picks up his sandwich again. "I think I'm going to ask him to prom," he says, like it's no big deal.

"I'm sorry, *what?*" I yelp. "I don't want to yuck your yum, but should we maybe start smaller? You can barely speak to the man, and you're going to ask him to the biggest social event of the year?"

"Go big or go home," Ezra says, a glint of determination in his eye. It's the same look he gets when he's underestimated by a visiting team because he's the shortest guy on the court, or at the start of a track meet lined up with longer-legged kids who think he's a joke: all big nerve and bigger heart.

I shrug. "Guess I can't argue with that."

"So Beau called you Charm, huh?"

"Oh, so you *did* hear me." I throw a fry at his head. It glances off his temple, and he retaliates with a wadded-up napkin.

"Not Monty? Or even Charmander? But *Charm*?" He fans his face and lets out a low whistle.

"Exactly," I say.

I haven't told Ezra that I think I'm crushing on Beau, but judging by the look on his face, he seems to have intuited it all on his own. I hope he hasn't, though. Whenever he gets a whiff of my crushes, he goes balls to the walls with encouraging me to pursue them. It's not a terrible quality to have in a bestie, but it can be an overwhelming one. Especially now, when I'm trying to focus all my energy on getting through the Plan.

I turn a little in my seat and gaze across the cafeteria at the table where Beau is sitting. She's been a bit of a lone wolf ever since that one friend of hers left town, but sometimes she hangs with the other kids who aren't really in an established clique—people who aren't exactly outsiders but aren't that popular, either, aren't burnouts or activists or nerds. Me and Ezra are kinda like that too, but he floats a bit closer to the jocks because of his athletic prowess, and sometimes with the artsy kids because of theater. I think my connection to Jada keeps me from being totally socially exiled, because even though she graduated, the dance team girlies still say hi to me in the halls. Ezra and I just . . . coast.

But Beau isn't stuck anywhere—she's confident enough to float everywhere. Today she's talking to Evie Perez, a cute girl who I know is on the debate team. Evie says something to her, and Beau shrugs before smiling her crooked Beau-smile. My heart just about jumps out of my chest when, at that very moment, Beau looks up and sees me staring. She's still smirking as she raises one of her eyebrows, and I pretty much feel like I'm dying.

To Ezra I say, "I have to take Maia to that show tonight, and I'm supposed to kiss her. It's the next step in the Plan. But . . ." I trail off.

"But . . . Beau calling you Charm has you questioning things?" Ezra guesses correctly.

My head snaps back to him. "No." I deny it, a bit too vehemently, probably. I shake my head, blink too quickly, look down at what's left of my lunch. "No, it's just, I'm not sure I know how." I'm trying to calculate how I got here, what steps or missteps led to this moment where these two impossible things are both true: I have to kiss Maia, but I *want* to kiss Beau.

"Is this a Jada thing?" Ezra asks.

"Huh?"

"Do you feel like you don't know how to kiss because of all that messed-up shit Jada said to you when you two broke up?"

For once, I wasn't even thinking about Jada. I haven't thought about Jada in a while, actually, but this feels like a truth that might save me—pull me out of or at least away from whatever I'm feeling for Beau. I know how to kiss a girl, but I want to know how to kiss *Beau*. I go with it.

"Yes?" I say.

"This might sound unhinged, but why not just tell Beau you need another lesson?" he says, so casually that I nearly choke on my water. Some actually dribbles down my chin.

"Attractive," Ezra says.

"A kissing lesson?" I ask. "Really?"

"Why not? How is it different from the flirting or the asking-someone-out lessons? Plus, it's pretty obvious Beau likes kissing. And she likes you. So why would she say no?"

Something in my chest swells. "Wait. You think she likes me?"

"I mean, yeah. You guys are friends, right?"

Friends. Right. So, Ezra *hasn't* guessed that I *like* like Beau. Or I've thrown him off. He's looking at his phone again, and I'm grateful because the thought of a kissing lesson with Beau makes me feel so many things at once, I'm sure my face is giving me away. I feel giddy and terrified; like I might puke or scream, cry or laugh. I let the possibility of it hang there, like everything I'm not telling him, and rearrange my features into a mask of calm when he looks back up.

We talk about what's been up lately at Roots, Enzo's upcoming show and the perfect bouquet he has in mind to give him, and then about how it looks like the track team might go to regionals this year. And when our conversation circles back to Beau, I let Ezra think he's convincing me to kiss my *friend*. "Let's be clear: Jada was a bitch, and I've been working on building you back up since her awful exit last summer. And if kissing Beau will help you feel good about kissing Maia, it'll probably help you feel good about you," he says.

This feels logical. I'm going to kiss Beau to build my confidence, to get better at kissing, so that I know how to kiss Maia for the good of the Plan.

Not because I like her.

"And you know me . . . ," Ezra continues.

"You're Team Charm?" I ask, grinning.

"I'm Team Charm."

So that's how I end up standing outside Beau's house a few hours later.

Bree and Chauncey are still in town, staying in a cute Airstream B and B while they wait for their loan to clear, and when Aunt Miki said she needed her car, so I couldn't borrow it, they offered up their sleek black SUV. At first I vehemently refused (my affection will not be bought!), but then Ezra told me it would be a cool car to pick Maia up in, and that they owe me, like, their *lives*, so taking their car wasn't that big of a deal. He also wanted me to drop him off at Roots, so his motives weren't pure, but still. He had a point.

When we got to Roots, Ezra gave me a peony for Maia, but after standing at Beau's door for a couple of seconds empty-handed, I go back to the car and get the flower to give to her.

I didn't tell Beau I was coming. I was too nervous, too worried I would overthink anything she said if I asked first. She gave me her address a few weeks ago, "for emergencies," and this feels like one, only I'm not sure what exactly I'll say if she asks me what the problem is. Maybe, *I needed your lips*?

I look at my phone to check the time: 4:49 p.m. I need to leave here by five forty-five at the latest to get Maia and drive to Sligo for the Oranges show at seven. But a time constraint is good, I think. If I have time to linger, I'll have time to lose my nerve. I swallow hard, and I'm just about to finally press the bell when the door swings open.

A girl who looks like Beau in drag is standing in front of me. Like, good drag. She has the same face as Beau, so she's beautiful, but her hair is wavy and shoulder-length, her lashes have a few coats of mascara on them, and she's wearing a long rose-colored dress and holding a half-eaten donut. The singer, I suddenly realize, from Favorite Daughter. Beau's sister.

"Was getting a little worried aboutcha," she says, chewing. Her voice is high and floaty—nothing at all like Beau's. "You've been standing out here for ages."

I cringe. "It hasn't been that long, has it?"

"Well, when you first got here, this donut was whole. And it's a cake donut. And I'm a slow chewer."

"Oh god, did Beau see me drive up?"

Fuck, fuck, fuck.

She looks me up and down. "Who are you, exactly?"

"Oh, right, sorry. I'm so rude. I'm Charm. I assume you're Beau's sister. Celine, right? Hi. Did I say hi? Sorry, hi. Is Beau home?"

She leans against the doorframe and takes another bite of her donut. "You got a boyfriend?" she asks.

I blink at her. "Uh, no. I, um, mostly like girls?"

It feels a little weird to come out to someone I just met, but even though she seems suspicious of me, I can feel that it's not because I'm queer. I think her energy has more to do with something about Beau than anything about me.

Celine looks like she's doing some mental math, and she must decide I'm harmless because she smiles a little, turns, and screams into the house, "Beau, a cute girl is here for you!"

A second later Beau screams back, "Haha, Celine, you're so funny. I don't have time to play this game. I'm busy!"

And then Celine is screaming again, "I'm not joking, someone is here for you!"

Beau says, "You're so annoying. You tell me to work on the damn songs, and as soon as I start, you or Daniel want to—"

Beau rounds the corner, sees me, and freezes. She's barefoot in denim cutoffs I've never seen before and a T-shirt that has the sleeves chopped off. The armholes are wide enough for me to see the sports bra she's wearing under it. It has a rainbow band along the bottom and she has . . . freckles . . . along her rib cage.

"Monty?" she says in disbelief. "What are you doing here?"

Celine walks toward her sister and bops her on the head with the hand holding what's left of the donut. A light shower of powdered sugar lands in Beau's hair. "Don't be a dick, Beau. Invite her in!"

"Why didn't you?" Beau shouts as Celine disappears down the hall. "Sorry, Charm, come on in."

Charm.

I step inside, and Beau looks at me for so long, I clear my throat. Then she clears hers. "You look . . . nice," she says. And that's when I remember I'm kind of dressed up for the Oranges show.

I'm in a thrifted leather jacket with a midriff tank top underneath, a pair of short jean shorts with fishnets, and combat boots. I tied my braids up and applied a ton of eyeliner, and I'm wearing contacts instead of my glasses. I put on a little extra lip gloss right before I got out of my car. I did consider that looking cute might make Beau more likely to accept my request. And by the way, her dark eyes seem unable to stay still—bouncing from my hair to my exposed middle, to my feet, back to my face, only to dart away again—I think I might have been right.

"The show is tonight," I remind her. "The Oranges, at Sligo. I gotta pick up Maia in, like, forty minutes."

She nods, then seems to remember where she is. "My bad. Let's, um, go to my room."

I follow her down the hall and into her bedroom. It's small and tidy, with blue walls and a tie-dyed rug. Her shoes are everywhere, and her drum practice pad is in one corner, but the bed is made, and other than a notebook and some crumpled pages on a desk against a wall with a window, it's neater than I was expecting. Apparently, her hair is the messiest thing about her.

"So, what's up?" she asks, flopping down on her bed. I stand across from her and take a deep breath.

"Here," I say awkwardly. I thrust the peony at her.

She looks down at it, grinning. "Um, thanks?" She scans her

room like she doesn't know what to do with it, then plops it in a cup with pencils, highlighters, and pens on the corner of her desk. Weirdly, it looks like it belongs there.

"I was thinking, before I go to this show with Maia, I need one more lesson."

Beau grins. "Oh yeah?" she asks.

"Yeah," I say. I can feel my heart pounding, but I try to ignore it as I stand up and take the few steps required to close the space between us. I sit down on the bed beside her, trying to remember all the things she taught me, because suddenly I want this more than I've wanted anything in a while. Eye contact and tone and intention and attention. I want to make it sound like a suggestion, like she said to do with the date, so I'll have an out if she says no. I touch her hand, just tap each of her knuckles like I'm playing a tiny xylophone. And I actually get it right. Unlike with Maia, I don't make a single mistake. I look into her deep blue eyes, and even though my voice shakes a little, I don't look away as I say, "You should teach me how to kiss."

19
Beau

Charm has a great sense of humor. The word "banter" has been beaten into the ground: sometimes when you talk to someone who thinks they're witty, conversations feel like jumping on a trampoline, and you have to make sure you find your feet before you land so you can hurry up and jump again. But Charm is just chill funny. It's why I like talking to her. And why at first I think she's joking.

But when I laugh, she does that thing where she drops her chin. If she were wearing her glasses, they would have slipped down just a little. But since she isn't, I have a clear view and . . . Jesus, her eyes. I can't even hold her gaze, which sends my eyes around my room and makes me realize . . . she's in my room. I've never had a girl in my room before. Not Maia, not anyone. Girls never want to come to my place—makes it feel too real for them. They like parking lots mostly. Their house when they're home alone and can sneak me in and out the back door. But here's Charm, sitting in my room. Not smiling.

"Wait, you're serious?" I say.

"I wouldn't ask if I didn't think it was necessary," she says. "If this wasn't kind of an emergency. Time is running out." She lifts her chin now, like she's trying to be cool and businesslike. *She's focused on the Plan*, I think. I know it's true—it's literally what we agreed to do. So I can be businesslike too. I just need to get a grip first.

"I mean, sure, Monty, I know," I say. "And, uh, I'll help however I can."

That didn't quite sound like I got a grip.

"Shall we?" I add, in the chillest business-casual voice I can muster.

"Should I sit? Stand? A secret third thing?"

I turn my head to my desk, where I have two chairs. The one dragged in from the dining room is where Celine sits when she's whisper-singing my lyrics after I've labored over them. Charm follows my eyes. Then smiles.

"Is that a typewriter?" she says, moving toward the desk.

"Oh," I say. "Yeah."

"Where you pen your masterpieces," she says. "Well, except not *pen*. Where you . . . tap out your masterpieces?"

I point at the trash can, which is piled high with balled-up papers.

"You mean my graveyard of clichés?"

"Death begets life," she says. "Or something like that."

She sits down in the chair that's usually mine, not looking at me but still smiling. There's a blank piece of paper in the typewriter. I had just put it in when Celine called me to say someone was at the door. Charm leans forward and then glances at me. Her eyes say, *May I?*

"Be my guest," I say. "You'll probably write something better than all the bullshit I've written today. Celebrating three weeks of writer's block, if you wanna bake me a cake."

She taps out a few letters, and I force myself to sit in the other chair nearby, scooting it a couple of inches closer. Our arms don't quite touch. Usually with girls I know exactly what to do. I know what they expect, and I can step into the role like broken-in sneakers. But Charm is starting to set me off-balance. Her even being here makes my axis wobble.

"There," she says, and leans back from the typewriter.

I glance at it, then away, then do a double take. She's typed two words:

Kiss me

My heart feels like it grabbed an electric fence. I'm glad I was already sitting down, because I'm not sure how I could have stayed standing or been smooth after that, but it doesn't really matter in the end, because it's Charm who leans in, who presses her lips against mine first.

But then she stops. It's like her brain has caught up with what she's doing, because she doesn't kiss me, she just freezes, our mouths touching.

Get a fucking grip, Beau!

I part my lips, and hers respond in kind. My hands remember they're hands. They lift and find their way to her face. I know I'm supposed to be giving her a lesson, but for a moment I'm distracted by how smooth her skin is under my fingers. I've noticed how smooth it looks so many times, wondered what it would feel like. And now I know. Cool and soft. She's wearing perfume, but I also smell whatever it is she puts in her hair, too. Her lip gloss. I can even pick up the faint smell of her laundry detergent. Marshmallow, melon, linen. Charm smells like all the good things in the world. It's kind of overwhelming, and I pull back.

"You should probably close your eyes when you kiss her," I say. I hope my voice sounds normal. And not like I'm thinking about kissing her. Even though I'm supposed to be thinking about kissing her. But not the way *I'm* thinking about kissing her.

"Close my eyes?" she says. "Talk about cliché!"

"It's not cliché to close your eyes when you kiss a girl," I say, laughing. "And besides, clichés are cliché because they're true."

"I feel like if my eyes are closed, I'll miss her lips," she says doubtfully.

I laugh, and then my hands find her face again and pull her closer, tracing her lips with my finger. "So use your hands." I blink at her to remind her about her eyes. I watch them flutter closed. Then this time, I kiss her.

"Soft at first," I say, between kisses. "Take your time."

Her eyes stay closed, but her lips respond, matching my slow pace. So she's listening.

"Now touch my neck," I tell her.

Her lips pause, and she doesn't move her hands from her lap right away. So mine come down from her face and rest on top of hers. I lift them, guiding them to my neck. "Like this," I say, and reach for her neck.

My right hand is on the side of her neck, its thumb on her throat. My left hand is farther back on the other side, thumb under her ear.

Her hands start to mimic mine, and a wave of goose bumps rushes down my back. Straight girls don't usually want to touch me. They want to be touched, but not do the touching—too much commitment to being queer. Fine if you go down on them. Taking is okay. But giving? Giving admits something. It wasn't until the last two times with Maia that she had gotten brave, reached under my shirt. But then she ghosted.

Charm's thumb moves in a circle under my ear. I didn't tell her to do that . . . but then I realize I'm already doing it to her. Is she mimicking me? Or is she doing it because she wants to, and I'm mimicking *her* without realizing it? My heartbeat is faster than it's supposed to be, but I can't think about slowing it down and kissing her at the same time.

I opt for kissing her.

The tip of my tongue slides between her lips. It feels like I could get lost in kissing her. I remind myself that this is a lesson and pull it back.

"Slowly," I say, pausing. "Not too much too fast."

She nods the quickest nod, almost like she wants me to shut up. This time her tongue meets mine. My hand creeps around to the back of her neck. She inhales sharply, and I know what it means. There's a string that extends from her mouth down through her body to the space between her legs, and I just strummed it.

Her tongue wanders deeper into my mouth, and somehow my hand finds its way to her rib cage and gently pulls her closer. Her mouth is so warm. Her body is so warm. God, she's wearing this cropped shirt. I stroke her skin. She makes a noise in the back of her throat that sounds like a whimper. It makes my heart beat even faster. I want to make her make that sound again. My mouth leaves her mouth, and I kiss her jaw on my way to her neck. Her hands are gripping my neck hard . . . so hard that it makes me pause.

I look at her. Her eyes are still closed. Closed tight.

Fuck. What am I *doing*? This isn't what she came for. She came for kissing lessons for *Maia Moon*, and here I am getting lost in it.

The arrival of that thought is like a sudden wind howling through my brain.

This is exactly what happened with Maia.

I hadn't seen it while it was happening. I started with my guard up, but she talked and giggled and kissed her way past it. Then as soon as she made it inside, she disappeared. Maia was never actually into me, not the way I realized too late I was starting to be into her. She was there for her own reasons, not for me. And so is Charm.

I stop immediately. I loosen my hands from her body and pull away quickly. Her eyes snap open. I can barely look at her. I'm afraid of what I'll see.

"So yeah, that pretty much covers it, I'd say?" I try to sound clear and chill, but inside it feels like I'm scrambling. "Definitely touch her ears. That drives her crazy."

I realize as soon as it leaves my mouth that it sounds a little bitter. I wince internally. Then I can't avoid it anymore—I look Charm in the eyes.

I catch the tail end of whatever it was that crossed her face. She has the dazed look of someone who was about to skydive and stepped back just in time to realize their parachute was stuck.

"Wow," she says.

"What?"

"Nothing." She stands a little abruptly. "Thanks for the intel."

"I mean, sure. Anything for the mission, right?"

And there it is again, that bitter tone, even if I hide it a little better this time. What is my problem?

"Anyway," I add, "I know you don't want to be late, so . . ."

She's turned, looking at the Little Dragon poster on my wall, and doesn't reply at first. But then she turns back to me.

"I feel like you're getting close to a constitutional violation."

"Huh?"

"I can tell you still have feelings for Maia," she says in a rush.

"And, like, that's fine. But just remember what we agreed to."

"Thou shalt not . . . tell you not to be late for your date?"

She rolls those perfect eyes.

"The 'thou shalts' are commandments, Beau. Commandments aren't in the Constitution."

"Oh. Right."

"And I'm talking about *our* constitution." She pauses before she says the rest: "We can do this without you hating me. We can still stay friends."

Stay friends. My lips are still wet with her saliva. The words "stay friends" feel like she bit my tongue.

20
Charm

Friends.

Even as I say the word, I know it doesn't fit what I'm feeling. The way my heart is racing. The way my face is burning. The way certain places are tingling.

But I'm also stung. I know Beau knows how to be sexy, but she's also honest. And if she pulled away that fast, like she couldn't bear to kiss me for a second longer . . . maybe she really couldn't. Bear it, I mean. And just like that, I'm back in that bedroom with Jada, back in Andi's house with Maia. I'm ten years old again and my parents are saying, "We want you to come live with us," in the same breath they're saying, "We're pregnant!" I'm back in every place I've ever been made to feel like I wasn't enough. My face is hot with shame, but in the same moment I feel something else.

With Beau, being embarrassed by my inexperience isn't the worst thing I can imagine. And I was laying it on a little thick anyway, letting her take the lead, pretending to be more clueless about kissing than I actually am. But I realize I'm worried her move to the other side of the room is more than one kind of rejection—romantic, yes, but platonic, too.

So I panic. And ever since Jada, when I panic because I'm feeling rejected, I act like a bitch.

"Friends?" Beau asks.

"Yes, *friends*, Beau. We agreed," I say, staring right at her. "We agreed we wouldn't do this."

"Do what, Monty?"

I try not to dwell on how she hasn't said my first name since we closed the door to her bedroom. I try not to notice how I can still feel the ghost of her pulse in my fingertips.

"Hurt each other," I say.

"What are you even talking about?"

She seems exasperated with me, like I'm being irrational or trying to confuse her on purpose, and I hate when people act like I'm being purposely obtuse when I'm being very, very clear. I groan and start looking for the notebook where we wrote everything down that day in the diner.

"You're doing the thing, Beau!"

"What thing?"

"The . . . the turtle thing! Where you won't even stick your head out of your shell to have a real conversation!"

"Wait, *turtle* thing?"

But once again, I was clear. I know I was clear. So I don't repeat myself. I stomp over to her backpack, furious that the whole room smells like a coming storm, earthy and fresh and clean like her. I unzip it, but the small green notebook isn't in there. I don't think about the soft feel of the hair at the nape of Beau's neck as I go back to the desk and start moving things around, catching sight of phrases she's thrown away like *sullen shadows* and *lots of knots* and *nothing hurts like home* winking up at me through the creases in balled-up sheets of paper.

"Where's the notebook?" I ask her, ignoring how the kissing instructions she whispered into my mouth are still echoing around in my brain. *Not too much too fast.* How they remind me of things Jada said: *Move like butter melting in a pan.*

"What notebook?" she says. And then she's standing, coming over to where I am. Touching me. "Just wait a minute. I think you should calm down." Her eyes go wide, like she knows she's said the wrong thing. "I mean, *slow* down."

But I don't want to slow down. I'm tired of all the voices in my head telling me to slow down! I regret not reaching under her shirt. I regret that I don't know what her freckles feel like against my fingertips. I regret not asking her more about her writing, how she thinks of the hooks for her songs, what inspires her. I regret not going faster, not doing more. . . . But the possibility that I might lose her entirely crowds out everything else.

I glare at her and pull away. "I *am* calm, Beau. Where is the notebook where we wrote the Plan? Where we wrote the constitution? Is it in here?" I ask.

I pull open her desk drawer, but it's shallow and neat. Pencils and Wite-Out and Post-its slide around a bit. I close the drawer and spin, my eyes scanning the room until they land on her small bedside table.

I step over a pair of her shoes, hand already reaching for the drawer handle, and I realize as I do it that I have no business riffling around in her room. But it's like I can't stop myself. I need to show her the words we wrote. Remind her of the promises we made. Because the thought of losing her makes my throat feel tight and achy. This feels like the only way I can stop her from . . . I don't know. Doing what Jada did when she found me lacking.

Leaving.

I pull the drawer open and I freeze. The green notebook is there. But sitting on top of it is a pair of lacy underwear that I know, just by looking, don't belong to Beau.

"Um . . . ," I say. I swallow hard and back away, and it's like Beau knows what I've found before I say anything, because she's jumping over shoes, vaulting to the nightstand, and positioning herself in front of it, like if I don't *see* the panties anymore, I'll forget they're there.

"Right," I say. "Sorry. God, that was so rude and weird of me to just go through your things. I don't know what I was thinking." I'm blinking too much and not looking at Beau because I can't, and I don't know whose underwear those are, but they make something in my chest ache.

"I was going to give them back," Beau says. "I swear. I actually came to that party to give them back to her. But then I walked in and saw you two about to kiss and—"

"Wait," I say, my brain doing a painful and slow kind of calculation. And then I do look up at Beau. Her expression is tight and her thick brows are furrowed, and she is so beautiful.

But that's not why I feel like I can't breathe. Like I'm maybe going to be sick.

"Those . . . are Maia's?"

21
Beau

How do you tell a girl that having another girl's panties in your drawer doesn't always mean what it looks like it means? *It's not what it looks like* is the stalest excuse for anything since forever, but . . . it's *not* what it looks like. Or at least, it's not anymore.

"I mean, yeah. She gave them to me. But I only still have them because I haven't been able to give them back yet. Which, like I said, I wanted to. But . . ."

I hear myself tripping over my words, and even though Charm is still standing in front of me, she somehow looks farther and farther away.

"You just . . . keep girls' panties in your drawer?"

I pause. "Not girls, plural."

"Oh."

Why did I stop kissing her? I feel like I had all these reasons five seconds ago, and maybe they're still good ones, but somehow everything feels much worse than what any of those reasons could have played out as.

"She gave them to me," I explain.

"You said that already," she deadpans with empty eyes.

I look away. Then it's like a balloon inflates in my head, and I don't know why I didn't think of it before: oh shit, Charm is falling for Maia again. The Plan is the Plan, but our rules do say we can call it off at any time, so there's nothing to say Charm still has to dump her. Maybe Maia's panties in my drawer pissed Charm off because she thinks this means she'll have less of a shot. I gesture at the underwear and try to sound casual.

"Well, this was all before the Plan, obviously. So, like, don't worry. It won't mess anything up for you."

Charm's lips part like she's going to say something, but instead she waves her hand like she's clearing the air of smoke.

"Oh, it doesn't matter. None of my business, right?" She takes a step back that makes me want to reach out and grab her before she can get any farther away. But I shove my hands in my pockets—my fists are a pair of turtles too, and my pants are the shell. I can see a decision passing over her face. I don't know what it is or where exactly it's coming from, but it's like watching her step onto an iceberg and float away.

"Monty—" I start.

"Don't want to be late to pick up Maia, like you said," she interrupts, talking fast. She's turning toward my door in a sudden rush. "Thanks for the lesson. Very instructive. Thanks for being a . . . um . . . team player."

Where are my words? I'm stuck staring between her back and Maia's panties, tossed in the still-open drawer. Why the fuck do I still have them? I'm suddenly furious at Maia for ever giving them to me to begin with. At myself for not just throwing them away.

"Charm!" I finally say just as she's walking down the hall outside my room.

She pauses but doesn't look back.

"What?" she says.

"I just . . ."

I don't know what to say. Now all I can think about is how smooth her skin felt under my hands. And how when she was touching mine, she was thinking about Maia's.

"Good luck tonight," I say finally.

I wish I could see her face. But she doesn't turn back. She disappears around the corner, and by the time I make my feet move to follow, she's already out the door.

Celine appears, Daniel just behind her. They both peer out through the glass of the front door, where Charm marches to her car, gets in, and immediately drives away.

Then, like they choreographed it, Celine and Daniel both look back at me.

"What did *you* do?" Celine says.

"I don't know."

"Oh, you know," Daniel says. "You always get that look on your face when you know you fucked up."

I never should have agreed to the kissing lesson. Just like with Maia, I let things go too far.

"Yeah, well, maybe I did," I mutter.

"Call her," Daniel says. "Apologize."

"It's not that simple."

Celine looks at me appraisingly. "Are we sure it's not that simple, or are you making things complicated and then saying, 'It's not that simple'?"

"Trust me, this is anything but simple."

"That's not Panty Girl, is it?" Daniel says, cocking his head.

"Don't call her Panty Girl! And no!"

"I didn't think it was," Celine says. Her little smile makes me want to put her in a headlock. "This girl doesn't have something that we know PG does—a boyfriend."

"Why *do* you always go for chicks with boyfriends?" Daniel says. A donut has materialized from seemingly nowhere and he's eating it, staring at me earnestly.

"I don't go for them, they go for *me*!" I protest.

"You're not helpless, Bowie," Celine says, laughing. "You have agency or whatever. Have you ever thought that maybe you only entertain girls with boyfriends because they're unavailable? You deserve more than that. More time. More attention. Not just getting squeezed in when . . ."

She trails off before she finishes the sentence, and Daniel sets his donut down and places his hand on the back of her neck. The gesture and the way she trails off make me wonder if she's not just talking about me. If this is about Mom not coming to any of our shows this year. I never expect her to, but I think Celine still does. Funny how the people in your life teach you how to treat them, but the lessons vary person to person. Me? Mom has taught me to keep my expectations low, to expect to get squeezed in, or no time at all. But the same Mom has taught Celine to keep hoping for more. I'd never say it out loud—at least not within Celine's earshot—but maybe I *am* used to feeling like a part-time everything. Daughter, friend, lover.

"Well, *personally*," Daniel says in the TV show announcer voice he does when he's trying to make Celine smile. It's already working. "I think you both deserve the world, and I *personally* think anyone with a brain in their head would rearrange their entire schedule to bask in your presence."

He's talking about girls. He's talking about Mom. But all I can think about is Charm. The way her shoulders suddenly stiffened when I called her Monty.

"You okay?" Celine asks, nudging me.

This conversation honestly needs to be over. This is why I don't do feelings. Is this . . . avoidance what Charm was talking about when she called me a turtle?

"It's fine," I say. "Me and Charm are just friends. She's actually on her way to a date with so-called PG right now."

Celine's eyes widen, then narrow. There are one hundred gnomes in her skull-factory putting all the pieces together. I brace myself, but miraculously she manages to reel herself in before going full sister-mom.

"You're right," she says. "Anything but simple."

"We're just friends," I say again.

She gives me a look that makes me want to hide under the blankets on my bed.

"If you say so, Beau. Now, go finish that song."

I go back to my room, but now that Charm has been here, the whole space feels occupied. I pace for a while before I realize the drawer is still open, with Maia's panties still lying there, red and lacy. I slam the drawer shut and throw my phone on the bed so I don't use it to text Charm, then storm over to my desk to finish the song.

But there's the paper, still with Charm's two words: *Kiss me*.

I type two more:

Goddamn it.

22
Charm

"I'm so stupid," I say out loud as I sit at a traffic light.

I pull over when I'm a mile away from Beau's to clean up my face. I reapply my eye makeup, because of course I started crying the minute I drove away from her. Those panties really threw me, and in the few seconds I was staring at them, all I could think about was how little I know about girls, how much Beau does. And then to find out they were Maia's . . .

I was so stupid. To think I could use Beau's own lessons on her. To think she could be over Maia Moon—or even if she was, that kissing *me* would excite her. What a joke. I never asked *exactly* what was up with her and Maia. Now I guess I kind of know.

I want to call Ezra, but admitting to him how I really feel will just make me start sobbing again.

I don't have time to start sobbing again.

"I'm okay," I say to myself as I resume driving. "This is what I get for letting my heart take over, for letting myself want Beau." I'm done, I decide. Really done. Done with wanting anything and anyone. I turn up the radio and breathe deeply in and out with the window down. Crumpled makeup wipes and tissues are all over the passenger seat, so I sweep them into the glove box at the stop sign on the corner, one block before I get to Maia's.

I had planned to go inside. But when I pull up in front of her house (it's much bigger than mine and Beau's but way smaller than Andi's—this town is so weird), I see Tate climbing into his candy-apple-red Dodge Charger, which is sitting, obnoxiously, in the center of her driveway. It's the kind of car cops love to pull over, but I've heard that because his dad is a sergeant at the local precinct, his back seat is full of written warnings, not actual tickets. He's petting a big, goofy-looking golden retriever, who is attempting to climb into the car with him—Maia's dog, I'm guessing—when she runs out and grabs the dog by the collar to drag him away. Before she gets the dog back to the house, Tate closes his door and leans through his open window, and Maia looks around before she kisses him. They don't see me because of the tree-lined street's landscaping and the neighbor's unkempt hedges.

And suddenly, instead of feeling sorry for myself, my whole body is a lit match.

I flip down my mirror. I stare into my slightly bloodshot eyes. *If Maia wants to use me,* I think, feeling like the Plan makes more sense than ever, *I'm gonna use her, too.* I open my purse. Pull out a tube of lipstick Ezra bought me for just this occasion. I look at the bottom and the shade is called Siren. It's as red as Tate's douchey car.

I can't have Beau. I don't want Maia anymore. And since I can't straight-up say, *Call your boyfriend, it's time you had the talk,* my actions will have to do the talking for me.

I apply the lipstick and put another cuff in my already short shorts. I wait long enough to text Maia to make it seem like I didn't see Tate leave.

Here.

Coming, she sends back, and I look at myself in the mirror again, practicing the serious, not-shy expression Beau told me to use when I'm flirting, trying to emulate the steady way she holds her dark eyes without smiling. I think about Jada describing looks like that as ones that would turn men to stone. Then adding, "But they're the best kind to turn girls on."

There are too many voices in my head. And that's when a text comes in from Ezra.

How'd it go?

I can't get into everything I'm thinking and feeling.

Can you do that thing? I text him instead. **The thing where you make me tell you good stuff about myself?**

His reply comes back immediately: **Tell me something true.**

I'm funny.

He sends a green check mark.

I'm cute.

He sends the 100 emoji.

I'm awkward, I send, thinking about the Benadryl, the way I took that photo with the flash on, then add, **But it seems like maybe people think that's cute too?**

Not to be punny, but the word you're looking for, Charm, is charming, he replies.

I'm charming?

You are, he says.

Oh.

Oh.

I can follow Beau's rules. I'm a great rule follower. But as I think back to what happened in Beau's bedroom, what happened in Jada's—I realize all the times when I followed other people's rules perfectly are precisely the times when things didn't work out for me. And anyway, I'm tired of following instructions.

Tonight, I'm going to do my own thing.

Love you, I send Ezra.

To the moon, baby! he sends back.

When Maia climbs into the car, she smells different. Under her usual syrupy sweetness is a hint of something else—something masculine. I wonder if it's whatever bro-y deodorant Tate uses or some shitty body spray he keeps in his car and mists in an X across his chest after his workouts like the walking cliché he is.

"Hey," she says, and she leans over like she's going to kiss me on the cheek. It seems more like a reflex, and it may even be something she does with her friends, so I don't jerk away, just casually turn to buckle my seat belt at the moment her lips would have made contact, like I didn't notice her coming my way. It's smooth, if I do say so myself. I think about Aunt Miki saying you can only control yourself. If we're going to kiss, even on the cheek, I'll be the one who decides when and where it happens.

Then I just start talking. Talking way more than Beau would say I should.

"I made a playlist," I tell her. "It's not all Oranges, but it's the songs they're gonna play tonight, according to the set list I saw online, plus some other artists I think you might like." I grab my phone to cue up the music, and as the first song eases through the speakers, I look over at Maia. She's in a fitted denim romper with stars all over it and has an orange scarf tied around her neck. Her curls are pulled up in a high ponytail, and she's wearing dangling earrings that brush her shoulders.

"You look good," I say, like it's a fact, because it is. I look her in the eye as I say it, and I smile wide—the opposite of what my lessons have taught me. "These earrings." I reach for them, letting my knuckles trail along her neck as the chains fall through my fingers. I giggle. "Are everything!" I might sound like a friend, but

I somehow know Maia won't friend-zone me tonight. I turn the music up and start driving.

"I don't think I've ever seen you in lipstick," Maia says. I shrug and keep my eyes on the road.

"I don't think I've ever worn it around you. Like it?" I glance over at her, and she's grinning, with a pink blush creeping up her neck. She clears her throat the same way Beau did when she saw me standing at her front door.

Maybe Jada had a point. I think I like surprising people.

"Yeah," she says, and her voice cracks a little. "You know it looks good."

"I do," I agree. "I wanted to look good tonight. For the Oranges. For you, too."

I don't look over at her, but I can feel Maia shift in her seat. She lets out a soft laugh. "Mission accomplished," she whispers.

When we get to Sligo, it's a little after seven, so the doors are already open and we don't have to wait in a line to get inside. I'm grateful to be out of the car, to be out of the intense (sexual?) tension that made the air inside my parents' SUV feel thick as butter. *It's working,* I think as I touch Maia's arm and ask if I can put my lipstick in her tiny shoulder bag. She takes it from me and I put my hand on the small of her back, ushering her ahead of me through the venue's doors.

The Oranges aren't on yet, but their opener is good, and me and Maia are able to push our way through the dense crowd to stand right up against the stage. I take her hand so we don't get separated, and it feels natural and easy to intertwine our fingers. For once I don't overthink it or worry about it seeming too eager.

After a few songs, the opening band finishes their set, and

Maia says she's going to grab a drink from the bar. When she comes back, she has two cups and she hands one to me.

I take a sip and taste something cloying under what I thought was just Coke.

I press my lips against her ear. "Is there alcohol in here?" I ask her.

"Yeah, it's a rum and Coke."

"How'd you even get it?"

"Fake ID," she says with a wink.

"Thanks, but I'm way too much of a lightweight to drink if I'm driving," I say.

She shrugs, downs her drink, then takes mine and drops the whole cup into her empty one. She watches me over the rim as she places her lips directly over the print my lipstick left behind. I feel like it's an opportunity to do something, to say something to get closer to the possibility of a kiss. So I lean forward.

"We should take a selfie!" I say. And Maia nods quickly, pulling out her phone and angling it toward us, her long, slender arm instinctively framing us perfectly. We both smile, and just before she snaps the photo, I turn to kiss her cheek. The result is a sweet shot: Maia smiling with squinty eyes, my face a blur due to the low light and the swift way I turned. Before I can read her expression, the lights get even lower and everyone in the crowd pushes in a little closer. I end up flush against Maia, my entire front against her entire back. I put my chin on her shoulder. "Is this okay?" I ask her, and she nods. I put my arms around her waist, and I don't think I imagine the shift in her weight. She's leaning into me.

The Oranges walk out, three women in wildly different all-black outfits, and Maia starts screaming. As the first song starts, she sings along loudly, closing her eyes during certain parts and lifting her arms into the air. I can't help but smile at the way she is here. She seems raw and open. It's clear she's being the realest version of herself.

"I've been listening to them since I was a geeky middle schooler," Maia shouts into my ear. I have no trouble imagining it—a smaller, quieter version of Maia with braces on her teeth, maybe a few pimples. How she might have lain on a rug in the center of her bedroom with her headphones on, volume turned all the way up.

"Which song is your favorite?" I shout back.

"I'll tell you if they play it," she replies, and then, when a faster song starts, she grabs ahold of my hand as the audience loosens a little, allowing us to move a bit more freely. She jumps up and down until I'm jumping too.

The music is good. I get lost in the way the lead singer—a Black girl with a buzz cut in ripped black jeans and a torn black tank top—whispers and screams the catchy hooks; how the curly-haired guitarist's maxi dress swings as she shreds unexpected solos; the energetic rhythms beat out by the muscular drummer, a white girl with dimple piercings who is wearing a black leather skirt. Nothing about her reminds me of Beau, but even this close to Maia, that's who's on my mind—the way her soft hair seemed to float as she banged on the drums at her show; the way her serious brows were so still and her tattooed arms were a blur. Then the singer says something about how the next song was inspired by her ex, and Maia shouts, "This one!" so loud it snaps me out of my Beau haze. "This one is my favorite."

"This is 'A Girl I Used to Know,'" the singer says into the mic. "If you know the words, sing 'em with me."

I dance with Maia as the Oranges sing thinly veiled metaphors about what it's like to find out the woman you love has fallen for someone else, and the irony makes me giggle. It hits me that a lot of the Oranges' songs are low-key gay. And this one is queer as hell. I want to text Beau and ask if she knew this was Maia's favorite Oranges song, if she knew that the Oranges are as queer as they are, if she knew how deep in denial Maia is, or debate with her about how compulsory heteronormativity has to be for anyone to miss this many signs. But then I hear her calling me Monty, and pushing me away mid-makeout, and saying, *She gave them to me* over and over again. And my heart turns to ice.

I look at Maia, and the lights from the show are dancing all over her sandy-brown skin. Her eyes are closed and she's belting out the chorus to this song and I wonder if she's thinking about someone specific as she sings these lyrics—if the girl she used to know is Beau, or someone else. I want her to open her eyes. To be here with me. I want to be the girl she's thinking about now. I step closer to her, touch her cheek until her eyes open, then look into the gray while the music riots all around us. I tilt her chin down, mine up, and I kiss Maia Moon fast and hard, doing the exact opposite of everything Beau taught me.

PART FOUR
Two Weeks till Prom

23
Beau

Everyone assumed me and Kay were fucking before she moved to Toledo. And by "everyone," I mean all her band friends, given I don't really have friends beyond Celine and Daniel. Which, on its face, makes me sound like a pathetic dweeb bricked up in a tower of loneliness. But honestly, I liked it like that—it was uncomplicated. Plus, Kay loved leaving things early, which is a great passion of mine. We'd go to a party for a half hour, and then she'd give me the look that meant *abort* and we'd fuck off.

But we weren't fucking. In fact, I think the thing I liked best about her was that she was one of the only girls who never asked to kiss me "just to see." And when her friends would insinuate that we were hooking up, she wouldn't do the frantic *no we're not!* thing that girls do when they're afraid people will think they're queer, which was refreshing as hell. We still text every now and then, but she got a boyfriend when she moved to Toledo, which keeps her busy. It's fine. I do miss her sometimes. She knew who she was, and she knew who I was.

"You're doing it again," Celine says, and bounces a Raisinet off my head.

"Hey!"

I hunch over to look for it on the floor of the car. It's barely light outside, so I use the flashlight on my phone, determined to find it. Any time there's a shred of a mess in the car, Mom adds it to the tally of Reasons Beyond Almost-But-Not-Really Killing Pedestrians That Beau Can't Drive. I don't even like Raisinets.

"You know you've never even taken this car to the car wash," I tell her. "I'm not allowed to drive it and I've gotten it washed more than you."

"She'll come around eventually," Celine says.

"Yeah when I'm, like, done with college and living in Amsterdam."

"Amsterdam??"

"Or wherever," I say, shrugging, still digging for the Raisinet.

"Don't go too far," she says.

I don't reply—this is a borderline mom thing to say, and a confusing one. Celine wants me to go to college but doesn't want me to go too far. No winning. Sometimes I want to ask flat out: *Is the college thing about me or about you? Are you afraid of what would happen if we both said fuck it? Or are you just worried about what Mom would think? Because, dude, how would she even know? The back-to-back shifts were only supposed to be for a year. It's been three.*

Things are almost always so easy between me and Celine—but there's a whole category of shit we don't touch, and Celine being my sister-mom is one. It became no-man's-land when she caught me drinking once and freaked out on me. I'd said, *I can take care of myself* and she'd said, *But we shouldn't have to*, and the "we" had felt really weird, Mom's absence sprayed like graffiti over the whole conversation. And even though we never really talked about it again, it's hard to act like something like that was never said. Especially in the long stretches of Mom's double shifts. We haven't seen her awake in eight days.

Thankfully, I find the candy and toss it out the window. "It's not littering," I say before she can yell at me. "It's *food*!"

"But someone behind us might *think* it's littering," she says. "What if we got a ticket? You'd never drive then!"

"I'm never going to drive as it is," I grumble.

"Anyway," she said. "Let's return to the matter at hand, which is the fact that you're doing it again."

I don't even ask what she means, because I know what she's going to say. She calls it ruminating and/or brooding.

"I'm just *thinking*, Celine, Christ. Not everybody says all the things that cross their mind out loud all the time."

I stare at her pointedly.

"I'm going to choose to ignore that," she says. "And also going to choose to ignore the fact that you're acting super fucking weird lately."

I can't help but laugh.

"But you're *not* ignoring it. You bring it up every chance you get!"

"Oops," she says. And bounces another Raisinet off my head.

"I'm not looking for that one," I say defiantly.

But one stoplight later I'm hunched down again, searching. It's six a.m. on a school day and we're on an errand for the bakery, because Celine said if I wanted a ride to school, I had to do the egg run with her. Sometimes the five a.m. delivery truck forgets the eggs, so we go out to this farm just outside town, the only place Daniel's parents trust for the Good Shit, as Daniel calls it. The Good Shit is from free-range chickens, who lay the best eggs ever. At first it seemed unlikely that eggs could really taste that much better, but now that I've sampled the difference, I can attest that they can. I could've still been sleeping and taken the bus, but honestly, I like going out there. It's cool to see them all living free. Being chickens. And once you see the farm and see how happy those fucking birds are wandering all over the place and scratching up the dirt, it makes sense that their eggs are way better.

"Just give me a clue," Celine says as we turn off the main road to the long dirt one that will take us to the farm. "A single word."

I yawn.

"Kay."

Her eyebrows shoot up.

"Kay," she says. "I haven't heard about her since she moved. Have you guys talked?"

"Nah, we weren't really that type of friends."

"What kind of friends were you?"

"Casual, I guess?"

"Did you . . . ?"

"No," I say, rolling my eyes. "Why does everybody think that?"

"The Lesbian Burden," she says with dramatic flair. "Is she a friend? Is she a lover? Is she both? The world can only guess!"

"The world can mind their business," I say.

"Fine, fine. So you were thinking about Kay."

"Yeah. Just how she never wanted anything from me. So the *opposite* of what you're asking, actually," I say, glaring at her. "She was chill about me being gay and I was chill about her being straight. There was no guessing."

"Like with Panty Girl," she says slowly. "With the boyfriend."

I sigh deeply. "Yeah. I guess."

"And Trina."

"Um, yeah."

"And—"

"Are you slut-shaming me??" I yell, laughing.

"No, bonehead, I'm saying what you already know and what

I am pretty sure I've already said: Date a gay girl for once! Date someone like . . ."

She pauses and shoots me a sly look.

"Like . . . ?" I demand.

"Like that cute girl who was at our house the other night."

I groan.

"Charm doesn't want to date me, dude. She's . . ."

I pause, thinking about how to explain this. The Plan and . . . everything. I don't even know how to explain it to myself at this point, honestly, especially since the kissing lesson. Charm has acted weird since that and her date with Maia. She's been . . . distant. Like her mind is somewhere else. I'll send her a text in the morning and she'll barely reply. I have to assume they kissed at the show, but while I expected her to talk about it, she didn't. That plus her distraction lately . . . it has to mean she and Maia are getting closer. I lean back against the headrest. It's why I haven't even mentioned the Plan to Charm since. If she's falling for Maia, that kind of changes things.

"Jesus, Beau, would it kill you to say it out loud?" Celine says. "I swear to god I'll dump this whole box of Raisinets on your lap!"

"It's six a.m.! Why are you eating Raisinets anyway?!"

"Because I'm an adult, that's why," she says triumphantly. "Now fucking say it!"

"It's just not an option, okay?" I say. "Charm, I mean. I'm pretty sure she's into this other girl. And we kind of made this promise that I wouldn't hate her for whatever happened with her and the other girl. Like not letting bullshit get in the way of being friends."

"Feelings aren't bullshit," Celine says. "If you have feelings for her, maybe you should tell her. Do you?"

"Do I what?"

"Have feelings for Charm?"

We're pulling into the farm now. The chickens are way more awake than I am. Already out scratching and looking for worms.

"We're friends," I say firmly. "And that means I have to keep my promise and be a good friend. Nothing else."

Celine parks by the barn and turns off the car. I can tell by her energy that she wants to say something, is on the verge of crossing over from sister to mother. I tense, waiting. Part of me wishes she would. But part of me wishes Celine would tell me her fucking problems for once too. And as if she can hear my thoughts, she just sighs and unbuckles her seat belt.

"You're the boss, Beau. Now let's go get the Good Shit."

The whole way from the farm to my school, our trunk packed with the Good Shit, I pretend to sleep so Celine will leave me alone. But instead I'm planning what I'm going to say to Charm. She was right. We wrote the constitution for a reason. If she and Maia are getting closer, then whatever feelings I might—or might not!—have are on me to deal with. I think about the conversations Charm and I have when we're not talking about Maia: about college and whether it even matters. About carving out a place for ourselves. The reason Kay was a good friend was because she knew who she was. And so does Charm. She questions a lot of things, but she doesn't question herself. And for some reason it makes me question myself . . . more? Like, sure, I'm used to preferring my own company, but sticking my head out of the Batcave with her (and yes, Ezra) is nicer than I thought. Not to mention all the other things about Charm that make the idea of *not* being around her anymore feel like swallowing a hot coal. The way she looks at you intensely when she's anxious. The way her hands end up playing with your hair like they have minds of their own. The way her laugh borders on a snort when something is *really* funny. The way she frowns when she's worried about Ezra. Or me. It occurs to me that she's been doing a lot of worrying. Here I am worried about my feelings, when it's Charm who is face-to-face with Maia all the time, doing the heavy lifting with the Plan. I take a deep breath. Fuck Maia Moon. I'm *not* going to let her get between me and Charm. And I'm not going to let myself, either.

Once I get to school, I find her leaving her locker, she and Ezra going separate ways. Her smile with Ezra is one of my favorite Charm smiles—relaxed and soft and sunlit. I'm a goddamn songwriter, I should be able to think up better imagery when I see that smile. But the only thing that ever comes to mind is *light*.

"Charm!" I call to her before she can get lost in the hallway rush. She half turns, as if she isn't sure she actually heard me.

I catch up quickly.

"Hey," I say. And I know I'm not imagining it. The way she tucks something away in her face. There was a flash of something—something like that light—but then it's like she zips it into a pocket.

"Oh, hey, Beau," she says smoothly.

It knocks me off-balance. And now I'm thinking about the Batcave again. It's nice and chill in here! The decor is top-notch! Great soundtrack! But Charm tucking herself away makes me want to come out of the cave and chase her down in the Batmobile. Doing the speed limit and not hitting carts, of course.

"The panties," I say, and her eyes widen slightly, but she doesn't look around to see who heard. "I just wanted to actually explain."

"Beau, you don't—"

I take a risk and pinch the edge of her hoodie, towing her through the river of people on the way to class to a quiet pocket by the water fountains.

"Listen, okay? She gave them to me at work one day. She was there with Tate and his friends. She came over pretending to get a different pair of shoes, and she reached under the counter and put them in my pocket. And I didn't know what to do with them. I just put them in a drawer because it made me feel weird, you know? That she wouldn't talk to me in front of any of these people, but she could stick her panties in my pocket on the low. So that night that I saw y'all . . . at the party, I literally had them in my pocket to give back to her. But then everything got messed up, obviously. It's not like I'm . . . keeping them, though. You know? And I realized it's not fair that you, like, are doing this Plan and don't know anything about any of this. You're so . . . exposed? From the very beginning. And it probably seems like I'm just hiding everything. A turtle, like you said. And maybe I am. Maia hurt me, you know? Her hiding me felt like shit. I think I had it in my head that she needed to know I was over her and her bullshit, and that's why I was going to give her panties back. But after you left the other night, I just threw them away. Because she doesn't need to know. I'm the only one who needs to know that. Does that make sense?"

I'm out of breath. Jesus, since when do I talk so much? And this was . . . not the speech I planned. This doesn't sound like an *I'm gonna be a better friend* speech. It sounds like the speech you give to the girl you hurt and don't want to walk away. I feel the blood rush to my face. *Jesus Christ, Beau, you're really fucking this up.* And I can't read her face at all. When did she get so smooth? Not her skin—that's always like . . . achingly smooth. But her expression. She's like a goddamn sphinx.

"Sorry, I know you didn't ask for that. I just wanted to explain. I don't like people making assumptions, you know? I just want that to be . . . understood." I take a deep breath. "Now, that's not even what I wanted to talk to you about. The main thing is . . . well, I know shit has been weird and I want you to know you were right about the constitution. And I'm gonna keep that promise. So I wanted to ask if we could plan a hangout. You know, friend shit—not revenge shit. We can go bowling and just eat nachos or whatever."

That sphinx face. Those sparkling brown eyes. Even as the words *friend shit* come out of my mouth, I'm looking at her lips and remembering what they tasted like. *Some friend, Beau, you absolute liar.*

"Well," she says slowly, "here's the thing."

My heart starts to pound. She's going to tell me to fuck off.

"You're always in your comfort zone," she says. "That's what you're saying in a way. I'm having to do all this shit with Maia and wear my heart on my sleeve, and meanwhile you've had the luxury of . . . not. So, bowling? You work at a bowling alley. Lesbian Lessons? You're the lesbian supreme."

I kinda wanna throw up. But then she goes on.

"If we're going to do a friend hang, it has to be something out of your comfort zone. Something that isn't easy for you."

I still can't quite read her. But then I see it. The tiny lift of the corner of that perfect mouth. An unfolding somewhere in her eyes. My heart is still pounding, but now it swoops. Airborne.

"Oh," I say. Now I'm smiling too, a smile I can't really get a grip on. "I think I get it. You want to see me suck at something. You want to see me at my worst? Hold on to your ass, Monty, do I have a date for you."

24
Charm

"She called it 'friend shit,' but then she called it a date," I tell Aunt Miki. It's early evening, and she's driving me to a private pool in one of her yoga students' buildings. She started giving swim lessons a few months back after mentioning casually, at the end of one of her yoga classes, that she is a lifeguard in the summer. One student asked if that meant she was CPR certified and if she gave lessons, and even though she hadn't before, she said it was something she could figure out. Now Miki has keys to pools all over town, a rotating roster of swim students of all ages, and one particular client who told her she can use the pool key whenever she wants in exchange for teaching her cranky elderly mother to swim.

"So what you're saying is you don't know if this is a friend date or a *date* date?" Miki asks.

"No. It's definitely a friend date. Which is good." My voice comes out all weird and wobbly.

Miki glances at me before tossing a few braids over her shoulder—a new style I did for her last night that I can tell she loves—and turning back to the road. "Sounds like you want it to be a *date* date."

I've been playing it real cool with Beau lately because I want to stay friends, and Beau says she does too. She gave me that long explanation about being over Maia, and then told me she'd go swimming even though she's terrible at it, so I believe her. But there's something extra in her eyes now when she looks at me, something searching and the opposite of detached. Her shoulders don't have the same nonchalant lean, and she always seems kinda happy to see me.

But maybe that *is* just friend shit. Caring what the other person thinks. Being happy that they're around.

I haven't made a new close friend in forever. Ezra is basically my brother, so I don't have anyone to compare her to. And she's too *Beau* to compare to anyone else anyway.

I look at my hands. "I don't want it to be anything except what it is," I say. "And friends are what we agreed we'd be." Then I get busy doing what I've been doing lately every time I know I'm about to see her: I lock my heart in a cage. Put away the softest parts of me that I don't want her to see. An unintended lesson Beau taught me? How to be a turtle. I now know how to hide in plain sight.

When we get there, I see Beau climbing out of the driver's side of an old Buick, and my heart immediately starts beating faster. After Aunt Miki and I park and head to the door of the luxury complex in front of us, my stomach feels like it's full of tiny tornados. Beau has a fluffy blue towel around her neck and a small green duffel thrown over her shoulder, and it's only at that moment I realize I'm about to see her in a swimsuit.

"So," Miki says after she's said hey to Beau. "This key card will give you access to the indoor pool on the rooftop. No one really uses it after hours, so Ms. Rosie, the seventy-eight-year-old I give lessons to, is really the only person you'll need to worry about. She's nosy as hell, and when her daughter is away and her nurse dozes off in front of the TV, she likes to wander around the complex."

Beau cracks up at this. "She sounds like my nana," she says, and Miki nods.

"She has big nana energy, but she's probably a little meaner."

Miki waves to the doorman, who lets us pass, and then she hands the key card over. "Have fun," she says. "I'll be back to pick you up in, like, two hours." When Beau turns to press the elevator button, Aunt Miki winks at me.

"So can you really not swim at all?" I ask Beau as soon as we're enclosed in the mirror-walled elevator.

"Not really?" she says. "My mom couldn't afford summer camp when I was a kid, and when we went to the beach, I'd always end up running around with the boys, playing football in the sand. Then, when I got older, I worked in the surf shop and played volleyball with cute girls after my shifts, so I was too busy flirting to get in the water." She shrugs. "Celine tried to teach me one summer, but she's not the most patient, and as you so astutely pointed out, I'm not the best at . . . being bad at things."

She looks back at me in the mirror and smirks, but not in a flirty way. In a sheepish way. It's so damn cute that I'm grateful when the doors slide open, and the reflected image of her disappears.

We step out onto the roof, and I gasp. The whole pool is enclosed in glass, like a greenhouse, and the water is glowing because of bright lights shining below the surface. As we open one of the glass doors and step inside, I realize it's climate-controlled—my glasses fog up because it's humid and warm. Beau immediately tosses her towel and bag on a lounge chair, slips out of her denim jacket, and pulls off her T-shirt too. I look away before she starts wiggling out of her jeans.

I drop my stuff and take off my glasses, and when I turn back around, all I can say is, "Oh." She's wearing a tangerine bandeau two-piece, and I don't know shit about color theory, but this shade of orange must be complementary to midnight blue, because I'm standing close enough to see that her eyes look like freaking sapphires in the light from the pool, even without my glasses on. I have to do something to diffuse the heat filling my body like mercury rising in a thermometer, so I brush past where she's standing and hip-check her hard as hell so she loses her balance and plunges, ass first, into the shallow end of the pool.

"Oops," I say before cracking up. I take off my pants and shrug as Beau resurfaces, sputtering and spitting and cursing my name.

"You bitch!" she says, and I'm still laughing while pulling my shirt over my head when I feel cold, wet arms wrap around my thighs.

Before I can get the shirt all the way off, Beau lifts (*lifts!*) me from the side of the pool and tosses me backward into the water. I peel the wet cotton off my face and throw the shirt at her head, and we're both cracking up for the next five minutes.

Once we catch our breath, I tell Beau to lie on her back and try to relax so I can show her how to float, belly up. She is hesitant and so stiff the first few times we try it that she sinks the moment she begins to lift her feet.

"Beau," I say. "You have to trust me." I end up with my whole arm under her back before she's able to relax enough to float. And while I'm holding her this way, completely in control, her whole body on display, I almost drop her because Beau all at once is . . . a lot.

"Like this?" she asks, and I swallow hard before I whisper, "Uh-huh, yeah."

Once she's upright again, I have to swim a lap away from her just to get a break from the smooth plane of her tummy—so I can stop thinking about the way her muscular arms picked me up so easily.

"Did you ever finish that song?" I ask her, once I'm a safe distance away, treading water. She's a little blurry since I'm not wearing my glasses, but I can tell her eyebrows are doing that thing they do when she doesn't want to answer a question.

"I'm working on it," she says. "Celine's giving me so much shit, it's making it harder. There's a reviewer who might be at a show soon, and Celine wants to have something fresh. So, like, I get it. But I can't work under these conditions!"

I swim a little closer. "How do you decide what you want to write about?"

Beau splashes a little awkwardly, and I smile a little. When she sees me watching her, she backs up and leans against the side of the pool, trying to regain her cool.

"It depends," she says. She pushes the wet hair out of her eyes and does her serious Beau stare where she's looking at you but her head is clearly somewhere else. "Sometimes it's something simple, like a thing that pisses me off. Those are the easiest ones to write."

"Because it's harder to admit when you're sad?" I ask.

She bites her lip. "Yeah, Monty. Pretty much anything other than mad is kinda hard for me."

"If I'm gonna be Monty," I say, grinning and giving her an out because I can tell that was difficult for her to say, "I think I wanna call you Carlo."

She raises an eyebrow. "Carlo?"

I shrug. "I thought about Carly." Beau does a full-body cringe, and I giggle. "Yeah, I figured that wouldn't be your favorite. So Carlo it is."

Beau sinks into the water so that all of her is below the surface except her eyes, and I swim closer.

"What's wrong, Carlo?" I ask, and she goes all the way under. I lose her despite the lights, so I swim over, scanning the water with my eyes. I feel her before I see her, strong arms around my shins, and then I'm airborne, flying up and splashing down and screaming with laughter. She comes up with a huge grin on her face, and I send a giant splash her way, using my whole arm to make a mini tidal wave. She shakes it off and her hair sweeps over her forehead in a way that makes me lose my breath. I lift myself up onto the edge of the pool and look down at her. It's too much—the water and me and her—and I shake my head.

"What?" she says. But I know I can't be honest. I can't tell her that kissing Maia was like kissing ice compared to the heat I felt kissing her. Can't say I want to know everything that's going on behind those tricky too-blue eyes. Can't reveal that before I met her, I was like a chalkboard covered in insecurities, and that her lessons and the way she never doubted that a girl I thought was completely out of my league would fall for me have erased so many of the doubts I have about myself. So I just tilt my head and say, "So do you want to keep harassing me, or do you want to learn how to swim?"

I spend the better part of the next hour teaching Beau the basics. We hold on to the edge of the pool and flutter-kick while I tell her I want to go to cosmetology school after graduation but that I don't think Aunt Miki will let me, and I tell her I get it because I worry about Miki working so much. "She never seems tired, but I know she is." I show her the rotating arm stroke as she tells me more about Favorite Daughter and how they want to tour this summer. She actually lets me hold her waist as she tries to put the two together, kicking and moving her arms before we decide we'll need to do this again so I can show her the best ways to breathe.

She tells me how Celine can't seem to decide if she wants to be her sister or her mom. "My dad died when I was little, and we've been struggling ever since. My mom works her ass off, and Celine thinks she needs to raise me or something," Beau says. "I think she wants me to go to college so she can stop worrying about me. But there's something else there too I haven't figured out yet."

When Beau asks me about my parents, I feel myself letting her in despite the locked door I tend to hide my heart behind when she's around. We're trading secrets, and it feels like it's my turn.

"I low-key self-destructed when I had to move in with them. I was so anxious and insecure and they were so distracted by the new baby. Eleven and hormonal as hell, I'd just gotten my period, was starting to grow boobs, and I was thinking too much about girls and the ways I wanted to touch them. Over the course of that year I lost all my friends, some because I had crushes on them, some because I was afraid they'd *think* I had crushes on them, and the rest because we lost touch when I moved away. And I was too scared of the same thing happening again to try to become friends with new girls. When I moved back in with Aunt Miki, I realized she had always been my home—and the only real parent I'd ever had. And once I met Ezra a few months after coming back, I felt like I didn't need anyone else."

"Are you angry with them?" Beau asks me. And I nod.

"Sometimes. Especially right now. They try to jump on board with everything I say because they want to be friends. Like them saying I should follow my dreams and go to cosmetology school. I don't know. I don't trust them. But I don't agree with Miki saying the only way to find success is college."

Beau nods. "I get that," she says.

"I think mostly I just wish things were different. Or, if they can't be, that I could get to a place where I didn't feel anything when it comes to dealing with them."

"Feeling nothing is my favorite," Beau says. I splash her and laugh.

Beau's awkward and fumbling in the water, and she seems less confident than I've ever seen her, but she laughs a lot too—especially when I tell her about an ice cream shop I used to love as a kid, which has a big cow with ice cream coming out of its teats on its awning. She says, "That is not a real place," and when I reply that I swear it is, that if she remembers, Bree even mentioned it at dinner, she lets out a real Beau laugh that's big and too loud, and I wonder why she doesn't show this side of herself more often. If girls like cool Beau, they'd love this unveiled version of her. It's like as I tuck pieces of myself away, she pulls back her curtain more and more.

"Remember when you said everybody needs to suck at something at first?" she asks me as she practices kicking.

I think I know where this is going, so I don't answer, waiting.

"Consider my character built," she says. "The character, it is constructed."

"Oh please, you weren't that bad," I say, giggling.

"You are the architect of my character."

"Well, we all have our strengths. And you're very good at other things."

199

"Like what?"

I almost say *kissing*. Almost. But she's so much more than that.

"You're a good friend."

"Yeah, okay," she scoffs.

"You are. You think I didn't notice at my house? When you turned all the attention to *Pizza Rat* instead of the awkwardness of my parents-not-parents?"

She sinks down into the water again, mouth barely above the surface.

"Happy to be of service," she bubbles.

"You're getting better already," I say, nodding to her. "If the band doesn't work out, you can join the navy."

"Gross. I'd become an actual seal first."

Just then I hear a small splash at the far side of the pool. I turn to see an old lady in a swim cap and a suit that I'd only want to refer to as a "swimming costume" dipping her feet into the water.

"Well, hello, dears," she says. "Mind if I join you? Just one quick lap to help me sleep."

"Uhhhh," Beau says.

"Only if you stay in the shallow end, Ms. Rosie," I say, remembering that Aunt Miki had said to expect her. "There's no lifeguard on duty, and I can't save you both."

Ms. Rosie eases into the water and does a slow lap. Which gives me too much time to look at Beau. Her slick hair, and illustrated arms, and the way her brows move more than her mouth sometimes. She watches me across the water, and it's the quietest we've been the whole time. But the way our eyes linger on each other makes it feel like we're still talking.

• • •

When we step back into the mirrored elevator, Beau's eyelashes are shining because they're still a little bit wet.

"Successful friend shit, Monty?" she asks. I nod, even as the word "friend" stabs and twists at something deep in my belly, the part of me that wishes I could kiss her good night. I push the button for the lobby and tuck my hands into my pockets so I won't be tempted to brush away the wet hair on her forehead. I look at my shoes.

"Yeah, Carlo. Let's do it again soon."

25

Beau

In exchange for using the car—and buying her silence—I promised Celine a pedicure and that I'd clean the bathroom we share. Though really the bathroom cleaning would have been sufficient, because Jesus Christ that girl has as much hair as Lassie and sheds like her too. Celine has never rescued me from a well, but letting me have the car tonight *has* saved me from having to part from Charm right away. At least, I hope. I haven't asked yet.

We walk out of the building and Miki pulls up in her car.

"You ready to get out of here?" she calls to Charm.

Charm starts to reply, but I interrupt as politely as I can.

"Actually, I was gonna ask—" I start, but then Charm's phone pings loudly.

"I'm on Do Not Disturb," she complains, though she's smiling. "Why is Ezra doing 'notify anyway'? So rude!"

But then she frowns. "Emergency?" she reads out loud.

When her phone rings, she answers immediately, and Miki and I watch with concern.

"Ezra? Are you okay?"

Damn, I think. I hope Ezra is okay, but also . . . this fucks things up. I had a plan, depending on how the swim went. Finishing swimming and then casually asking if she wanted a ride home. Saying goodbye to Charm always feels like too soon, and yes, it's just friend shit, but also friends hang out and friends give each other rides! (Why am I making a mental alibi for myself?) But whatever's going on with Ezra seems likely to divert things.

"Wait, slow down," Charm says. "All I heard was 'gay panic.'"

"Oh, *that* kind of emergency," Miki says from inside the car, relieved. "Charmy, Beau is going to take you home after you handle whatever chaos has arisen. I have an eyebrow appointment I can't miss for gay panic."

Charm looks like she's going to argue, but then I hear the sound of Ezra's wail, and she goes back to listening. *Oh hell yes,* I think. Miki winks directly at me. Now that's a wing-woman.

"You *can* drive, can't you?" she says, leaning out her window.

I decide it's best to leave out my reputation as a killer of carts.

"I'll keep her safe," I say, grinning.

"Okay, good, byyye!" Miki says, waving, then stomps on the gas.

"Sorry," Charm whispers, looking embarrassed and moving the phone away from her face. "I can't believe she stuck you with me like that! Are you busy? I can take the bus or . . ."

I snort. "I'm not letting you take the bus."

She widens those doe eyes, and for a moment she stops listening to Ezra, focused on me. I notice the tiny freckle underneath her left eye. *I wonder if I could kiss it without making her blink.* It crosses my mind over and over, like an intrusive thought.

"Let?" she says. "I do what I want, Carlo."

"Except hitchhike," I say, then put my hand on her back, propelling her toward my car. "Now let's find out what horror has been unleashed on Ezra."

She crosses in front of me as she heads for my passenger door, and I swear I don't mean to look at her ass. But directly in my line of vision? Sure, I have a choice, but I just spent the last hour having to avoid staring at her body while she swam around me like a mermaid. Her body is so beautiful. Her soft belly, her strong legs. How her skin felt when I picked her up to toss her—warm and cold at the same time. Slippery.

Jesus, Beau.

I open the door for her before she can grab the handle and she rolls her eyes, embarrassed, before sliding in. I know she's thinking this is probably a Lesbian Lesson, but truthfully, I need a second before I get in next to her. I walk slowly around the back of the car, telling myself to get my shit together. For some reason I'm thinking of all the questions I've asked other girls, mostly just to make them shy: *Has anyone ever eaten you out? Do you like two fingers or one?* I want to ask Charm, but not to make her shy. It feels like I need to know. All I can think about is touching her. And if she ever let me, I'd want to touch her exactly how she likes.

But these are *the exact last fucking things* I should be thinking about the girl I swore I'd be just a good friend to.

"Get it together," I mutter again, then open the car door.

She doesn't even have to put it on speaker. Ezra's voice is loud anyway, and it's even louder now as he wails into the phone.

"Okay, okay, so it couldn't be much worse?" he says. "Like, they say A for effort, right, but no, no, Charm, *effort* gets you exactly fuck all! I picked out roses and lilies. For contrast, you know? Plain roses—too boring. Plain lilies are too friendly. I wanted to make an *impression*!"

"On who?" I whisper.

"Enzo, obviously," she whispers back. "He has a show tonight. Ezra was going."

Ezra hears.

"Is that Beau Carl? Beau, goddamn it, it's a disaster!"

"What actually happened?" I call, and now Charm puts the phone on speaker.

"Did you hear the flower blend? Roses and lilies? They were fucking beautiful. I decided enough was enough: in practice the other day Coach said, 'You miss a hundred percent of the shots you don't take,' and I don't know why it took me so long to translate this from sports to romance, but better late than goddamn never, Charm! So I planned ahead. I thought, okay, I won't drive. I'll take an Uber. Two reasons. One, so I can hold the flowers and they won't fall on the floor. I'm a planner, right? And two, so Enzo can ask if I drove and I can say no and he can offer to take me home. Obviously! A strategy! I'm a *planner*!"

Charm and I both nod, impressed. It's brilliant, really.

"Sooo what happened?" Charm prods.

"I took the Uber! But as I was getting out, the driver let off the brake and the door swung shut!"

Charm gasps. "The flowers were still inside?"

"No! Worse, Charm! Worse! The flowers were in the *door*! So do you know what I have in my hand right now, Charm?"

"No . . . ," she says slowly.

"Guess, Charm!" he shrieks.

"A vase?"

"STEMS." He wails again, and I clap a hand over my mouth to stop the laugh that explodes from my throat. Charm slaps my arm but mutes herself just in time to scream-laugh too.

"Hello? Hello?" Ezra says. Charm is working hard to collect herself and points at me threateningly to tell me to stop laughing. "You better not be fucking laughing, Charm Montgomery!"

She quickly unmutes herself.

"No, no, never! Oh my god, Ezra. So you have . . . stems. What are you going to do?"

"I'm carless! With raggedy-ass stems! And the play starts in exactly two minutes. Charm, you have to help me. Please, please, please go find me flowers. My mom is probably still at Roots! Can you? Please. I'll name my firstborn child Charmaine."

"Charmaine?"

"Well, yeah, it can't just be Charm."

"What's wrong with Charm?!" she demands.

"*Please*, Charm, it's about to start and I gotta go to my seat. Please get me new flowers. . . . I have to ask Enzo to prom tonight—it's my night, I can feel it! I played pickup at Warwick Park on Saturday and shot the lights out. I'm not missing!"

"When do I need to be there?"

"Intermission," he says. "One hour!"

And then there's the flurried sound of the phone going into his pocket without hanging up. Charm ends the call.

I already know she's going to do it. I can see the map unfolding in her brain. Flower selection, directions from here to there to the school, where Ezra is sitting in the auditorium watching Enzo prance in the limelight. She sighs.

"Well," she says, "you're the driver, but . . . wanna go on a mission?"

She could ask me to drive her to Montana and I'd say yes.

"Always."

26
Charm

"I don't think I've ever heard Ezra's voice that high-pitched," I say, still laughing.

Beau is smiling too, but she looks mischievous, so I cross my arms and look at her.

"What?" I ask.

"You didn't want to ride with me," she says in her flirty voice.

It flusters me a little bit.

"How do you know that?" I ask.

She rolls her eyes. "I saw the way you were looking at Miki. Like, 'Save me, save me.'"

I turn to look out the window, face hot. "It's not that. It's more that Miki deserves rest, you know? But I didn't want to, like, inconvenience you."

"Suuuure," Beau says, still grinning.

"Whatever. Just drive."

She cracks up.

I think Roots closes soon, but Ezra's mom will let us in even if it's after hours, and she'll probably help us assemble the bouquet, too. I tell Beau as much.

"It's over on Parsons and Fifth," I add. "The brick building with the mural of green vines morphing into a mix of curls and big black braids on the side of it?"

Beau throws her arm over the back of my seat, and it makes

me feel small and protected in a way I can't exactly explain. "Oh, I've driven past there so many times! I had no idea that was where Ezra's mom worked."

"I worked there for a while too. Only left when school started because Miki wanted me to focus on 'grades instead of braids.'"

Beau lifts her heavy eyebrows. "Did she actually say it like that?" she asks. "Because . . . bars."

I smile and shake my head.

In the small parking lot, I hop out of the car and walk up to one of the dark windows of Roots to peer inside. Most of the lights are off, but I see Ms. King trimming some leaves off the stems of a few roses. It looks like she's twisting them into a flower crown. I tap on the window.

She looks up, and a wide grin splits her face. She looks so much like Ezra, with her sugar-cookie complexion flecked with freckles, that every time I see her it makes me wonder what Ezra's dad looks like. She could have spawned him and his brother Ezekiel all on her own.

I wave Beau over, and when Ms. King opens the door, she says, "You here to rescue my baby?"

"How does one even close the top of an entire bouquet in a car door?" I say as I walk past her into the shop. She shakes her head, and the smell of the place—all Black hair care products and flower perfume—makes me feel heady and romantic for some reason, like I've stepped into a movie moment. Ms. King has soft R & B playing too, which only adds to the atmospheric feel of the place.

She's the florist, and her longtime friend, Izzy Turner, is the hairstylist. When I worked here last summer, I was supposed to just sweep up and shampoo clients, but Izzy also showed me how to feed in extensions for knotless braids smoothly, how to trim split ends, how to detangle and condition naturally curly and kinky hair. The rhythmic movements of my hands as I braided or cleaned helped me forget about Jada for a few hours every day. Part of me misses the rush of water over my fingers, the way rose petals and hair clippings would mix together under the broom. I forgot how it felt to spend time in a real salon—I wish I could stay forever.

"Hi, Ms. King. I'm Beau Carl," Beau says in her most charming voice. I've been kinda trying not to look at her, and the moment I glance back, she tosses her head to get her bangs out of her eyes. "It's so nice to meet you." She gently touches a few petals that are scattered across the worktable closest to the door. The way her hands move shouldn't affect me as much as it does.

"Nice to meet you, Beau Carl," Ms. King says. "Do y'all need help figuring out what to get for that boy of mine? I'm just finishing up an order, but then I can be of assistance."

"That would be great," I say, just as Beau says, "Nah, I think we can handle it."

And then she's walking past me, running her fingers over the various cut flowers and sniffing the blooms.

Ms. King makes a face like she's impressed. "Well, excuse me, Beau Carl. Stick to the leftovers on those three tables back there. I need the rest of the ones over here for these flower crowns."

Beau has an air of confidence as she eyes the assortments.

"You have some kind of hidden bouquet-building talent?" I ask her. She reaches for a peony and brings it up to her nose. She sniffs, then looks up at me through the fringe of her lashes, dark blue peeking through the dark brown, and nods.

"I help Daniel pick stuff out for Celine all the time," she says, like it's nothing.

"Okay, but this bouquet needs to be a really good one, since it's for his promposal."

She nods seriously, then lowers the flower and makes a face like she's just thought of something brilliant. "Maybe this can be another lesson. How to make a bouquet."

I don't mean to look surprised, but the intrusive thoughts must win. Flowers aren't part of the Plan, and just as I'm about to point that out, Beau says, "Maia loves flowers. Might be helpful to have some for her when you . . . ask *her* to prom?"

I shift on my feet and clear my throat. I hadn't realized it, but neither of us has mentioned Maia all day, and now that her name is floating between us, it feels like poison in the perfumed air. "Oh, okay," I say softly.

"So first, you pick a few flowers to be the centerpiece," Beau says. She puts away the peony she was holding to her nose and picks up a rose. "I like to use bright flowers for the middle, because it sorta helps your eyes know where to go." She picks up a few more roses and hands all of them to me. "Hold them like this," she says as she moves my fingers around the stems. Her hands are warm and gentle, and I keep my eyes on the flowers, but I can feel hers on me. She picks up some lilies and arranges them around the roses, turning the growing bouquet in my hands.

"What kind of flowers do you like?" Beau asks as she continues moving around the room.

"I think I like dried flowers more than fresh," I say. "And wildflowers more than anything I know the name of. Give me something beautiful and weird and that will last over any of this other stuff."

Beau bites her lip and picks out a few more flowers. She mutters something that I don't quite catch, but when she walks back over to me with new blooms in hand, she continues on like she didn't say anything.

"Then you just keep adding, Monty. Flower by flower." She's standing right on the other side of the bouquet, so our noses are inches away from touching, the only thing between us petals and fragrant air. "If you think about it," she says as she moves around and behind me, "you can kinda say with flowers things you can't say with words."

"Oh yeah?" I ask. "Does this one say, 'Uber doors suck'?"

Beau presses her lips together. "I was kinda going for, 'These flowers are nothing compared to how I feel when I see you, but they're the best I got. I hope they make you smile.'"

Standing beside Beau in the low light, listening to her low voice, I can't get a read on her. Is she flirting or teaching? Am I wishing for one more than the other?

"You mean, you hope they make Enzo smile," I say, "when Ezra gives them to him?" Because her eyes are all over me. She holds my gaze for a moment too long before she nods. "Yeah," she says. "Enzo."

She adds and adds until the bouquet is big and beautiful, garnished with baby's breath and leafy green pieces I don't know the names of, and then she wraps it with twine and brown paper. She hands the flowers back to me, gentle as if she's handling a baby, before we wave goodbye to Ms. King, who compliments Beau's work.

Beau jogs ahead of me to the car and opens the door for me. Her eyes seem distracted, but then she grins and puts her hand through her hair in that way of hers: cool and casual. After we each climb inside, she turns on the radio and cracks a joke, and I wonder if I imagined something more than just the stiff parchment paper on the bouquet crackling between us.

27
Beau

The parking lot at school is packed—there are absolutely no spots left, but that's okay because Ezra is waiting at the curb, his anxiety evident even from a hundred yards away. He shifts from foot to foot, looking over his shoulder or at his phone from time to time. Inside, through the big windows, I can see people milling around, standing and talking in groups.

"Intermission," Charm says. "Perfect. He would have been freaking out if he had to step out in the middle of the last act."

"Are all these people here to see the play?" I say, my head swiveling as I steer us toward Ezra. "People like *plays*?"

"Yes, people like *plays*," she says, laughing. "This may come as a shock, but people do social things sometimes. Things that lead them to engage with the rest of the student body."

"Sounds gross," I say.

"Shut it, Carlo," she says lightly. "Plays are great, and ya know, so is occasionally socializing."

"Yeah? Then why weren't you at said play?"

"I had plans," she says, shooting me a look that's so sly it makes me blush.

Thankfully, I don't have to say anything else because we're pulling up to the curb. Charm hops out with the flowers, and I crane my neck to see if Ezra is still clutching the decapitated bouquet because that would be hilarious, but he's disposed of it already, and eagerly takes the flowers I put together with Charm. I can't quite hear his reaction, but I can tell he's pleased with the arrangement, and that feels satisfying in a weird way. Ezra being pleased means Charm will be pleased, and that means Charm will be pleased with me.

Since when do I give a fuck whether anyone is pleased with me? I find myself picking lint off my shirt, like that will help me pick off the feeling.

Then Ezra is beelining back toward the school and the few people other who were outside vaping—bleh—are heading back inside too. Intermission over. Charm plops back into my car.

"Mission accomplished," she says. "He says he's still hoping to finagle his way into a ride with Enzo. The cast usually goes out to eat together afterward, and you know how Ezra helps out as a stagehand—"

"Does he? Wow, he's committed to this crush," I interject.

"Very," she says, smiling. "But yes, Enzo told him at rehearsal, 'Hey, the cast is going out after the show, you should come.'"

"A good sign."

"Exactly. But I think Ezra has a bit of . . . I dunno, crush dysmorphia going on."

"I'm sorry, what?" I say, laughing.

"You know, his brain is seeing it through a warped lens. Twisting even the most obvious flirting into a platonic nightmare."

"Are we sure it's *not* a platonic nightmare?" I ask, hell-bent on not overthinking this conversation.

"Enzo would be a simple bitch if he didn't like Ezra back," she says. "And Enzo may be cute and silly, but he's not simple. Either way, we should hang out just in case it doesn't work out and Ezra needs a ride."

God, she's so sweet. She gets this glow when she does something for someone. Like it truly makes her happy to do things for people. I have a sudden impulse to grab her, tell her how amazing she is. But because I'm not a lunatic, I grip the steering wheel instead and steer toward the side of the building.

"The cast usually comes out the stage door," I say. "Same for band performances, so Ezra will probably meet Enzo here."

"Do you do performances with the band?" she says, sounding surprised.

"Not since Favorite Daughter, but yes, Monty, I used to. This may come as a shock, but I do social things sometimes."

Me echoing her words makes her laugh sharply, but then she gasps, and the laugh stops as soon as it started.

"Ohmygod," she says. "I'm not driving. And here I am telling you *I want to hang out and wait for Ezra in case he needs a ride!* Like you're my chauffeur! You can drop me off. I'm sorry, I can take an Uber, or Ezra and I can!"

I snort.

"What do you mean? I *am* your chauffeur."

"I feel like such a douche!" she says, and when I glance at her, she actually is so embarrassed she looks like she's wilting. "Assuming you don't have plans and expecting you to just—"

I cut her off.

"I do have plans. To hang out with you while we wait for Ezra."

She looks at me—Jesus, the doe eyes—but then looks away quickly.

"Are you sure?"

"Don't ask me if I'm sure," I say. "I don't do things I don't wanna do. I don't go places I don't wanna go. I'm doing what I want to do where I want to do it, right now."

I can't tell if she's still embarrassed or if she's overthinking, but I talk to fill the space.

"Besides, it's what friends do, and you're such a good friend. Bringing Ezra flowers. Waiting for him. Like, fuck, how did you get to be so great?"

But now I've filled the space with something even more awkward, and I inwardly press not one but both palms against my face.

"Oh look, someone spray-painted the dumpster again," I continue, desperate.

"'Principal Walken voted for Trump,'" Charm reads. "Well, that's unsurprising."

"Have you seen his wife? She has a TikTok account."

"No she doesn't," Charm says, laughing.

"She does!" I insist. "She does line dances and posts them. Ask me if she's ever on beat."

She's laughing and laughing, that musical laugh that sounds like it should be part of a song.

"Ask me!" I cry.

"Is she . . . is she ever on beat?"

"Charm," I say seriously. "She is a vampire. And the beat is garlic."

We sit there in my car—well, not *my* car but mine for right now—for an hour, just laughing and talking, and as far as I'm concerned, we could do this all night. Kissing her was amazing. And would I do it again right now? You're goddamn right. But sitting here making her laugh and listening to her talk about going to beauty school . . . this is somehow just as good. Wow, imagine that. A world outside the cave. I think back to our conversation at the bowling alley—the single name she told me. Jada. I knew then that the string of insecurity I sometimes see thrumming in Charm is tied directly to whoever Jada was to her. And whoever she is, I hate her instinctively for hurting Charm.

This train of thought is interrupted, though, by the sound of a crowd. Double doors clanging open, other people laughing and talking. The play is over and the masses are exiting the building.

"Oh, finally," Charm says, and she swings her door open. And I can't help it, I wince a little. Has she just been counting down the minutes? I almost reach for her wrist, say, *Let's stay here a little longer*, but she's climbing out of the car, and so I do too. We lean on it, watching people leave. It's a smaller crowd than a football game, of course. But still, lots of people came to see this play. It's not exactly that I wish I did things like this. I don't, really. Even when Kay was here, we laughed about organized school activities, especially prom. Going somewhere to be around assholes from school *on purpose*? But I kind of get it now. How being "out" can feel—not out of the closet, but just *out*. It's never really felt like it's worth all the bullshit until now.

"There's Ezra!" Charm says. He comes around the front of the building and angles nervously toward the cast door, where a few people are already waiting. The bouquet looks huge in his arms. But not too huge. We chose well. It makes a statement but isn't over-the-top. He glances over and sees me and Charm, raises his eyebrows high as if to say, *Here it goes?!* She gives him a double thumbs-up, grinning widely. She's such a good fucking friend.

Then I hear a familiar laugh. It rises above the noise of the people leaving the theater. I'd know it anywhere—it's a scaled laugh. Three notes: each escalating above the previous one.

Maia.

Charm hears it at the same time.

"Oh shit," she says.

And there she is, walking with her gaggle of friends. Tate and his boys mingle with them. It's chilly out, and none of them are wearing jackets. I watch as Tate says something and Maia shoves him. There's that laugh again.

Charm looks at me sharply. She says nothing, but I see it in her face loud and clear: *she cannot see us together!*

A reminder of the obvious and unspoken rule in the Plan. Maia can never know that me and Charm hang out—it would ring the alarm bells that she is so sensitive to, breach the carefully designed perimeter that ensured no one ever knew we were hooking up. If she knew me and Charm were friends, it would jeopardize everything—her two secrets (one former, one current) hanging out? That head is full of a lot of things but not air. Little Miss Paranoid would smell a conspiracy right away.

I immediately turn and get back into the car, hunkering down in the driver's seat. At this distance Maia will never see me, and she's never seen Celine's car. She's never been in here, or to my house. That would have been too intimate. No: just bowling alley break rooms and supply closets.

I peek, staying low. Maia is at the edge of the parking lot, headed in the opposite direction, when she happens to glance back. She sees Charm, and Charm raises a hand, gives a flirty wave. Good for her. Maia shoots a look at her friends, and I can almost see the gears in her brain cranking. *(Tate nearby) + (will people notice/wonder) = [strategy].* It's the kind of calculating you have to do when you're Maia Moon—or maybe any girl who worries what people will think if she's queer. As someone who has been girl-crazy since first grade, I can't imagine throwing "gay" in a box and keeping it in my basement. Then again, my mom used to actually be home sometimes when I was that young, and she bought me my first rainbow T-shirt. Being another thing Maia keeps in her basement, I never met her parents. I don't know what they're like.

Maia's math reaches a surprising sum. She slaps the palm of her well-manicured hand against her lips and blows Charm a kiss. Not sneaky, but not blatantly flirty, either. Hollywood, like maybe she's greeting a fan. But it's something, and I'm not expecting the stab to my heart that it produces. Damn, just when I think I'm over all that shit. Am I actually?

Maia carries on with her friends—no one even seemed to notice the blown kiss—but I can't bear to look at Charm. I just stay hunched in the car, imagining myself morphing into a floor mat.

I'm glad when I hear the commotion of the cast bursting out from the side door of the school.

I peek again before I sit up, ensuring that Maia is really gone. (She is.) When I get out again, Charm says nothing, and the awkwardness of it is like a big gay elephant sitting on the hood of the car. Thank god for Ezra and his bouquet.

He's at the front of the small crowd, and I see Enzo's smile as he takes in the flowers and Ezra's face. He has his stage makeup on still, glittering in the glow from the streetlights while Ezra, always so certain and confident, stands there with a soft posture, offering the flowers shyly.

Enzo's bright mouth forms the words *Thank you!* And I can see Ezra inflate.

But then there are other flowers, other bouquets. More people have joined the congratulatory group and they're pressing in for their turn, roses and carnations and baby's breath all piling on top of our masterpiece. And as Enzo is surrounded, Ezra is squeezed backward. Eventually he's on the outskirts of the group that has formed around the cast, hands empty as their chatter and laughter splash through the night.

I recognize Ezra's body, the way expectation and reality crash into each other and throw him through the windshield.

Goddamn it. I know *exactly* how that feels.

Charm hasn't realized it yet, though. She stands there looking uncertain, waiting, maybe, for Ezra to make his move back toward Enzo. But I know defeat when I see it. He'll be too crushed to go out with the cast afterward. There's only one move left to be made.

"Ezra!" I call over the top of the car. His head jerks up and I motion him over. He casts just one glance back at Enzo and the crowd of admirers before he walks toward us. He gets in the back seat silently while Charm slides back into the front passenger side.

"Ready?" I say, addressing Ezra through the rearview.

"For what?" he answers.

"Fucking ice cream."

28
Charm

For the first few minutes as Beau navigates the overcrowded school parking lot, the energy in the car is . . . tense. I can tell Ezra is disappointed because he didn't have more time with Enzo, and that Beau feels some type of way about having to hide from Maia. I still haven't told her that Maia and I kissed, that the Plan is working exactly as we hoped it would and Maia seems like she's inching closer to being putty in our hands. I also haven't told her that I've gone totally rogue. But this doesn't seem like the time or place.

"The worst part of the world is all the people," Beau says, breaking the silence.

"Amen to that," Ezra agrees.

"Except me. Right, guys?" I say, trying to lighten the mood. I glance over my shoulder at Ezra, who is staring longingly through the window in the direction of the cast door, where there's still a crowd of humans. I pat his knee, then look back at Beau, who is frowning at the windshield. I poke her in the side, and she wriggles away from me seconds before laying the majority of her upper body on the horn.

"Get out of my *way!*" she says, then looks over at me. "Of course you're the exception, Monty. You're like . . . a cotton-candy human. Not a regular one."

I squint at her and laugh a little. "What? What does that mean?"

Ezra pipes up from the back. "It means you're like, soft and sweet and melty. A dessert of a person. Simply a delight." He says it all in a bored voice, like this is my dictionary definition. Waves a hand dismissively.

"Aww," I say, reaching for the radio. "They like me!"

"We clearly more than like you," Beau says, but then her eyes go a little wide, like she's surprised at her own words. She reaches for the radio too, and when our fingers collide, she pulls her hand back quickly, like my skin is hot to the touch. She tells me to turn up the music and then immediately asks Ezra how the play was, her eyes focused hard on the long, dark road ahead of us.

When a Beyoncé song comes on a few minutes later, Ezra's still lamenting his loss. Beau turns the radio up even louder, and she starts singing at the top of her lungs. "C'mon, Ez!" she says, giving him a nickname the way I'm realizing she only does with people she really likes. I hold my phone to Beau's mouth like it's a mic during the chorus, and when the next verse starts, I take my seat belt off so I can turn around and aim the phone at Ezra. He finally cracks a smile, leans forward, and joins us. Then we're all dancing and singing and I feel full of something like love for both of them.

I assumed we'd be going to Oscar's, but when we take a left on Crenshaw, it looks like we're heading somewhere else. Beau knows all the places to avoid after big school events if you want to avoid people, like the beach and Warwick Park, Andi Patterson's house and the bowling alley, so I'm not worried we'll end up somewhere where Maia might be. Still, my mind keeps circling back to how Beau's face looked when we both heard Maia laugh—the way Beau immediately understood she couldn't be seen with me. Seeing her duck down in her own car made my chest hurt a little, like I did something wrong and she was having to pay the price.

Maia made her hide. But I'm proud to be Beau's friend. I don't want to make her do that too. To be honest, more and more lately, Beau's lessons and the Plan feel like they're just an excuse to hang out. And now that we're making an effort to hang out more, to be real friends, do we really still need to do revenge?

Maybe I should tell Beau I don't want to do any of this Maia shit anymore. Especially if the Plan could be hurting her.

"So, since my plans went to shit this evening, how's everything going with yours?" Ezra asks. It's the only thing that pulls me out of my thoughts and plants me firmly back in the front seat of the car.

"Huh?" I ask, still tuning back in.

"The Plan. How's it going? I feel like I haven't gotten an update in a while."

I look at Beau, but her eyes don't move from the road. We haven't talked about this on our own yet since our fight, and it feels strange to do it in front of someone else first. But Ezra is leaning forward so his head pokes between us and he's looking back and forth from me to Beau. I know he won't let it go.

"Well, let's look," I start. I rummage in my backpack and pull out my notebook. I rewrote the steps of the Plan on the first page before any of the notes I took during my lessons with Beau. Ezra grabs the notebook from my hand before I can stop him. My stomach churns as he reads the steps out loud.

"Ask Maia out," he reads. "You did that. And she said yes. That was the Oranges show."

I nod. "Yep."

"Amazing!" Ezra says, looking back down at the list. "Oh my god. But did you guys kiss yet? Did you kiss at the show? If you kissed Maia Moon and didn't tell me, I will pass the fuck out right now."

I swallow hard. I glance at Beau, but her face is unreadable. When I finally told Ezra about the kissing "lesson" with Beau, I mentioned that I'd felt . . . things. But I didn't want to admit I felt nothing with Maia—couldn't afford to, not with the Plan and, more importantly, our friendship on the line. I didn't tell him about kissing Maia because I'm still processing how I feel about it. After kissing Beau, kissing Maia had fallen so flat I haven't known what to say.

"Ummmm," I begin.

"You did!" Ezra says. "You bitch. How was it?"

I look at Beau again. I wish she would look at me, but her blue eyes are vacant as an ocean and just as far away, though her knuckles seem to be going white with how tightly she's gripping the steering wheel. Or are they? She said she wanted to be friends. She just gave me a lesson on how to build a bouquet *for* Maia, for fuck's sake. *We're just friends,* I remind myself.

"It was a part of the Plan, so I did it. It wasn't bad, but I can't say it changed my life, either. It was . . . fine? For me. I gave it my all, so I hope it was better for Maia, since it was supposed to be a kiss she wouldn't forget."

Beau doesn't make a snarky comment. Beau doesn't say anything. *Friends,* I think. Still, something inside my body feels like a sieve—all the warm leaking out.

There's a moment of silence, and Ezra leans back and starts scrolling through his phone. I almost tell him not to—in this state of mind he's probably looking for a reason to believe Enzo was never a possibility. But then he gasps so hard it makes me jump.

"Oh shit!" he says. "Oh shit!"

"What?!" I demand.

"The Plan! Number Three—posting a picture! Look!" He pushes his phone into my hands. "That's totally you, right? It's a little blurry, but I can tell by the hair that that's totally you. You're halfway there!"

I yank his phone out of his hand and stare down at a photo Maia posted . . . seventeen minutes ago. A glance at the clock and some quick mental math tells me she must have put it up right after she saw me in the parking lot. The caption is just a bunch of orange emojis in a row. And I wonder if she's trying to send me some kind of message—I wonder if she's saying with actions instead of words that she wants to like me out loud. I look closer at the picture. It has over eight thousand likes.

"You can barely tell it's me," I say.

"You can tell it's not Tate," Ezra mutters.

When we stop at the next red light, Beau looks over at Ezra's phone too.

"Wow, Monty. She's into you."

Her voice reminds me of burnt coffee grounds, it's so bitter. I peer through the dark car, trying to see her face, but the only illumination is from the phone in my hand, and the headlights of the cars on the opposite side of the road. She moves in and out of shadow too often for me to see her clearly.

She says, "So that means . . ." and I already know what she's thinking. I nod and bite my lip as she says, "Dumping Tate's next."

"You think that could really happen before prom? We're only, like, eight days out," Ezra says.

We've been driving for a while, and I haven't paid much attention to where, but now the glow of a sign catches my attention. A giant wooden cow with ice cream coming out of its teats stands atop the red-and-white-striped awning. Milk It.

Ezra gags and says, "That is disgusting."

"Holy shit. I haven't been here since I was a kid," I say. And that's when Beau cracks. She finally looks at me.

"I know," she says, one hand on the steering wheel, one across the back of my seat. "You told me."

I can't imagine sitting in this car alone with Beau looking at me like this after she just found out about the kiss and the picture, and with Ezra's question about the likelihood of Maia dumping Tate in the next week still floating in the air unanswered. So after we park and Ezra moves to open his door, I yank him back. "I'll get it. Text me your orders."

"You already know mine," Ezra says. "Dairy-free, baby."

Then I'm out of the car, queuing, looking over my notes like I'll be able to find the meaning of Beau's heavy gaze somewhere in these pages.

29
Beau

Charm really *is* a cotton-candy human. Some people just stand in line. But not Charm. She sort of . . . floats there. Not air floating, but water floating. Like a sea anemone. In documentaries the camera goes into the ocean and we see the anemones and the urchins and the coral all doing the under-the-ocean shit they do, and they're never moving fast, but they're never quite still, either. There's a rhythm to them, and Charm has that same movement. And just like that, my mind is back in the pool. How I gripped her hips to throw her backward in the water. Any other girl and I'd have held her ass instead, but it's Charm, and I avoid all the parts of her that, if touched, would throw the whole Plan out the fucking window. But did it really matter? Hips might have been just hips on another girl. But they were *Charm's* hips, so I still wanted to throw the whole Plan out the fucking window.

"It's hard to avoid, huh?" Ezra says, and I'm suddenly so terrified that I said something out loud, or worse, that he read my mind, that I jerk in my seat.

"Wh-what did you say?" I stammer.

But Ezra isn't looking at me. He's pointing out through the windshield. I follow his finger—two girls from school are in line a few people behind Charm. They look around, not nervously but . . . warily. Then their fingers brush. My heart skips a beat. There's still always a special thrill that comes with seeing other queer girls. It's like being a bird zooming around nothing but lizards and suddenly seeing something with wings. It's like the Spider-Man meme. *Hey! You! And me! Us!*

"You're always going to see *somebody* from school," he says. "Unavoidable. Who do you think they're hiding from?"

He has his gossipy voice on. I can tell he's pushing down his bummed-outness about Enzo. I want to ask him about it, but I don't. Sometimes hurt feelings have to be soothed in private first; I know that all too well. Which is why I'd been so pissed when I ran into Charm at Oscar's that night after the party.

It's hard to imagine ever being mad at Charm for anything now, but after the confirmation that she kissed Maia, I feel that urge again to retreat and process it alone. At least she said it was "fine." It "wasn't bad." It didn't change her life. Maybe, like Ezra, I'll cry about it later. Or maybe I'll just keep thinking about what kind of kiss *would* change her life. And who would give it to her if not Maia.

"Maybe parents," I say, answering Ezra. We both study the girls, who are fully holding hands now. One leans her head on the other's shoulder. No, I've never been what I'd consider closeted, but I've never done *that*, either. I've never held a girl's hand in public. Never kissed in public. Does that count as being in the closet? Well, *I'm* not hiding—so am I in everybody else's closet? I think of Charm's frantic gaze, wordlessly propelling me into the car to hide. That makes my chest hurt more than her kissing Maia. I know it's not the same—it's just part of the Plan. But fuck.

"Could be everybody," Ezra says. "You know what I saw the other day? Somebody on TikTok said that the concept of 'the closet' was extinct, because being gay is so generally accepted now."

I snort, loudly, and Ezra pushes my shoulder. I guess he's coming around to actually liking me.

"Exactly!" he cries. "I think people think that because queer shit is all over the internet, that means the whole country is a Pride parade. Must be nice to live in whatever fantasy he was living in."

Ezra's trying hard to change the subject. He's picking something to put some outrage in his voice and distract him from Enzo. I can help. I am an acolyte in the church of outrage.

"If not parents or *everybody*, there's another possibility," I say, pointing at the two girls. "Maybe one of them is, like, embarking on a secret plan of revenge to make the other one fall in love with her so she'll dump her douchey boyfriend to complete her evil plot."

"Who would do *that*?" he says, straight-faced. We look at each other and grin, but then he's pointing at Charm next.

"Look at our girl go," he says.

It's Charm's turn at the window, and there is somebody very cute working tonight. They're soft masc, curly hair, big earrings. I can tell by the way they look at Charm that they've been waiting for her to reach the front of the line. I wonder if she'll use our lessons not just for revenge. Something about it makes my stomach twist.

"Look at her not following *any* of your rules!" Ezra cries, laughing.

She's definitely being shy. I can tell from here that she's doing that thing where her eyes are avoiding any single landing place, twisting her lips to the side like she's trying to kiss her own cheek. And yet the cashier is riveted, a smile creeping across their face. It makes me want to get out and stride to the front of the line, loop my arm around Charm's waist.

What a dick move that would be.

I root myself to the driver's seat, then look out the window, up at the sky. At anything else.

"Think she'll give them her number?" Ezra says.

"Probably," I say, internally miserable. "Why wouldn't she, right?"

Ezra blows in my ear. It makes me shriek.

"Dude!" I laugh.

"Jealous?" he says with a smirky little laugh.

"Yeah right."

"You are."

"We're just friends."

We both look out again at Charm, who's now somehow balancing three ice cream cones on her way back to the car.

"We're *just* friends," I repeat.

"Sure," he says in an easy voice, but doesn't look at me. "And I don't care at all that I'm sitting in this car and not at the afterparty with Enzo."

I lean over the console, open Charm's door, and shove it outward. Then we wait for Charm, preparing our smiles.

PART FIVE
One Week till Prom

30
Charm

After I knock on Maia's door three days later, I have a moment where I consider running back to the car and driving away. I'm only here because the library is closed while they look for Mx. Anderson's tarantula, which some of the seniors let loose on the third floor as a prank. I silently wonder if it was Tate's idea, even though he knows Maia loves that thing, as I wait for the door to open.

I'm in a weird mood, and I'm still second-guessing continuing the Plan, but I haven't had a chance to talk to Beau about it. Maia's been blowing up my phone since the concert and the kiss, saying she wants to see me again, but "wanting to see me" feels galaxies away from wanting to *be* with me. Which is what we need. For the Plan. And I still have no idea how to make Step Four happen. I didn't say this to Beau, because the way she looked ducking into the car after the play still haunts me, but this part isn't something she can help me with. She's good at flirting, excellent at kissing, and is generally a pro at getting girls to be into her, but so far I don't think she's ever gotten a girl to dump her boyfriend. To really choose her. The thought makes an unfamiliar feeling churn in my belly, but I push it away. Point is, for this step, I think I'm on my own.

Just as I'm taking out my phone to panic-text Ezra, Maia's door swings open.

I don't see anyone at first, then I hear a small voice say, "Who are you?" and I look down.

A tiny girl with bread-brown skin and the same curls and gray eyes as Maia is frowning up at me. There's what looks like chocolate frosting around her mouth, and she's holding a LEGO truck in the hand that isn't on the door. She's wearing a cape, a leotard and a tutu, and no shoes. She's cute as hell.

"Oh. Hi, I'm Charm, Maia's tutor. She home?"

Before the kid, who I'm guessing is Maia's little sister, can answer, the giant golden retriever I saw all over Tate the day of the Oranges show bounds out of the house and nearly knocks me down. He plants his paws on my shoulders and licks my neck as I squeal, more from surprise than anything. "Well, hello to you too, sir!" I say.

"Getty! Down!" the kid yells. Impressively, even though the dog—Getty, it seems—is twice the size of Maia's sister, she's able to grab him by the collar and drag him inside the second he's back on all fours.

"Maia!" the girl screams next. "A brown girl is here for you!"

I snort at her description of me, and at the absurdity of the last two and a half minutes, but then Maia is there, and she's clearly embarrassed. "Maisie, I told you. You can't just *say* shit like that."

"Mom!" Maisie shouts, running down the hall after the dog, who has already lost interest in me. "Maia said shit!"

"Sorry, Charm. My dog is nuts and my sister is too. She just turned five and is, like, trying to figure out race stuff. Come in."

"Well, I mean, I *am* brown," I say, laughing.

"Ughhhh," Maia groans. "She just started noticing that, like, she and our dad have dark skin and that I'm more light, like our mom. And we had cousins over from both sides a few days ago, and so she started calling them 'brown cousins' and 'beige cousins' like they were on teams. Then she was asking me if I was brown or beige, and since I'm kinda in between, looks-wise, she started calling me 'swirl,' like the vanilla and chocolate soft serve? It was so awkward."

I crack up. "What did you tell her?"

Maia shrugs. "That it's not okay to call me that! That yeah, I'm both—half Mom, half Dad—but so is she."

"Is that like, a rite of passage for biracial kids?" I ask her as we walk deeper into the house. I'm genuinely curious about this stuff, but I'm also so relieved to be talking about something that isn't related to what's going on between us that I could cry.

We pass photos of Maia as a kid with frizzy hair and braces, of Getty as a puppy, of a tiny, newborn Maisie wrapped up in a muslin blanket, eyes closed with a bow on her head. I smile at a photo of Maia's whole family in matching outfits, which had to have been taken in the last couple of years. There's an older boy in the photo who is paler than both the girls, so I guess Maia has a brother, too. Maisie is a toddler in the photo, and she looks like she's being held hostage. "I guess I never thought about how that happens. Like how kids start to make those kinds of connections in their heads. I don't remember a moment when I realized I was Black, but maybe that's because my whole family is?"

Maia shrugs. "I don't think I thought about it very much until like middle school. But Maisie is intense about everything, including this."

Maia leads me up her stairs and down a long hallway, and then we're at her bedroom door. She pushes it open without much hesitation, and I can't help but remember that the last bedroom I was in that wasn't mine was Beau's.

I can't afford to think about that right now.

Maia's room, unlike Beau's, is kind of exactly what I expected it to be. Most of it looks like a room from a movie, all tidy bookshelves and white furniture, makeup and fragrances stacked along the back of her vanity like a city skyline. There's a ring light on a tripod, a small table and chair in front of a backdrop in the corner where she records her videos. But the ceiling is dark indigo and covered with an extensive network of constellations and planets. I can't tell if it's wallpaper or paint, but it's pretty and complicated and a little shimmery, just like Maia herself.

"Nerd," I say, pointing to the ceiling.

"Duh," she replies, smiling.

I kneel on her floor to unpack my bag, and I know I should be gearing up to flirt, to move toward bringing up Tate, but I'm still thinking about Maisie. Something about Maia calling her intense is rubbing me the wrong way. Maybe it's because I can tell that Maisie is full of big, wild feelings in a way that reminds me of myself. Maybe it's the way she handled me and that dog—fearless, like a girl who knows how to be bold and boldly herself. Maybe it's the way Maia seems to be her opposite in every way—unsure of who she is; a little too scared to look at herself closely enough to figure it out. But also . . .

"Maybe your sister has to think about race more because she's darker-skinned than you," I say. I'm almost certain this isn't the right time or place for this conversation, but it's like, as usual, I'm having a hard time controlling what I'm feeling from spilling out. "The world reacts to you differently when you look unambiguously Black." I pause only for a second before the rest of it clicks into place—why Maia's dismissal of Maisie is bugging me. I think of Beau hiding in her car as I add, "The same way you have to be aware of how the world perceives you when you're visibly queer."

Maia was on the other side of her room clearing off her desk so we could work on it together. But at the sound of that word, "queer," she turns and looks at me like she's nervous.

"You're right," she says. "But I've never felt like I really fit in anywhere. I've never felt Black enough, or smart enough, or skinny enough." The *queer or straight enough* feels tucked into the air between us, though she doesn't say it. "I was never brave and wild like Maisie or perfect like my older brother, Jude. Hell, I'm not even brown *or* beige enough for Maisie to figure out where I belong. I don't know how the world sees me, so it's hard to know how to see myself." And there she is again: real Maia. The more of her true self she shows me, the harder it is to hate her.

She picks up a comb from her dresser and turns it over in her hands. "I've been watching all these videos, trying to figure out how to do my own hair. I have a good stylist now, but I'm nervous about what it will be like when I go to college if I don't know how to do some basic things myself. And that's only a tiny part of the stuff I need to know about myself, you know?" She looks up at me. Pulls a face. "Sorry. I don't know why I'm saying all this. We should get to the homework."

"I know how it is to feel like there are parts of you that are a secret, even from yourself."

Maia just looks at me. I think I've said too much again.

"Have you ever worn your hair in braids?" I ask her.

Maia blinks. "No. Why?"

I grin. Keep my eyes steady on hers because I have an idea. "You should let me do your hair."

"You don't think I'd look weird? Like I'm trying too hard to be someone I'm not?"

I frown at her. "Maia. You're Black. You're white, too, but you're a Black girl. Wearing braids is a part of that." She turns and looks at herself in the mirror like she isn't so sure, but I just smile at her reflection. "Welcome home," I say. "You've always belonged here."

So that's how I end up sitting on Maia's bed, her on the floor with her head between my thighs (a much tamer variation on my wildest Maia fantasies). Her curls smell sweet and fruity, like strawberry shampoo, and even though she doesn't have most of the products I usually use, we're making smooth progress.

I showed her a few different options for styles, and she picked Fulani braids. As my fingers weave the cornrows into her hair, we go silent for a bit. She puts on music and hums while working on her trig homework, only asking me the occasional question when she gets really stuck. And then I'm thinking about Beau without really deciding to. I'm thinking about her dark eyes, and how my fingers felt in *her* hair, and the way she said, *I hope they make you smile* when she was twisting together the stems of the flowers in Enzo's bouquet. I'm just beginning to picture Beau's lean body in her swimsuit as I finish the last braid in Maia's hair. I spray mousse over her scalp and I'm smoothing it all down with my fingers, when Maia's soft voice shatters the silence.

"This is random, but . . . I've been thinking. I'm not so sure I want to go to prom with Tate."

Of all the things Maia could have said in this moment, I never would have seen that coming. Even though it's been our goal all along.

"Why?" I ask her, and for some reason my hands start trembling. I stop smoothing out the mousse and tuck one of the braids hanging in front of her ear behind it. I like that the braid has a little spiral at the end.

Maia turns to look up at me. Trails her finger along my thigh. The braids look good, and she looks different, but still like herself. It would be easy to take this moment in my hands. Ask her to call her boyfriend right now and dump him. Tell her that the why doesn't matter and say she should go to prom with me. But I stay still and quiet, giving her the space to figure out what she's feeling.

"I've just been . . . questioning some things. I'm not sure it's fair to Tate to string him along when . . . I don't know what I want."

I'm trying very hard to control my face as Maia continues to give me whiplash. Not fair to *Tate*? But totally fine to fuck around with Beau and me? She hasn't even mentioned our kiss the whole time I've been here.

I understand having questions and needing time to figure yourself out. I went through that too. But I didn't conduct romantic experiments that involved other people. I pushed everyone away specifically to avoid that. Maia needs to understand that she doesn't get a pass to be a manipulative bitch just because she's a pretty girl who is unsure about her attractions.

I'm seconds from saying that out loud, which would ruin the Plan to the point of no return, when Getty bursts into the room, a brown, bikinied Barbie in his mouth. And then Maisie is right behind him, shrieking. Getty jumps up onto the bed beside me, slamming his soft, furry body into mine, and I fall backward onto the duvet. He scampers over me, and then Maisie is on the bed too, leaping over my prone body, grabbing for the doll, while Maia is screaming at them both to "Get the hell out!"

"Mom," Maisie shouts, "Maia said hell!" And then Maisie yells at Getty, "Baguette Duane Milo Moon, if you don't drop that right now, it's gonna be bathtime!" At the mention of the bath (and maybe his full government name too), Getty instantly drops the Barbie and leans down so his head is right next to mine. He sniffs, and then he's licking my whole face like it's an ice cream cone and I'm squealing and laughing and Maia is trying to yank him off, but he is very insistent.

When Maia is finally able to herd her sister and dog through her door and out of her room, I'm still smiling. Which is better, I think, than how I felt moments before their intrusion, when I was about to tell Maia the fuck off.

"I should go," I say now, and Maia's face falls but I don't care. I need to get out of here before I say something I regret. She's already thinking about not taking Tate to prom, and that feels like a win. I grab my stuff. "See you at school?"

"Not tomorrow," she says. "Professional development day or whatever it is."

I almost say, *Oh, that's right, because Beau has a show tomorrow night.* Maia is looking at me, waiting for me to say something. I should ask if she has plans. I should be thinking about the Plan. But I feel flustered, and not in the way being around Maia used to make me.

"Okay, so the day after," I say, trying to smile.

"Yeah," she says as she follows me down the stairs. She stands at the door, watching me until I drive away.

As soon as my phone connects to Bluetooth, I'm saying, "Call Beau," and when her deep voice fills my car, I say what I've been afraid to say out loud for at least the last week: "I think the Plan is working a little too well."

"Well, hi to you too, Monty," she says. "And . . . isn't that a good thing?"

"I don't know!" I say, hoping she'll give me some kind of hint that she's thinking what I'm thinking . . . or better yet, feeling anything like what I'm feeling. "Is it?"

"Are you having second thoughts? We said we'd stop if either of us didn't want to do it anymore."

And there it is, I realize. What I was calling her for: I wanted Beau to give me an out. But I don't want to take it unless there's something, or rather some*one*, waiting for me on the other side.

"Are you just afraid you won't be able to get Maia to dump Tate?" Beau continues before I say anything. "Because I get that, but—"

"No, it's not that. Maia just told me she isn't sure she even wants to take Tate to prom, so we're well on our way."

"Oh," Beau says. It's a complete sentence, that single syllable. And I'm suddenly worried I shouldn't have told her about Tate. "Well," she continues, "I guess Step Four's done. You're . . . efficient."

"She hasn't dumped him," I say, and then a little quieter: "Gentle reminder about the constitution. Please don't hate me. I don't think I could handle it if you hated me."

My heart feels bruised as it strains against the cage where I've locked it away.

She's quiet for a beat too long. "I don't hate you, Charm."

In the background, I hear two random clicks of the typewriter. Knowing that means she's sitting at her desk makes my head spin. Knowing exactly where she is, what her room looks like, how she looks slouched in that chair. She kissed me right there.

"Are you working on a song?" I ask, not wanting to hang up yet.

"I actually just finished one last night," she answers.

"The writer's block is broken?" I ask. "Are you going to celebrate?"

"Well, let's not get ahead of ourselves," she says in that voice. "We have to see if the song sucks or not first."

"There's no way," I say.

A couple more clicks sound on the typewriter, like she's idling. I remember typing *Kiss me*.

"The Plan," I say bluntly. "Do *you* want to call it off?" Now I offer *her* the out. I take and hold a big breath while I wait for her to speak.

But instead of answering my question, Beau laughs as she says, "Maia's gonna lose her shit when you prompose."

31

Beau

No school today, and thank fuck.

The show is tonight—*Elicktric* may or may not be in attendance—and Celine is being a rehearsal tyrant disguised as a nonchalant benign empress. She clearly cares, and yet insists on the front.

"I mean, it would be cool if they did a review," she said earlier today. "But it's no biggie if they don't."

Me and Daniel exchanged the look that confirmed we both knew that it *is*, in fact, a biggie.

As confusing as it is, I think I've started to understand. In some ways it's easier to pretend not to want something—and it's not about what other people think. It's about what you're willing to admit to yourself.

"Let's do the new song one more time," she says. "Just for fun."

"I'm already sick of hearing it," I say.

"Can it, Cart Killer," she snaps. "Now drum!"

Me and Daniel exchange the look.

I'm not actually sick of hearing the song—it's actually the best song I've ever written. Celine doesn't say so, but when she sang it for the first time yesterday, we could all tell. There are a lot of lines I really like, but there are two that, when Celine sang them to the melody she and Daniel had been working on, made goose bumps rise on my arms.

I've been calling to the other side, the space seemed so unbridgeable.
Shadows are made for the dark—is this how it feels to be visible?

After Celine sang it, we were all quiet for a while. I prayed she wouldn't say anything. Not to me. Not about the song. And she didn't. She just said, "This is going to be a good show."

And it will be.

If I can get my shit together.

My drum kit is usually where I feel most relaxed, but today it feels like it's a Fisher-Price toy and I'm folded up behind it like a big, weird grasshopper. The sticks keep falling out of my hands and—twice—I fuck up the transition. With my first couple of mistakes, Celine side-eyes me and we begin again. After the fourth one, her glances start slowly escalating into glares. Finally she breaks.

"Jesus, fuck!" she says right into the mic. It echoes around the garage, even with the levels turned to low. "Beau! What the hell is going on with you?"

"Ooh," Daniel says. He lowers his guitar so it's resting against his pelvis. He has the alert, amused, but still slightly nervous face of a guy getting strapped into a ride at the theme park. "Should I go get snacks or . . . ?"

"No snacks for Beau!" Celine cries. "Beau doesn't deserve snacks!"

"Hey!" I protest. "We have a Universal Snack Rule, I thought! You can't jam hungry!"

"You're not hungry, you're distracted!" Celine snaps. "You don't get snacks when you're just fucking up!"

I groan, leaning back on my stupid stool to press my back against the garage wall. It's cool. All winter long I've avoided touching it like an electric fence, because with no insulation, it was cold as hell. But no, now it's cool, not cold. Because it's actually spring. Prom's a week away.

"Fuck my liiiiiiiife!"

My eyes were closed, but when I open them, Daniel and Celine are both staring at me.

"That was supposed to be quieter," I say softly.

Daniel gently sets his guitar down, turns the chair beside him around, and sits on it backward, his arms on top of the backrest. His forehead crinkles.

"Is there something you want to talk about?" he says.

"You look like a youth pastor," I reply.

"Now, Beau," he says, "your defensiveness tells me you need to share."

"Like a youth pastor who is trying to talk to me about how Jesus thinks drugs are uncool."

"Jesus would never say that," Celine cuts in.

"Celine!" Daniel cries. "Do you mind?! I'm trying to talk to Beau about her problems."

"I don't have problems," I say, rolling my eyes.

"Oh you do," Celine cuts in again. "Huge ones. Otherwise you wouldn't be flopping around like a salmon on the day an *Elicktric* reviewer could be watching us play."

"This is a safe space," Daniel says soothingly, ignoring her. "If you're nervous about the show tonight . . ."

"Oh my god, I'm not nervous. We've been rehearsing for days, and we've played Pack of Eight like six times."

"Not in front of a potential reviewer," he counters.

"I'm not nervous!" I shout.

"Then why can't you get the song right?" Celine says over his shoulder. She's walked away from the mic and leans against Daniel's back. The sight of them together always makes me smile. Even when she's being a cuntasaurus. They're so easy with each other. I haven't seen my mom in days, and maybe it will matter at some point, but right now it doesn't.

"I don't know," I say. "It will be fine by tonight. Have I ever fucked up onstage?"

"There was that one time," Daniel says.

"What time?!" I demand.

"To her credit, that girl she had a crush on was there."

"What girl?!"

She and Daniel go on having the conversation like I'm not sitting right there. I watch in disbelief.

"Remember her face?" Celine says, laughing. "Oh my god. She was like a little baby beet. And when I asked her about it later, she said she was just hot from the stage lights."

"There were no stage lights," Daniel says. "That place was a dump."

"The girl was so cute, though," Celine says, pondering. "I get it. If you'd been standing at the edge of the stage staring at me like that, I might have missed a note or two."

"She had to skip the drum solo," Daniel says. His shoulders move up and down as he laughs. What a dork. "A small mercy. That girl's crush would have evaporated."

"Okay, clowns," I interrupt, and mime throwing a drumstick like a spear. "Thanks for the intermission! Can we get back to rehcarsal now?"

"No," says Celine blithely. "I just wanted us to fine-tune some shit, but there's no point in overdoing it. It'd be wasted time anyway, because you're on another planet in your little undeveloped brain."

"In case you forgot," I say, pointing at her, "your brain isn't fully developed either. You can't even rent a car."

"But . . . ," Daniel says, grinning.

Goddamn it. I basically teed it up for him.

". . . at least she's never committed vehicular manslaughter against a cart!"

"I can't be a cart murderer *and* a cart . . . manslaughterer, okay!" I yell. "Those are separate charges."

"You would know," says Celine. She sounds bored, but there's something sharp underneath it. "But I digress. And so do you. On purpose. Like always."

"Wait, what?"

"What's going on with you?" she says, ignoring my question. "You've been weird for weeks. We keep talking about it but not talking about it, and you've got a real talent for slithering out of actual conversations like a goddamn eel. At what point are you going to stop keeping things from me?"

I've been thinking for days about Charm calling me a turtle. I don't stick my neck out, I don't make myself vulnerable. Now Celine is essentially saying the same thing with yet another creature metaphor. I'm fucking over it.

"Has it occurred to you that you are not, in fact, a parent and that I'm allowed to keep whatever I want from you?" I snap.

Celine rarely yells. But she does now.

"Has it occurred to you that *neither of us* really has an active parent and that I'm doing the best I can to be a good role model? To teach you not to keep your feelings inside? Has it occurred to you that I don't want to be a fucking role model at *all*, Beau? That there's shit I want to do with my life?"

There's a long moment of silence. When it settles, Celine echoes my words:

"That was supposed to be quieter."

I'm staring at the floor, but out of the corner of my eye I see Daniel rest his hand on the back of my sister's neck, just like after Charm left my house the night we kissed. They've talked about this before, I realize. Just the two of them. And even though I can't decide if I'm furious or sad, in this moment I'm glad they have each other. But I still feel like crying.

"I'm hungry," Celine says. "I'll make us something before it gets too close to the show."

And just like that, I'm neither furious nor sad. I'm just hungry. I follow her to the kitchen silently.

She pulls out a bag of pancake mix. When we were younger, Mom would make them from scratch—I even kind of remember the recipe. Flour. Baking powder. Egg. Blah, blah, blah. But when she started working around the clock, Celine started asking her to get the mix so she could make them for us when Mom wasn't home. Which, as it turned out, came to be all the time. Now it's our go-to. Except Celine puts the batter in the blender and adds spinach.

"Do you think when you're grown and living on your own you'll make them without spinach?" she asks me when the grass-colored moons are sizzling on the stove.

"Absolutely not."

"I hope not," Daniel chimes in. "It's the only way she'll eat a vegetable."

I could protest—tell them I eat carrots and cucumbers and sometimes broccoli. It's just the stuff with leaves I can't stand. But I don't say anything. God, they really know me. Daniel like the dad I never had and Celine like the mom I only have a fraction of. Celine luring my heartache out with food. Feeding me because she loves me. Feeding me even though she just told me a secret: that sometimes she wishes she could care a little less. Feeding me because she's my sister, *not* because she's my mom. Suddenly, being in this small, hot kitchen feels like the only place in the world where I'm understood. I haven't kept this shit to myself because of Celine acting like a mom. I've kept it to myself because I'm a spineless toad (creature metaphor number three).

"Say it," Celine says.

"I think I'm in love," I say immediately.

"With Charm," she says decisively.

I think of our conversation in the car on the way to get eggs for the bakery, how Celine had been trying to nudge me toward this epiphany, and it makes my face even hotter than the kitchen. Being out of denial is so annoying because when you get over the hump of it, it's like running straight into a mirror where a new version of yourself is saying, *LOL, told you so, dumbass*.

"Yeah."

"Does she know?"

"No," I say miserably. "I've been agreeing we're friends and all that bullshit."

"You mean all that bullshit you were saying in the car to me," she says cheerfully, flipping a pancake.

"Ugh, shut up." Turns out the mirror on the other side of denial can also have your sister in it. Thank god.

"I'll save my told-you-so's for after you bag the babe," she says.

"Misogynist," Daniel calls without looking up from his phone, like he's reading a sign we're passing on the highway.

Celine ignores him.

"Invite her to the show," she says. "Tonight. You'll play your gay little heart out and she'll be enraptured and then you can confess your love under the neon lights. It will be so romantic."

"You saw that in a movie," I say, groaning. "This isn't like that."

"I didn't see it in a movie!" Celine says.

"Yes, you did," Daniel says, again without looking up. When he feels her glaring at him, he looks up with only his eyes and adds, "Love you. You're perfect."

Satisfied, she turns back to me.

"Text her," she demands. "Right now. Ask her to go."

She slips the spatula under the cooked pancakes and transfers them to a plate, where they lie steaming.

"I can't do it in a text," I argue. "I know Charm. She'll start overthinking it and figure out some reason to say no."

"Do you think she would *want* to say yes?"

I bite my lip, staring at the little bubbles in the next set of pancakes as they cook through. The same little bubbles cook in my chest. Little hopeful bubbles.

"Maybe?"

"You gotta ask her in person," she says. "Look her in the eye!"

"That kind of makes me want to die," I say.

"All the more reason! Love is torment! *Go to her!*"

"Have you been watching period dramas again?" I ask suspiciously.

"Go to her!" she shouts. "It will be so romantic! Right, Daniel?"

"So romantic," he says in a monotone, completely absorbed now in playing a block-shifting game on his phone.

She smacks him with the spatula, which he ignores.

"Okay, I'm gonna eat a pancake first," I say.

"No pancakes for you!" Celine shouts. "Love calls!"

"Dude, I'm starving!" I cry.

"Text first," she says, brandishing the spatula like a weapon.

"Ugh, fine."

Charm's number is, of course, at the top of my texts, so I tap out:

Hey where are you? I gotta come talk to you if that's okay.

I send it before I can talk myself out of it.

"There, happy?" I say. "Can I have a pancake now?"

Celine frisbees one at me, which I barely hold on to.

"Go to her!" she proclaims again.

"Jesus, Shakespeare, thanks for the help. This is hot, by the way."

I take a bite of the pancake and look at her from the open kitchen door.

"Thank you," I say. We have a lot more to say to each other. But she'll be here. And so will I. "The show tonight is gonna be really good."

"Prayers up for *Elicktric*," she says. "Love you. Now go. And don't manslaughter any carts."

"Oh, fuck you!" But it means *I love you*, and she knows it.

I chew the pancake on the way to her car. The hope in my heart cooks.

32
Charm

I hand Maia a bouquet of pink and white flowers the second I see her, and a moment later, a kid wearing a glow-in-the-dark shirt that says F*CK YEAH! SPACE! escorts us to our seats at the planetarium. As soon as we sit down, Maia brings the bouquet to her nose.

"These are beautiful," she says. "What kind of flower is this?"

I grin, feeling a little overly proud of myself. When I asked Ms. King what kind of flowers to use in a bouquet for a NASA lover, she said there was only one answer. "They're called 'Stargazer' lilies."

"Shut up. They are *not*," she mutters with wide eyes.

I laugh a little. "They are, I swear."

She smells the flowers again with her eyes closed, then puts them down on the seat next to her and takes my hand. She strokes her thumb over mine. "I need that kid's shirt," she whispers, and I smile even though I honestly don't think she'd wear it outside of her own bedroom.

It's pretty dark and mostly empty inside the theater, since it's a random Tuesday morning. It was Beau's suggestion to see if Maia was free today—to try and seal the deal, since prom is on Saturday. She said the planetarium would be the perfect place to prompose, and when I saw there was a show about supernovas playing, I agreed. What could be better for a space nerd like Maia than to be asked out under the stars? But now that I'm here, and Maia is smiling at me in the dark, I'm not so sure I actually want to go through with it.

When the show starts a few minutes later, there are four other people scattered around the big domed theater. But when the ceiling above our heads is suddenly filled with thousands of twinkling stars and a thunderous voice rattling off facts about the universe, it's easy to forget that we're not alone.

"Supernovas are powerful and luminous explosions of massive stars," the narrator booms. An animation that looks like fireworks on steroids blooms overhead, and I look at Maia, who is staring straight up, grinning. We learn that they only happen a few times a century in our galaxy, and that they have two major causes: the core of a star collapsing, or a dying star being reignited.

My phone lights up in the dark, and all I see is Beau's name. I flip the phone over. She must be checking to see if I proposed yet. She'll want to know how it went. And that's when I feel my own core collapsing, my heart and everything inside it getting heavy enough to pull me under. I turn to ask Maia what I came here to ask her, just so I can tell Beau that I did, because even though it pains me, I don't want to let Beau down.

It almost feels poetic that Maia decides, at that precise moment, to squeeze my hand. With the blazing light of a supernova shining all around us, I ask the question simply, in a way that's real and soft and all me: "Maia, would you like to go to prom with me?"

Instead of answering, though, she leans over and begins to whisper.

"The first girl I ever kissed was named Nova. She was my best friend in middle school. After I kissed her, she didn't say anything mean. She didn't even act surprised. We just kept playing with the makeup she'd brought over to show me. But the next day she stopped answering my texts, then she stopped liking my posts, and eventually she stopped talking to me at school. She just kind of slowly faded away. She'd look right through me, like I was invisible. I think it was the first time someone broke my heart. It kinda felt the way that looks."

We both stare at the dazzling, too-bright star folding in on itself.

"Wanna know why me and Andi aren't friends anymore? Over winter break I told her I had some questions about myself, and she was just so annoying about it. She was like, 'Okay? So? You don't get enough attention from all your stalkers on the internet? You gotta be gay, too?'"

"Ouch," I say. "That . . . doesn't sound like a real friend."

"Boys could never hurt me the way girls could," Maia says, looking back down, her gaze hard and steady on mine, the exploding stars reflecting like shattered glass in her eyes. "The way girls have."

I want to say she's not the only person in the world who's been hurt. That my heart's been broken a few times too, most recently by *her*.

But she hasn't moved, and her face seems to glow in the dark as she finally answers my question. "Yes, Charm. I'd love to go to prom with you."

She looks terrified. She looks thrilled. I nod, gently kiss her cheek, and watch the stars, holding Maia's hand until the show is over.

Once I'm back in my car alone, I text Ezra, **SSTC ASAP**, and he sends me his location. I can tell from the map it's not Oscar's, but I know Ezra wouldn't lead me astray. After Maia's story about Andi, I'm feeling more grateful for him than usual. He's always been my safe place, my safest person. I hit go on the turn-by-turn navigation, knowing he'll be at the destination, wherever it is, waiting for me.

I'm holding a calico cat with an uninspired name (Callie) when I finally check the messages that came in from Beau earlier. I breathe a little easier after I see that she's asking where I am, and not about Maia. I also happen to be crying a little, because I just finished telling Ezra everything that happened at the planetarium and how I've been feeling lately about Beau, so I wipe the tears off my face and blink a few times so I can see her texts clearly.

"Here's your purr-fect chai latte, and your cattuccino," says the server as she sets down our drinks. We're at Cathaus, the cat café where Ezra goes whenever he needs a little extra affection.

"What happened that landed you here?" I ask him.

"I tried to ask Enzo to prom again," he says. He clicks his teeth at a particularly elusive feline at the top of a carpeted cat tree. It looks pointedly away from him. "We were the last two people left in the auditorium after last night's performance, and right before I was about to leave, he asked me to run some lines with him. I thought that was super weird, because he had just rehearsed them with the literal other actors after getting some notes from Mr. Franklin. So I took it as a sign. He's into me, right?"

"That's what I've been telling you!" I say, my own tears disappearing momentarily.

"I read a line, he read one, and then I thought, 'Oh I can just ask him to prom, like it's part of the script.' So I was about to do it when Clay Paulson walks in looking for his physics textbook. And once Enzo started helping him search around for it,

I figured, no way he's into me if a physics book is enough of a distraction to pull his attention away."

I give him a look. "Or he's just nice, Ezra."

"Whatever. I chickened out. Again. So I came here to nurse my wounds."

"Shit," I say. "I'm so sorry, Ez. At least you're trying to ask a person you really care about."

"At least you actually asked."

I read Beau's text again. I think about what Maia told me, and I'm now less sure than ever about going through with the Plan—the goal of which is hurting her in the exact way she's most afraid of. This is all so much messier than I planned for it to be, and worst of all, I can't deny any longer what I've been feeling for weeks: I've fallen hard for Beau, and she's who I really want to take to prom.

This time I send a response before I think too hard about all the reasons I shouldn't want to see Beau right now. But the pathetic truth of my life is that I always want to see her.

At Cathaus with Ez. Why?

What's a cat house? is her immediate response.

"Who you texting? Maia or Beau?" Ezra asks, as he strokes the tabby lounging at his feet.

"Beau," I say to Ezra.

"Don't tell her where we are," he replies. He looks panicked.

"I kind of already did," I say, sniffing. "Sorry."

"Damn it. If she comes here, all the cats will like her better than me, and I need their love!"

He has a point.

"One of Beau's greenest flags is that Calypso liked her," I say, new tears filling my eyes. "Cats have boundaries," I tell him, thinking about Getty and Maia, who are just the opposite. "Cats require consent. Cats don't let just anyone touch them. Cats know vibes."

"Cats are ruled by the moon, like the ocean," Ezra says, giggling.

"Cats can hear our thoughts," I add, texting Beau back at the same time.

"Cats are descended from dragons," Ezra says. "It's why they have reptilian eyes."

"Cats are witches."

"It is known," Ezra adds.

"It is known," I repeat.

"Does Beau know you already asked Maia? And that she said yes?"

"No," I say. "She probably thinks I'm gonna take Maia to the planetarium later to ask her. So don't mention it, okay? But also . . ."

I swallow hard and pet Callie more. I look up at the ceiling, to keep the tears I feel burning the backs of my eyes inside my face. "Ughhhh!" I say.

"You want to go to prom with Beau," Ezra says, completing the sentence I never would have had the guts to say out loud. It makes me want to rage-cry.

"Maybe as friends," I say, my voice thick and tight.

"You both keep *saying* that you're just friends," Ezra says. "But I don't know who you're trying to convince."

"She said that? To you?" I ask. "That we're friends?"

Ezra nods.

"In the car the other day. When you were getting the ice cream."

"Oh," I say. I stare at the wall for a long minute before gently placing Callie back on the floor. She meows loudly, protesting. "I gotta go to the restroom."

"For the record, Charm," he says as I stand up. "I didn't believe her. I don't believe her. And I told her so."

In the bathroom, I take off my glasses and splash water on my face. Ezra doesn't believe her, but I can't afford not to.

"Good friends do nice things," I say to my reflection, like I'm explaining something simple to a kid. "She only flirted with you during your lessons," I tell myself, even as I try to ignore the memory of our pool "friend date"—the way she looked at me with her wet eyelashes, the way her arms felt wrapped around my legs. I brace my hands on the sink and let my head fall forward. "She warned you this would happen," I mutter in the direction of the drain. I can still see her sitting across from me at the diner, blushing as she said, *It's just that girls tend to . . . like me.* I take a deep breath, feeling things, all kinds of things. For her. But I have to play by the rules. I swallow hard to push the feelings down my own throat.

"Okay." I look at myself again. "Okay. I can do this. I can be friends with the girl I . . ."

The bathroom door creaks open, so I stop talking to myself. I put my glasses back on and check my phone.

A message from Ezra: **Your FRIEND Beau is here.**

"Go time," I whisper.

When I turn toward the door, Beau is standing there, watching me.

"Go time, huh?" she says. "Where you going?"

"Oh! Hey!" I say, my voice too loud. It echoes around the bathroom, filling the space.

Beau smiles widely.

"I told Ezra, I didn't even know this place was here. It's so cool that you can just hang out with cats! And that menu—the meow snack mix, the kitty cakes!"

I laugh. "Yeah it's pretty great."

Beau nods. Looks around like she's only just realized we're still in the bathroom. "Anyway. I was coming by because—"

"I asked Maia to prom," I blurt for some god-awful reason. Call it a weird defense mechanism, but invoking Maia (a girl I no longer care much about) seems like the right thing to do in this moment to protect my heart from Beau (a girl I care a little too much about).

"Already?" Beau asks.

"Um. Yeah. We went to a show at the planetarium. Like we talked about."

"Right," Beau says, scratching the back of her head. "Right. I guess I didn't realize they had stuff during the day. . . . And what did she say?" Her face is unreadable.

"She said yes," I whisper.

If Beau's face was unreadable before, now it's just straight-up blank. "Oh."

She doesn't look angry exactly, but she definitely doesn't seem happy. But shouldn't she be happy, since this means the Plan is working?

"Are you upset?" I ask her.

And then her hand is in her hair, pushing it back to reveal her incredulous brows. I want to smooth them down with my fingertips. She's shaking her head, and I think she's smiling a little at her shoes. Why is she smiling at her shoes?

"No, not upset. It's just . . . I told you it would work." We're still standing pretty far apart, but then Beau takes a few steps forward. "I knew it would work. That *you* would work."

I shake my head. Look at the floor like a story is written there. I laugh my hardest, meanest laugh just so I won't cry.

"I came by because I wanted to see if you'd come to the Favorite Daughter show tonight."

It's so far from what I was expecting her to say that for a second, I just stand there. But then I think about how she looks onstage, with her biceps on full display, sweat making her soft hair stick to her pretty forehead. I think about the last show I went to, and how her hands covered mine over the drumsticks. I don't think I could take any of that, let alone watching dozens of other girls flirt with her, their bodies pushed up against the edge of the stage, Beau grinning and leaning and touching their lovely, manicured hands instead of mine.

"I don't think I can?" I say. I'm too frazzled by our whole interaction to think of an excuse, but I really don't think I *can* watch her play without breaking my own heart.

"Oh," she says. "Okay."

"We should get back out there so you can steal all the cats from Ezra," I tell her, forcing a grin and feeling grateful she doesn't ask why I can't go to her show. "There's a ragamuffin named Beyoncé that he's particularly fond of, and she's been avoiding him since we got here. But if she gets one whiff of you, I'm sure she'll come down from where she's been lounging."

Beau bites her lip. Points to a stall. "I'm gonna use the litter box first, but then tell Ezra, Beyoncé's mine."

I laugh a little because Beau's blue gaze is playful and warm. But really I want to run away, just like a spooked cat, and hide.

33
Beau

I pull up at Pack of Eight at the same moment Daniel and Celine rumble up on his motorcycle, and finally I can let the tears out.

I didn't want to cry until this very second.

I'd gone into the bathroom stall at the cat café to get my shit together, and it had worked. For a moment.

In the small space, I took an inner iron to my brain. At first all the goop in my skull screamed, *Holy shit rejection hurts! Holy shit she's going to prom with Maia!!! Red alert*, like I needed to flee the whole building at top speed. But that would have been even more embarrassing, so I talked myself down. I didn't exactly ask in an explicitly *date-like* way, so maybe Charm wasn't saying no in an explicitly rejection-of-a-date way. But even if I didn't ask it that way . . . I meant it that way. Surely Charm knew that. Didn't she? Fuck. But duh, why *would* she say yes to the Favorite Daughter show? She's going to prom with Maia Moon. Yesterday I had the chance to call the whole Plan off. But denial is sticky. A day late and a dollar short.

And it hit me like a comet: this is what Celine meant about dating straight girls. Sure, those situationships didn't make me feel great. But they never put me in danger of feeling like . . . *this*.

I kept it together, though. I left the restroom. Smiled and petted the cats and joked with Ezra. Avoided Charm's eyes, which wasn't hard because she was avoiding mine, too. Then all I could think while I drove around town before the show was, *Wow, you really fucked this up* followed by *How could you be so stupid?* Charm had made it so clear we were just friends, and I kept telling myself I would follow the rules . . . and then I kept breaking them. Meanwhile Charm is always keeping them. She was the one who proposed them, after all. The founding mother of the constitution.

But now that the tears are stinging my eyes and Celine is taking off her helmet, I suddenly remember her Shakespeare pontifications, and how can I even tell her? Oh, how very fucking annoying.

"Hey—" she calls, but before she can say anything else, I wave and walk quickly toward the theater.

"I gotta pee, I'll meet you backstage!"

Pretending to be normal sucks, but it's worse if it doesn't even work—seeing the recognition on Celine's face and the quick look she tosses toward Daniel, who, as always, catches it. It makes me feel like throwing a tantrum. Like being a little kid and throwing myself on the ground and screaming, *Why can't everyone just leave me alone* while also praying they don't.

I close myself into the backstage bathroom, which is blessedly single-stall, lock the door, then lean against it and pull out my phone. I go to Charm's name.

Hey sorry if I made things weird. I totally didn't mean for you to come like a DATE, I know you're going to prom with Maia. I just meant you and Ezra might like the show and . . .

I delete it all. What the fuck am I doing? Trying too hard. Doing too much. I suddenly don't feel like crying anymore. I just want to hide. But I'm about to go onstage in—I check my phone—fifteen minutes. That means I need to put on my performance disguise. Tonight of all nights. I owe Celine a lot. The least I can do is be the best fucking drummer I can be if Favorite Daughter has eyeballs on it.

The disguise is chill, indifferent, distant. It has always been such an easy thing to put on, and honestly, sometimes I forget to take it off. A thought nags at me: Do I *forget*? Or does it feel too comfortable or safe to discard? Because the idea of putting it on right now feels like putting on a bulletproof vest.

"Get your shit together," I snap. I sound like a freak. I close out of my messages, shove my phone back in my pocket, and head to the stage.

"Hey," Celine says cautiously. "All good?"

"Yep," I say. I can feel the disguise starting to fall down over me like a curtain. But for some reason, it doesn't fit like it once did. I can't do it without thinking about it. Like there's a Charm-shaped hole right through the center. "Do you two feel good? Ready?"

"For sure," says Daniel. "Donut?"

He named his guitar Powder for this reason. There are always powdered donut fingerprints all along its case. And right now, a donut box on top.

"You're damn right," I say, and grab one. The sugar rushes to my brain. I've never done drugs in my life, because the idea of not knowing or remembering the shit I do sends me into a spiral just thinking about it. But sugar . . . sugar I can do. I finish the first one and then start on another.

"Slow down there, champ," Daniel says, laughing, pulling away the box like it's a bottle of whiskey.

"I know my limits!" I insist.

Celine crosses to the wing and pulls a bag of carrot sticks out of her purse.

"You need a chaser," she says. "You're going to have a headache otherwise."

I can feel myself on the verge of snarling. I can feel the words almost coming up: *Thanks, Mom*. But instead of words, a feeling; and instead of out, in: *guilt*. Everything Celine said in the garage at home. She shouldn't have to care this much.

"You're twenty-one," I say. "You could be carrying much better stuff in your bag than this."

"Like what? A disembodied arm? A fifty-pack of condoms? It's a big purse. It—and I—contain multitudes."

She shoves the bag of carrots at me. I grab it and dig out a handful, then stuff them in my mouth and chew obnoxiously.

"You should eat some too," I tell her, probably spitting carrot sawdust.

"You kind of look like a rabid rabbit," Daniel says seriously.

"A rabid rabbit who's ready to *jam*."

The stage manager, Kush, shows up then, clipboard and headset in hand. They slip the headset over their head. It's a small venue, but they take their shit seriously here. One of my favorite places, honestly. The crowd is always good, and the management will give us free food after.

"Y'all about ready?" Kush says. "Full house out there."

I toss the bag of carrots back to Celine, who stows them in her bag.

"We're ready," Celine says, moving toward the mic. "Sound check?"

"Already done," Kush says.

Like I said, they take their shit seriously. Especially Kush. This is their last year in this town—their cousin moved to Atlanta last spring and apparently started his own company doing sound for theaters. Kush can't wait to get down there and join. I suddenly want to ask if they'll take me with them. Fold me up like a shirt and pack me in their bag. Get me outta here.

"You're the shit, Kush," my sister says, adjusting the mic stand.

"Obviously," Kush says with their bright smile. Charm has a smile like that. A flash that grows and grows.

Oh, we're doing that now? I berate myself. *We're doing the whole everything reminds me of her thing? Get. Your. Shit. Together. She's going to prom with Maia.*

"Good on the set list? Everyone's cool?"

I can't help but think Celine is directing this at me. And . . . she is. She's addressing the band and I'm one-third of it. *Disguise,* I remind myself. *Get through this show and you can cry again later. Or maybe the disguise will settle into your bones and you won't need to cry at all.* This idea feels comforting. I grab onto it.

"Yep," I say. "All good."

The old and raggedy curtain goes up and the audience cheers. I generally try not to look at the audience directly—it can be distracting. But tonight I let my eyes scan the crowd. Maybe some part of me wonders if Charm will still show up. Will have changed her mind about whatever it was that made her say no.

But when I cast my eyes over the audience, I don't find Charm. There is a gaze that's turned toward me, though, focus riveted. My eyes pass over it, but then snap back.

Maia.

Maia?

What the hell is *she* doing here?

It's not like there's another band playing. It's just Favorite Daughter. So why is Maia Moon in the audience? God, does that mean Charm is here too? *With* her?

I stare just a moment too long. Long enough for one side of her mouth to start to curve up in that smile I know so well. Or used to.

I look away quickly and immerse myself in the music. For Celine. I love drumming, but this thing wouldn't exist if it wasn't for my sister. She doesn't see parts: she sees the whole. Me drumming and her singing could have been separate trails, separate lives. Daniel could have just been the cool boyfriend who loves music as much as she does. But Celine envisioned it all synthesizing. As the rhythm travels through my body, I think of the hours she spends editing our clips, posting them on Instagram, responding to comments, scouring the area for gigs. If that reviewer from *Elicktric* is in the audience, I hope they hear everything she puts into this music. My lyrics are just words until she sings them, and tonight I feel like I'm hearing them for the first time. She puts a private, special something into this. The one thing she reserves just for her. It makes me want to lift it all the way to heaven.

I play as hard and as well as I can, sweat running down my back. Everything sounds perfect. Daniel rocks the fuck out. Celine's voice is as clear and full as it's ever been. And when we're playing the last song of our set, half the audience knows it well and sings along, their voices lifting the whole theater. It might make me want to cry if I weren't so deep in my armor.

After the show, Daniel and Celine are ecstatic. They felt it too—the energy, the way every song landed exactly how we wanted, every note just right. We won't know if there was a reviewer in the audience until they publish the hypothetical write-up. It's the kind of thing that will eat me alive with preoccupation until I know for sure, but Celine just seems happy that we played so well. After all that she said today, it feels good to see her feeling so light.

Once I've packed up, I sit on the edge of the stage alone, rubbing cream on my hands where my calluses feel dry. Celine and Daniel are chatting with friends who came, putting their own shit away. Sitting here like this invites conversation, and part of me hates myself for knowing and doing it anyway. But I put everything into tonight's show. All that's left are the thoughts of Charm: Did she come tonight? Were she and Maia holding hands while I played? I scan the venue but don't see Charm. My eye lands on the girl with a Mohawk over by the bar who's been looking my way—I know it's only a matter of time before she winds a path through the crowd to say hello.

But it's Maia who comes. Alone.

There's no way I can smell her perfume, but part of me imagines I can. She smells like danger. I'm still rubbing my calluses when her hand appears on my knee.

"Great show," she says in that slithery voice.

"Yeah? Thanks."

"I haven't seen you in a while," she says.

I've seen you, I want to say.

"We've both been pretty busy, I think," I say instead.

I scoot off the stage so her hand slides off my knee.

"Are you okay?" she asks. She's standing a little too close and tries to catch my eye.

How can she even ask? I wish I could tell her I know she's going to prom with Charm. That she should be ashamed of herself, coming here mere hours after accepting Charm's promposal. I want to ask if she's even told Tate she's not going with him anymore, or if she's still deciding which of them she's going to disappoint. Like she disappointed me. And now she's here, in my face, back again—I can assume what she wants. Chances of her actually wondering how I am? Slim to none. By *Are you okay?* she really means *Why aren't you taking me to a dark corner backstage and putting your hand up my skirt like before?*

"I'm glorious," I reply.

"Glorious?"

"Excuse me," I say. I don't look at her. "Someone is waiting for me."

I scoot out from between her and the stage and head straight for the bar, where the girl with the Mohawk still sits. She looked away when Maia approached, but now she watches me coming. Her eyes are wide but not nervous. She's curious. Interested. She's older than me, but I don't care.

"Hey," I say, standing directly in front of her. A little too close for casual.

"Hey," she says. She has sleepy-lidded eyes. Bright pink lips. She reaches out a finger and plucks at the collar of my shirt. "You played your ass off."

I reach behind my back and pat my jeans pocket.

"Nah, still there."

She laughs.

"Mind if I check?"

"Be my guest."

She leans forward and wraps her arms around me. She doesn't actually grab my ass, just holds on to me, her smiling mouth close to mine.

"Can I?" she asks, pink lips curving.

"What did I say? You're my guest."

She presses her mouth against mine, and her tongue tastes like sour apple candy. Surprise washes over me—not good or bad, just a feeling like *oh*. Her friends giggle. All the times straight girls have used me in secret . . . this time it feels like I'm the one doing the using. And it's the most public kiss I've ever had. It makes me want to iron out my brain again.

Underneath it all I can feel eyes on my back, and when the girl stops kissing me, I look over my shoulder and catch a glimpse of Maia's face. Cloudy. Hurt. I feel a little jolt of remorse, but why should I? How is this any different from her kissing me in the back room, then making out with Tate at a party? She turns away, headed for the door. I still can't believe she came here at all.

I force myself to stop thinking about her and chat with the Mohawk girl and her friends for a little bit. At the end of the conversation, she gives me her number. She's cute and funny, and honestly, it was nice that her friends were fine with her publicly kissing a girl—even if it was a girl she didn't even know. At one point the context didn't matter: every time I kissed a girl it felt like a thrill. A token of validation. It made me feel like I existed. But something has changed and I'm not sure what or how. But it feels . . . shallow. And even though this isn't a secret, something about it *still* feels shallow, just in a different way. So when I get a chance to extricate myself, I take it.

Celine and Daniel are still hanging out with the friends who came to see the show, and I'm suddenly glad Celine let me drive—it'll be so much better to hide in a silent dark car than a damp bathroom that smells like piss and copper.

I go out to the car and hunch down in the front seat to watch people mill around and talk through the club windows. I'm thinking about Maia and what she did, but not what she did to me. I'm angry at her, but not for me. For Charm. Maia said she'd go to prom with her, then shows up here. Looking for what? Fuck, do I even tell Charm?

I pull out my phone and pull up her number. *Friends,* I think. A friend would tell her.

Did anything else happen with your prom date?

I sit waiting for her to reply, staring up at the night sky through the windshield. A DJ is playing music inside the venue now. I could still go back in and dance, hang out, kiss. Instead I stare at the text I sent to Charm, rethinking it. What if it seems like I'm trying to sow doubt?

I hope you're excited, I add.

I wait some more. No reply. Fuck, but what if that sounds bitter or sarcastic? Am I really going to triple text?

You should be. Prom will be really fun.

Jesus, Beau. *Now* I sound jealous.

Still no reply. And why would she? I'm not even saying what I mean. Maia is lurking in the back of my brain like a boogeyman I should be warning Charm about, but I don't want to hurt her, especially if she does have feelings for Maia again. And I'm starting to wonder if . . . maybe I'm the problem. Maybe girls don't keep me a secret because they don't want to be queer out loud; maybe they just don't want to be queer out loud with *me.* The Plan unexpectedly turned Maia into even more of a villain in my story, but maybe sometimes the villain gets the girl, and the creature from the Batcave is actually just standing in the way of someone's happily ever after.

I've sent three texts, all of which say nothing, and there's no way in hell I'm sending a fourth. I throw my phone onto the passenger-side floor, knowing I'll lunge for it if she texts back.

But she never does.

34

Charm

When I got my college acceptance letters a couple of months ago, I opened the envelopes with a thudding heart. Even being accepted to the two that I was kinda *meh* about had flooded me with a feeling of relief. Firm ground to stand on. A plan, backup or otherwise. Certainty.

My heart thuds that same way when I see three waiting texts from Beau.

But when I open them, it's like getting a letter that starts with *We regret to inform you* . . .

It's definitely firm ground. Firm with a sharp *f*. Just like "friend."

Aunt Miki slides the peach cobbler, shake, and waffles with the works in front of me. Ezra's order, cherry pie à la mode, is in her other hand, the ice cream already melting a little because the pie is still warm from the oven. (His lactose-intolerant ass is a masochist—I'll be dealing with his complaints about his stomach for the next two hours.) We came here specifically to eat our feelings—mine about Beau and Maia, his about Enzo and prom—and Beau's messages just make me want to choke down more sugar.

I smother my waffles in strawberry syrup and take a bite, making sure to scoop up a huge glob of whipped cream to chase it with.

"What just happened?" Ezra says with a mouthful of hot

cherries, flaky crust, and melty ice cream. He nods in the direction of my phone, which I may have violently slammed face down on the table before grabbing my fork.

"Honestly?" I ask. And I'm about to say, *A whole lot of nothing*, but that's when Aunt Miki circles back to our table and interrupts. "Probably something with Beau. I been waiting for that girl to ask you out since I saw the way she looked at you after your li'l pool date."

I'm seconds away from repeating our refrain, *We're just friends*, when I stop myself. I look at Ezra as he's stuffing his face with pie, and he reaches over and squeezes my hand with his free one, his eyes as soft as the vanilla scoop currently dripping over the edge of his plate. I smile at him, and something in my heart feels like a light switch that was just turned on. I look back over at Miki.

Ever since Beau and I kissed, I've been acting like being her friend is a bad thing—like I'm losing something instead of gaining access to a wonderful person who genuinely makes my life better. Beau listens to me. She is kind to me. I know now she would never do anything to intentionally hurt me. Beau *is* my friend. And there's nothing "just" about a friendship that feels as good as Beau makes me feel. Maybe it's the messy waffles, reminding me of Beau's secret, messy sweetness, but I suddenly feel like . . . I better snap out of it. Just because I can't love Beau the way I want to doesn't mean I can't love her at all.

"Beau's my friend," I say. "Do I also love her? Yes, I think so. But she's my friend first, and that's what I care about most right now. Aunt Miki, I have something to tell you."

I fill Miki in on what me and Beau have been up to the last couple of weeks. I say I didn't tell her sooner because I didn't want to bother her. "You already do so much for me," I say. "I didn't want to bug you with this, too." I tell her about Maia saying yes to my invitation to prom. And then I ask her what I should do.

Aunt Miki looks at Ezra, then back at me. "Well, you got yourself in one hell of a mess, haven't you?" she says. I let out a labored moan. "At this point," she says, "I think you have to go to prom with Maia. You can't leave that poor girl hanging, even if that was the original 'plan.'" She uses air quotes around the word "plan," and I cringe a little. "I know I raised you better than that."

"Ugh. God, Miki. I knew you'd say that."

"If you had asked me about this messy-ass scheme from the start, I would have told you not to do it in the first place!"

"Uh-oh," Ezra mutters. He throws back the rest of his pie and tries to excuse himself from the table. Aunt Miki catches him by the arm.

"I'm not going to lecture you guys, because I know it would be a waste of my breath. I'll just say this: the best revenge against any kind of wrong is simply letting them see you happy."

Ezra faux gags.

"But I'm not happy, Miki. That's the whole problem. She screwed me over and I feel like shit."

"Then you figure out what you need to do to get happy. And it *shouldn't* involve making someone else miserable." Aunt Miki taps her temple like she's given us something deep to think about and heads back to the counter.

I know I'm pushing it, and that this might not be the best moment, but I see an opening about something she and I have both been talking around for almost a year, and I can't ignore it.

"What if cosmetology school would make me happy?" I say in a small voice. "Happier than college would?" I add before I chicken out.

She stops walking abruptly, and when she turns back to us, her face is unreadable. There's some frustration there for sure, but also curiosity.

"Okay, you know what?" Miki says. "Between you and Chauncey and Bree, I'm going to lose my mind. So tell me, Charm: Why do you want to go to cosmetology school so badly?"

I swallow hard. "Because I want to make people feel beautiful."

She blinks. Smiles. "That's . . . not what I was expecting you to say."

I shrug. "When I ask if you need anything, you always say no. But when I do your hair, I know I'm giving you something you need that you would never ask for. You work so hard. You deserve to feel beautiful. I want to do that for other people, especially other Black women."

"Charmy!" Ezra says. "Cotton-candy human!"

"I know," Miki agrees.

"Protect her at all costs," Ozzy says, appearing at my side with a fresh shake, even though I haven't finished the first one.

"I *know*," Miki says again. She's quiet, but she looks like she's thinking. "Okay," she says. "How about this? You have to do at least a semester before we talk about beauty school again. Understood? Because I'm not paying for any school that doesn't have 'university' in its name until you've given college a *literal* college try. Got it?"

"Okay," I say as Ezra and I quietly smile at one another. Then I pick up my phone and reread Beau's messages.

My tortured heart ponders what her motives could be in sending these messages about Maia. Does she really want me to have a good time? Does she really think I can without her? *Think like a friend*, I tell myself. *Be a friend.*

Confession? I send to Beau. I'm nervous I'll blow it. I'm not sure I have it in me to break someone's heart.

I pause for a second, but when she doesn't text back immediately, I keep going.

I don't think I want to continue with it. The Plan, I mean, is what I send next.

I swallow hard and type out one last message.

I know you want revenge, but I don't think I do anymore. Please don't hate me.

I turn off my phone and shove it into the very bottom of my bag, because I can't bear waiting to hear back from her. Then I chug my shake so fast I get killer brain freeze. I have my eyes squeezed shut for so long that when I finally open them, Ezra's pie is gone and *his* eyes are all glassy.

"Ezzie," I say, using a nickname I only use when I can tell he's really hurting. I immediately stand up and walk around to the other side of the booth. I scoot in beside him and put my arm around his shoulder. "Wanna talk about Enzo now?"

"I guess I'm feeling like I missed my chance with him. Prom is in four days, and then there's, like, only a few weeks till graduation, and he's probably going to some amazing performing arts college and I'm never going to see him again."

He takes a shuddering breath, but I don't say anything because it seems like he might not be done. A second later, he speaks again. "I don't really . . . like people. You know that. So the fact that I like him, like *that*, is a big deal. I guess I'm wondering if I'll like anyone else . . . *ever*."

I pat his back and stare at a plant, thinking. "I'm sure that eventually, once you're out of this little town and out in the big wide world, you'll meet plenty of other people who you'll like.

But four days is still four days. . . . Do we actually know if Enzo has a date to prom?" I ask quietly. Ezra chews his bottom lip and then takes out his phone. Scrolls Enzo's social.

"I don't see anything . . . ," he says.

"And I haven't heard anything," I tell him, a plan beginning to form in my mind. "Do you want to try to ask him to prom one last time?" I lean forward so he'll look at me. I smile encouragingly. "I'll help you."

He looks hesitant, so I insist. "You're always worrying about me, helping me. Let me worry about you this time. Beau's Lesbian Lessons are probably applicable to gay boys too."

He looks down at his phone, then looks back up at me. I tap a few of my favorite freckles of his along the bridge of his nose. He shoves my hand away and I laugh. But then his eyes lock on mine and he nods his agreement.

"Okay," I tell him. "Here's what I'm thinking. . . ."

A half hour later, when Aunt Miki's about to take her break, we convince her to let us borrow the car to go the half mile to Party Town, the local party supply store. We buy a bundle of gold letter balloons that spell out *P-R-O-M-?* And then get a bunch of regular ones in white, and clear with gold confetti inside. We stuff them in Aunt Miki's car, being very careful when we shut the doors (no repeats of the flower incident), before we drive to Enzo's house. We blast "Formation" to get Ezra hyped up, and it seems to be working.

When we pull up out front, we roll down all the windows so the round balloons billow out, and we open the sunroof, so the ones that spell *PROM* can float right above the car. I queue up another Bey classic, "XO," so I'll be ready to hit play on the song as soon as Enzo comes to the door.

"Okay," I say after I hop out and make sure everything looks perfect. "Text him to come outside."

But Ezra, who has been uncharacteristically quiet ever since we hit the end of Enzo's block, seems frozen. I walk over to him. "Ezra, text him," I say. "Do you want me to do it?"

"No, no, no, no," Ezra says. "Shit, Charm, I don't think I can. What if he already has a date and I just don't know? What if he says no? What if he, like, sees me and immediately pukes?"

"Why would he puke?"

"I don't know! I'm just thinking about all the possibilities now, and there's only one good outcome while the bad ones are infinite! What if he's not home? What if he laughs? What if he looks at me like I'm nuts? What if he texts back, 'Hell no,' and just . . . doesn't come outside?"

I take both his hands in mine. "Ezra," I say. "Tell me something true."

"I'm an outstanding athlete," he says.

"You're a fucking star," I agree.

"I'm selfless," he says.

"Always putting others first," I add.

"I never give up," he concludes.

"Third time's a me?" I say, glancing over at Enzo's front door. Ezra frowns. "A charm, Ezra. Third time's a charm."

"God," Ezra says. "Please."

I cackle. "Go big or go home, right?" I remind him. But then I can see it, the fear in Ezra's eyes. I watch as he locks his heart down the same way I do with mine. "We should go home," he says.

I look back at Enzo's house again, remembering how I flirted with Noemi and how Enzo looked so excited when Ezra called me. "Enzo's right there," I say. "He's so close, the possibility of your happiness is inches away."

"I'll ask him, if you ask Beau," Ezra says, and I freeze.

"How is that even fair?" I ask him. "How's that even the same? I already asked Maia. I have a date to prom."

"Not the date you really want. Beau is your Enzo, not Maia."

He's being hard-ass Ezra—the version of himself he usually saves for the court, for the track. He has that look on his face—the deeply determined one, so I know he won't back down. It's all right there, what he's saying without saying it: that we're each too afraid of rejection to make the move with the most at stake. The people who can change our lives are also the ones who might break us beyond repair, and even though I love Ezra more than almost anyone, I'm not sure my heart can handle anything else tonight.

"Let's go, then," I say to him, my throat feeling suddenly tight. "Let's go quick."

I climb back into Aunt Miki's car. I try to reel the bouquet of balloons inside, and end up tucking the strings under my thighs and ass to keep them from floating away. Ezra stares through the window at Enzo's house, and I silently wonder if either of us will ever have the courage to let our hearts out of their cages.

35
Beau

I don't realize I fell asleep until Celine is tapping on my window. Or, actually, her window.

I jump, then sleepily open the door so I don't have to turn on the car.

"Wow, you're cool," she says, both eyebrows raised. "What a cool-ass rock star. Jamming out and then coming out to the parking lot and taking a nap."

I roll my eyes.

"No, seriously, this is good," she says. "Let's start doing shows at local nursing homes. The retirement home scene could be really good for us. Why crowd-surf when you can be a grandma?"

"I was tired!" I complain. "Damn!"

"Heartbreak is exhausting."

"What are you even talking about?" I say, sighing loudly. "Nobody is heartbroken."

Then why does it feel like it?

"You're not fooling me, asshole," Celine says. "But I won't push you about it. Not right now, anyway, because this is a parking lot and Daniel is hungry."

"Daniel is always hungry," I say. Which is true.

I look behind her at Daniel leaning against the motorcycle. All the leather padding and the black helmet—if you didn't know him, you'd think he was cool and dangerous, and not a goofy-ass, donut-chomping, hopeless romantic.

"The point," she says, "is that you were sleeping in a parking lot like a teenage runaway. Take your ass home. Or . . . you know. Somewhere. And once Daniel has food, we can talk. If you want."

I know she wants to ask about how my not-so-grand grand gesture turned out. She knows it was bad by the way I came to the concert, in the same black T-shirt from that morning. I admire her restraint. Just thinking about recounting what Charm said at the cat café still makes my stomach burn.

"Or we don't have to talk," Celine says. Look at her, making an effort.

"We could talk about something else," I say. "Like my gap year."

I watch her focus narrow in on me.

"What about it?"

"Celine," I say, staring her in the eye. I hope she sees a sister in mine. "You're so good at this. This is what we do."

"Beau . . . ," she starts.

But then it hits me. I see it in her face. She's been mothering me about my decisions—who's been mothering her?

"You could do this," I say quickly. "We could."

She's silent. I can't read her when she gets like this. But I think I see something glowing in there.

"I need to eat," she says. "And you need to get outta here."

"I'll go when I'm good and ready," I say grumpily, to be grumpy about something.

"Well, no you won't," she says, walking off toward Daniel, who is astride the bike now and starting it. "Because they're about to gate the lot. So . . . ya know. Unless you wanna *sleep* sleep here . . ."

Sure enough, I can see security guards heading toward the gates that will close the venue's lot off to traffic—in or out.

"Shit!" I yelp, and quickly start the car while Celine laughs maniacally. She and Daniel zip off, and I drive more slowly after them. Last thing I need is to hit something—anything—while they are there. Jesus, I'd never live it down.

But once I'm out, I have no idea where to go. Home isn't an option, not in this mood. And I rarely have the car. Maybe I'll just drive around and listen to music. Charm made that playlist. . . .

I pull over and look in the cupholder for my phone before remembering I tossed it on the floor. I stretch myself all the way over the console and find it in the dark. The screen wakes up and I see the expected notifications from Celine from when she was still in the venue.

And then texts from Charm.

I read them and then reread them. She sent them an hour after I texted her—I must have passed out right away. *Heartbreak is exhausting,* I think, and then wipe that thought away and read the texts a third time.

She doesn't think she can break Maia's heart.

She doesn't want to do the Plan.

And she still doesn't want me to hate her.

What the fuck?

I have to check that the car is in park because I feel like I'm in motion, my senses swimming a little in all the whys. But one surfaces above the others. *Why can't she break Maia's heart? Is it because she loves her?* It must be because she loves her.

I start to text Charm back, but I'm afraid of . . . everything. Of her confirming my worst fears, telling me some truth I'm not ready to hear. I'm afraid of responding and not saying what I mean again.

What is it about text messages that lets you get away with saying everything but the thing you're trying to say? Or reading things all wrong? You can get a lot from punctuation and word choice. But if you really want to hide, you can say just about anything and choose the most normal words and the most normal phrasing and it's like putting on a disguise when you feel anything but normal.

I don't want to do that.

And I don't want Charm to do that.

I want to see her. To say, *No, I don't hate you. How could I possibly hate you when I love you? Surely you know that?* But no, she doesn't, I realize, because how would she? She would have if I had actually done what Celine told me to do. I didn't go full Shakespeare. I went half turtle. Asking while peeking out of the shell. Just like Charm said.

And now the time has passed.

Hasn't it?

She doesn't want to break Maia's heart. But she does still want to go to prom with her.

At some point you've got to know when to quit.

And I will. But I know Charm: she's anxious and hates the idea that I could be mad at her. It floods me with clarity.

So what if we're just friends? Charm is an amazing friend. She's funny and cool and she notices *everything*. Which makes her fascinating to talk to and also makes her jokes extra hilarious, because she sees shit that no one else sees. She really only hangs out with Ezra, so to even be considered her friend is a high fucking honor.

But the ache. I can't get around it. I let my heart out of its pen like the goddamn chickens at that farm. Now my chicken-heart doesn't want to go back in. I wish I could stop being a little bitch about it—but would I blame the chickens? I guess I should just be glad I know what fresh air is like now. Somehow looking for the silver lining makes it hurt even more.

But right now there are more important things that need to be addressed. I don't trust myself not to say all the things if I text her, so I put the car in drive. Since I'm not going to reply to her messages, I can't just text her and ask her where she is. I've got to track her down to reassure her. Maybe by the time I come across her, I'll have swallowed all the things I really want to say again.

I'm not too far from her house, so I go by there first. It feels strange to look at a building I've been inside and be able to imagine her in there so easily. Doing something new with her hair like always, watching one of those silly-ass comedies she likes. But one look at the house tells me she's not home. I know which window is hers, and it's not only dark, but closed. Charm always sleeps with the window cracked, one of the many things I've learned about her that are etched in my brain like music notes. So I drive on.

I steer toward Ezra's house. (Jesus, at this rate Celine is going to demand I put gas in the car. And I will. Maybe.) But Ezra's house is quiet, and Charm's parents' black SUV isn't there, if by chance they'd let her drive it tonight. Where else would she be? There's nothing going on at school that I know of, no play or any random surprising social shit that Charm likes to do.

And then it hits me. I shake my head. The diner. Obviously. She's there, I'd bet this actual fucking car. I turn down Winthrop toward Upper, my heart suddenly beating a little faster.

When I pull up outside, I see Miki's car. But all that means is that Miki is working, not necessarily that Charm is there. Still, I quickly park and go inside, scanning the diner and trying not to breathe too fast.

At first I'm disappointed—I don't see her or Ezra anywhere. But then I realize that something is blocking my view. A huge bunch of balloons. At first I think they spell out *PORN* and I think, *Well then*. But it's an *M*, and the order is jumbled. *PROM*.

My heart no longer beats quickly—it freezes.

I was asleep and didn't get Charm's texts right away—did Maia get her those balloons? Did she prompose *back*? Fuck. The idea of walking over to what I know is Charm's favorite booth and seeing her cuddled up with Maia Moon makes me want to puke. But I go over anyway because I have to. Better to know than not know.

It's not Charm and Maia, though, and it only takes one look at Ezra to know that it wasn't Maia who was doing the promposing.

"What happened?" I ask, dismayed.

Ezra looks morose, and Charm is so focused on him that at first she doesn't even greet me. When she finally does realize I'm standing there, she looks surprised and then relieved.

"Beau," she says. Friends or not, I can't help it that my blood sings when she says my name. "Can you please tell Ezra that if he hates the idea of being told no, that *not* asking Enzo to prom is the equivalent of no because it leaves no possibility of yes?"

I parse through what I've been told. "Wait, you *didn't* ask? Why not?"

"Because he might've said no," Charm says, giving Ezra a gentle—but pointed—look.

"Mights are very scary!" Ezra wails.

"They sure the fuck are," I say, maybe a little too passionately.

Charm glances at me, but I focus on Ezra instead, hoping my presence alone at least says, *No, I'm not mad at you* and not all the . . . other stuff. It would be super helpful if I could get away with saying nothing about me and Charm at all, because who knows what will come out if I open my mouth.

"Guys, it's really okay," Ezra says. "I'm comfortable with the fact that I will die alone. These are the facts of life and I accept them."

"Oh my god, Ezra," Charm says in that fake-shocked voice she does sometimes. "You are not going to die alone."

"No, I'll just go to prom alone," Ezra says. "Which is almost the same thing."

Charm reaches over and touches his hand.

"How about we do this: we'll all get ready together at your place. We'll dance and you'll do my makeup and Beau can tell us how much prom is going to suck. I'll tell Maia I'll just meet her there. She'll understand a friend emergency. This is definitely a friend emergency."

Ezra seems to like this idea. He nods. I don't move a muscle because hearing her making plans with her date might as well be a jab followed by an uppercut, and maybe if I just hold really still it won't hurt so bad.

"And we can even dance together at prom," Charm goes on. "No one is only dancing with their dates there. It's not 1995."

Enzo looks like maybe he's no longer planning his funeral.

"I wouldn't mind not going with Enzo as much if I had two hot babes to dance with all night," he concedes.

"I don't really dance—" I start, but Charm interrupts.

"Yes, you do," she says, the verbal equivalent of a hand wave. "Ezra, that's what we'll do. It'll be great."

She casts her eyes down at her syrupy empty plate just briefly. I see the waffle wreckage. And the milkshake. And the cobbler. *Oh, she went big,* I think, impressed. She only does this when she's anxious or sad. Or both. But if she's got Maia, why is she choking down carbs? Commiseration with Ezra, I decide.

"Brilliant," I say, hoping my smile doesn't look as fake as it feels. The way it feels on my face, if someone even tapped it, it would shatter.

PART SIX
Prom Night

36
Charm

I've always loved Ezra's room. It's one of those bedrooms that just feels so much like the person it belongs to that it's borderline unreal. I could write a dissertation about teenage bedrooms and what they say about the people who inhabit them. Maia's was pretty and full of stars. Beau's was understated and filled with words. Maybe all rooms say more about their owners than meets the eye. But Ezra's room screams it. It's so *Ezra Jabari King* that stepping into it feels like entering a country my best friend founded.

The walls in Ezra's room are mirrored. All of them except the one behind his bed. So when his big brother Zeke walks me in, carrying my prom dress over the threshold like it's his bride, Ezra sees us coming without turning around. Still, Zeke announces our arrival.

"Princess Charming is here!" he says with a massive grin. It's the best nickname anyone has ever given me, and I'm so happy he's home from college to call me that tonight that I reach out to hug him. Then I bow.

The walls being floor-to-ceiling mirrors hasn't stopped Ezra from plastering them with everything from life-size Beyoncé posters to photos of his family and friends. Polaroids of us (mostly taken by Zeke, who's majoring in photography) are strung up like pennants along the crown molding.

"Boo thing!" Ezra says as Zeke deposits my dress on his brother's bed.

Then Zeke picks up a camera I hadn't noticed from Ezra's dresser. "Mama King essentially wants a docuseries about y'all getting ready since she had to work tonight, so I'mma be in and out," Zeke tells us. I smile and put up a peace sign, and he immediately drops the hand holding the camera. "Nah. No posed photos. I'm all about the candids."

"He's taking this way too seriously," Ezra says to me. "As usual."

Zeke picks that moment to snap a photo. Then he looks up. "The lighting in here really ain't giving what I need it to be giving," he says.

Ezra never turns on the round recessed lights embedded in his ceiling because, as he puts it, "Overhead lights are homophobic." So he has twinkle lights in every corner and three big paper lanterns that hang down over his bed. Zeke starts flipping switches, unplugging cords, and rearranging things, and soon the whole room glows like it's full of candlelight. If Ezra is intense about athletics, Zeke is the same way about art.

I climb into Ezra's bed and get under his duvet like I came over to nap, not to get dressed for prom. I'm even still wearing my bonnet. Zeke snaps another photo, looks down at his camera, nods, and disappears.

"Prom night," Ezra says. "Can you believe it?"

I roll onto my back and stare up at his ceiling. He flops down beside me. "I kinda just want to get it over with," I say. I feel his head turn to look at me, but I keep staring straight up.

"Come on, Charmy!" he says. He jumps up and runs over to his laptop. Puts on, to no one's surprise, Beyoncé's newest album, and rips his T-shirt over his head. He spins it around and starts twerking, and just as I let a smile slip across my lips and climb out of the bed to dance alongside him, Zeke reappears in the doorway with his camera. He takes another rapid series of photos, then steps aside, revealing a wide-eyed Beau.

She quickly shifts her features into mock anger. "You couldn't even wait for me to get here? This is bullying."

Zeke lifts his camera, capturing Beau's profile, and laughs.

I start dancing. Something about the music and the movement is helping me forget the weight of the moment, and I want to lean into that, get lost in it a little if I can. The fact that the person I want to be my date tonight will be with me but not *with* me feels like mist in the air when I'm moving like this, something I can see but that isn't solid enough to worry about yet.

Beau steps into the room and looks around. She nods, taking it all in, and says, "Yeah, this makes sense," more to herself than to either of us. I love that she's gotten to know Ezra enough in the last few weeks that she can see how *him* his room is. It makes me feel closer to her even as so much about tonight is pulling us apart.

I forget that Zeke is taking photos when I see her. Because all I can suddenly see is *her*.

"Come dance with us!" I shout in Beau's direction, and before I think too hard about it, I'm grabbing her hand and pulling her over to the empty, danceable space near the foot of the bed. I'm pulling her bag off her shoulder while still moving around her, sandwiching her body between mine and Ezra's.

Beau swears she doesn't dance, but here she is, dancing. She's a drummer, so I should have known her rhythm would be perfect, but I'm still a little surprised by just how smoothly her hips move, how easy it is to fall into step with her.

And then she's looking at me. And while I know she's not one for makeup, I wonder for a second if she let Celine pluck her eyebrows, because there's something smoother, or a little softer about her expression. I notice that she's gotten a haircut, too—an undercut, plus the longest pieces that had been flopping over her eyes are trimmed back a little—but she still looks hot and edgy.

"Okay, Carlo," I say softly. "I see you."

She looks away, eyes cast down so her lashes seem to brush her cheeks, and Jesus, I want to kiss her.

I spin away instead and skip to the next song just for something to do with my hands; just to give my eyes somewhere to land that isn't all over Beau. "Ez," I say, "where's your suit? And are you still gonna do my makeup? I saved that tutorial."

We spend the better part of the next hour getting ready. Beau is in one corner of Ezra's room with several different mousses and gels, doing something complicated to her hair, while I put in my contacts before Ezra gets started on my makeup. Since I'm Maia the makeup maven's date, it has to be perfect. By the time we both finish, Beau turns around and I immediately appreciate the care she's put into her do. The sides are smooth, the top is messy in a deliberate way, and she looks good enough to eat. She clears her throat, which makes me realize I'm staring, so I blink a few times before smiling at her.

"I like your hair," I say to her. (Understatement of the century.)

"Let's see yours," she says. And that's when I realize I'm still wearing my bonnet. I pull it off slowly, and the goddess braids I did on myself last night fall, like curtains, over my shoulders.

"How do I look?" I ask before I spin around to see myself in one of Ezra's many mirrors.

Beau clears her throat again. "Like a queen," she says, her voice husky and low. "As usual."

Zeke pops back in to capture our looks so far, moving silently around the room. I turn to check out the makeup that Ezra's still fussing with and I agree with Beau. My eyes well up a little, because I didn't know I could look like this—attractive in a way that's closer to sexy than cute. Ezra takes a cotton swab and dabs at the corners of my eyes. I swat his hand away.

"Ezra, it's perfect. Leave it alone!"

"I know it's perfect, so how about you don't cry and ruin it?"

I give him the finger and poke him in the ribs.

He leans closer to the mirror and starts plucking his own brows, so I grab my dress and head to his walk-in to change, but just as I reach for the handle, Ezra screams.

"No! Charm, not in there—"

But the doors are already open, and the prom balloon bouquet we got for Enzo's promposal floats out and up, filling the room and scaring the shit out of me. At that very moment, Zeke snaps a photo.

I jump back, trip over Beau's bag, and hit my head on the bench at the foot of his bed.

"Fuck. Ouch. Jesus!" I say, in rapid succession. Before I can even process what's happened, I see Beau's arms flying, as she fights through the balloons to get to me.

"Shit, Charm. Are you okay?" she asks, batting a final clear, confetti-filled one away from her face. She touches the right side of my forehead and I wince.

"God, of course this would happen to me. Of course I'm gonna have a freakin' goose egg on my face at prom!"

Beau tucks her lips in, like she's trying not to laugh, and I punch her in the shoulder. "This isn't funny, you jerk!"

"I didn't even laugh yet!" Beau screeches, but then she does laugh, and I hear Ezra laughing too from somewhere inside the Mylar, rubber, and strings forest that has swallowed us. "If one of you doesn't get me an ice pack or a bag of frozen veg in the next two minutes," I say, standing up and battling the balloons, "there's gonna be hell to pay."

A few minutes later, inside the now balloon-less closet, I put on my dress. It's hot pink, strapless, and has three tiers of ruffles. It hugs my curves all the way down. I pull on sheer socks, slip into my platform boots, and grab the bag of peas Ezra got for me from his kitchen for my face, taking care not to mess up my makeup, before I step back out into the room.

Ezra's suit is indigo and sparkling, like the fabric is made of the night sky. Soft music is playing, he's turned off all the lights except the paper lanterns, and because of the balloons the whole room feels romantic. He's spraying cologne into the air from a bottle shaped like a heart and stepping through it, moving his head and arms around to catch the floating particles. It looks like he's casting a spell.

"Damn," I say, walking over to him. I take one of his hands and spin him around.

"Right back atcha," he says, spinning me too. I go up on tiptoes to kiss his cheek because even with the bump on the head, thanks to him, the night is starting to feel like magic.

The door opens and we both turn at the sound. Beau walks back in from the hallway bathroom. She's in a blue suit—not quite cobalt, not quite royal—and she's wearing a soft-looking white shirt under the jacket. It's unbuttoned enough that a gold necklace with a pair of drumstick charms dangling between her cleavage is on full display. Which makes me think about . . . things. Too many things.

Her Vans are fresh and clean and she's wearing striped socks that peek out when she walks. When she gets closer, I see that her eyelids are shimmering a little, and that's what unravels me completely. That tiny touch of unexpected sparkle makes my heartbeat feel like stadium applause.

"Okay, Blue!" Ezra shouts at Beau, and she laughs and shakes her head.

Zeke says a final posed photo is acceptable, so we line up at the foot of Ezra's bed and smile. And just as I'm about to turn to Beau and maybe do or say something that is very *not* friend-like, I hear "XO" by Beyoncé start playing faintly from somewhere behind me. Not the speakers, though. Outside? I look at Ezra, who looks at Beau, who bats balloons out of the way and walks over to the window.

"Oh my god," she says. "Um, Ezra?" She points through the window at something we can't see.

Ezra races over, with me right behind him, and then he's yanking the window open, and the song gets ten times louder. Down below Enzo is hanging out of the sunroof of a limo, dressed in the kind of red bodysuit Freddie Mercury would wear, holding a sign that says:

> *We don't have forever*
> *Ooh, baby, daylight's wasting*
> *Come to prom with me?*
> *Before our time has run out?*

"Oh my god. Oh my GOD!" I shout. "Zeke, get back in here! Get this shit on video!"

Then Enzo is telling someone inside the limo to lower the music. Seconds later, he's shouting up to Ezra, "I tried to ask you to prom so many times, and something or someone always got in the way!"

Ezra is leaning so far out of the window I'm worried he'll fall. "Me too," he's shouting back. "I tried so many times too!"

"I thought maybe the universe was conspiring against me," Enzo continues. "Punishing me for flirting with too many people or something, by keeping me apart from the one person I really wanted. Then my sister just told me I was used to people coming to me. That I just wasn't trying hard enough.

"I got in my own head after that about the perfect promposal. I know how much I flirt with everyone, so I knew it had to be big for you to take it and me seriously. It had to be special. But nothing felt good enough. Or big enough! Then, when I saw you through my window a few days ago, with the balloons and everything, I thought, awesome. He's going to ask me. This is perfect—I'm off the hook. But then you didn't. And I was so much more disappointed than I expected to be. I knew I had to take a chance. Be the one to come to you.

"So here I am, finally really doing it. And doing it big." Enzo climbs out of the sunroof completely then and stands on the roof of the limo. "Ezra Jabari King," he shouts. "Will you go to prom with me?"

Ezra looks at me, looks at Beau, looks down at himself, then screams, "Yes!" A second later he's saying, "Wait, it's okay, right?" And then I'm screaming, "Yes, go!" and so is Beau, and he's sprinting out of his house, Zeke stumbling behind him with his camera, leaving me and Beau to watch them drive away through the window.

"Didn't have *that* on my prom-night bingo card," Beau says. I shake my head, still watching the limo until it disappears. I realize we're alone, and that Beau is watching me, at about the same time.

"How's your head?" she asks, and then reaches up to move the bag of peas away before I answer. "You def have a little bump, but it's not too bad." Her hands are warm where they trace the curve of my brow. And a second later, when our eyes lock, my mouth falls open, just a little. She looks at my lips. Then spins away so fast I wonder if I imagined it.

"Where are you meeting up with Maia?" Beau asks, her back still turned to me.

"At the door," I tell her. "She said she wants to walk in together. I kind of can't believe it."

"Me either," I think I hear her say softly. And then, "I got something for you," she adds a little louder. She digs into her bag and pulls out a small plastic container. A corsage, I realize, as she cracks it open.

"Beau, what?" I say. I put down the peas and step closer. It's dried and made of wildflowers, and it's too perfect for words.

I look up at her and she blinks a few times. "Friend flowers," she says before looking back down. "Is it weird to give you these when you have a real date?"

I shake my head hard, trying to hold in everything I'm feeling. The fact that she got this but she said, "Friend flowers." That we're alone and going to prom together but not.

"Thank you," I say. And her deep ocean eyes are serious and seem a little sad when she nods and touches my hand so softly.

"Anytime."

37

Beau

I never gave a shit about prom. Literally told my sister since freshman year that I'd never bother. Not just because I never pictured myself actually dating anyone, but also because the idea of getting dressed up for the sole purpose of going to school on a day I didn't *have* to be at school, to be around the people I didn't really want to be around, was at the bottom of my list of priorities. I still felt a little like that putting on my suit. *Why am I doing this? What is this for?* And then I saw Charm in her prom dress and I knew.

On the drive over, Charm is squirmy.

"So Celine let you borrow the car again," she says, glancing out the window, then down at her phone, then out the window again.

"Well, you know how she is," I say, managing a real smile. "She's a cuntasaurus, but a benevolent one. Also I pledged to make her dinner every Monday for a month."

My phone chimes.

"Speaking of Celine," I say. "That's her text tone. Can you check it for me?"

Charm scoops up my phone, peers at it, then squeals.

"What?" I cry. "You can't squeal while I'm driving! Driving is precarious!"

"Sorry! But! Squeal-worthy! This text . . . here, I'll read it: 'Don't respond until after prom: *Elicktric*,' then a million dots and four thumbs-up emojis. And a link!"

"Oh shit!" I squeal.

"Now who's squealing!"

"You gotta reply," I half shout. "Say 'Gap year'?"

Charm texts back quickly, and a second later the chime again.

"'I said after prom'—all caps," Charm says. "And then four winks."

"Goddamn," I say. "Give her so many fucking hearts."

My chest swells. Holy shit. Life is weird. On one hand, I feel full of possibility. But when I glance at Charm and see her in the prom dress she put on for another girl, all the balloons pop.

Plus, there's the expression on her face as she looks down at her phone.

"What's up?" I ask. "Everything cool with Maia?"

"I'm not sure," she says. "She's not texting back, and I don't know if she's there yet—she's the one who wanted to walk in together. You don't think she'd screw me over again, do you?"

I do, actually. But I don't say that to Charm. She killed the Plan because she didn't want to hurt Maia. If Maia hurts Charm again . . . well, my gap year will be spent on a revenge plan far more elaborate than this one.

"I'm sure she's just running late," I say instead. If anyone had told me a week ago I'd be making excuses for Maia Moon on prom night, I'd have punched them in the face. "You know how she is with the makeup and stuff. Probably making a video or something."

I want to drop Charm at the curb so she doesn't have to walk as far, but I don't like the idea of her feeling anxious about showing up alone. So I park as close as I can and we walk silently together, farther apart than we ever have, all the narratives my brain is building taking up the space between us: Charm and

Maia going on dates and inviting me as a third wheel; Charm asking for advice on what to get Maia for her birthday. By the time we get to the door of the school, I want to say, *All right, this was fun, peace out* and go bury my feelings at Wonderdough.

But how can I leave her standing there alone? Especially when Maia hasn't answered yet. Especially when the minutes tick by, and prom is in full swing, and the two of us become the only ones standing outside in the spring chill. I have a half worry that we shouldn't be seen together, but the Plan is off. And I refuse to leave her alone.

"I don't think she's going to show," Charm says quietly.

I curse Maia out in my head, but to Charm I say, "Let's give her five more minutes. Traffic, you know. Or maybe she caught her dress in an escalator and they're extricating it as we speak."

But ten minutes later Maia still hasn't come, and the only texts are from Ezra, with lots of question marks and exclamation points.

"Let's go in," Charm says. "This is dumb."

I listen closely for pain in her voice, but she seems to be hiding her disappointment well. Or maybe it hasn't sunk in yet, and she's holding out hope that Maia will come into prom and find her when she gets here. Worst-case scenarios run through my head as I follow Charm into school. What if Maia is already in there? Dancing with Tate? I don't know who I'd throw a punch at first, TBH.

But inside, there's no sign of Maia. Just everyone else, dressed up and sparkling. Walking behind Charm, I get to watch people watch her. Seeing their faces is almost as enjoyable as her actual face. She's fucking breathtaking, and watching her take breath after breath—in a non-serial-killer way—makes me feel like all the prom balloons we left floating in Ezra's room. He and Enzo are taking pictures in the photo booth, Ezra beaming like he swallowed an actual shooting star. All of it kind of makes me want to cry: I'm at the prom next to the most beautiful girl in my school. Ezra is happy. And the music is somehow, impossibly, against all odds, *not* terrible.

Even when we dance, it's not weird.

"Blue is your color," Charm shouts over the music. Then her eyes are closed and she's moving to the music. Her shoulders sway and she's just within arm's reach. I could put my hands around her waist.

But what do friends do?

I *am* her friend, right? So why the fuck don't I know what to do?

"I'm trying to think of what color *isn't* yours," I say back. She doesn't quite hear me. I'm suddenly transported back to that night at the party, when I came looking for Maia with her panties in my pocket. Charm was on the dance floor then, swaying like this with Ezra. Her eyes were closed just like this. She didn't see me, and I didn't really see her. Not the way I see her now.

"Charm, you look amazing!" someone shouts. "Your dress, oh my god!"

It's a girl whose name I don't know, stopping by as she and her date push through the crowd.

Charm opens her eyes, and Jesus, with those braids it's like watching a water goddess come alive. She turns to the girl, smiling, and they chat, while the boy looks bored. At least he's holding this girl's hand. It makes me itch, wanting to reach out and hold Charm's. What do friends do? Probably not that.

"I'm gonna grab you something to drink," I say to Charm. I rest my hand lightly on her shoulder when I say it, just to get her attention. Her skin is smooth and warm, and I can tell she put on body oil or whatever the girly girls do. She shimmers and I think, *Friends give massages, right?* Internally I punch myself in the face.

"Thank you," she says, smiling into my eyes. I just blink in reply and turn away.

As I start to cut through the crowd, I hear the girl ask: "Ooh, is that your date?"

I pause just long enough to hear Charm's answer.

"Oh, we just came as friends."

In my head, I punch myself one more time. Maybe I should just KO myself now and get it over with.

It's early enough in the night that moving through the crowd smells like cologne and the sweet, thick scent of hair products. I still haven't seen Maia. Or Tate, either, for that matter. Who knows what's happening in Delulu-ville, where Maia takes up residence? It seems hard to believe I ever gave a shit. The Plan feels like a distraction now. Something some asshole would do, not me. And certainly not Charm. But I remember the way Charm looked in the diner that first night. Heartbroken. It still makes me mad at Maia for hurting her but also mad at myself for standing in the way. What if Maia didn't come because she figured out what we'd been up to? Fuck, this is all my fault. A good friend would have tried to hook Charm up with Maia for real, not use her for revenge. Would Charm be here with Maia right now if I hadn't made it all about payback?

I realize I haven't even moved toward the tables of drinks and food. I stand at the perimeter of the dance floor, catching slices of Charm's bright pink dress as the crowd moves around her. I see her hands up high, and the bobbing of her braided head. A flash of red tells me Enzo has found her, which means Ezra is nearby.

It occurs to me that maybe I should just . . . go. This isn't really my scene.

"Wanna dance?" someone says close to my ear, and I jump.

It's . . . Trina?

"Hey," I say, sizing her up. She's wearing a dress that's floral and could look really old-fashioned, but it's cut asymmetrically, and with her hair done in this futuristic-looking tall style, it doesn't. "You look great. Cool dress."

"Thanks," she says. "I made it."

"You've gotten really good," I say. "I remember you telling me you made those headpieces for the theater kids last year. I saw pictures. Very cool."

She laughs. "The shrimp ones? I still don't know why they wanted shrimp headpieces. I never saw the play."

"Me neither."

"Shocker," she says. "Beau Carl not engaging in a social activity. Surprised you're here, actually."

"Yeah, well, even cave dwellers come out for daylight now and then."

She gives me a knowing smile.

"I like this song," she says. "Let's dance."

I'm reluctant, because part of me still really wants to get the fuck out of here. But whatever, I like this song too, so . . . we dance.

At first I feel stiff. Even though I know Charm and I are here as friends, I don't like the idea of her seeing me hugged up with Trina. Or anyone, really. It would feel like lying, when the only person I can think about touching is Charm. But Trina keeps her distance, even as she keeps giving me that same sly smile.

"What?" I say. "Do I have something on my face?"

"Yes," she says.

My hand rises to my cheek.

"What is it? Where?"

"A goofy-ass look," she says. "And a little eye shadow. Which looks very nice, actually."

I roll my eyes. "Yeah, yeah. Thanks, I guess."

I cast a glance in Charm's direction. She's dancing with the girl who was holding the boy's hand. He's disappeared. My heart squeezes. Maybe that wasn't the girl's date at all? Are she and Charm . . . ?

"I think it's time to tell her," Trina says.

She's moved a little closer so I can hear her, but I'm not sure I actually hear her correctly.

"What did you say?"

"I think it's time to tell her," Trina says. "Charm."

"What are you talking about?"

"Beau," she says patiently. "I only came and asked you for a dance so you wouldn't be standing there staring at her like a weirdo."

"I wasn't!" I cry.

"Oh, that's not up for debate," she says. "You definitely were. Let me guess. You guys came together as 'friends.'"

She air-quotes "friends" so hard that it seems like she'll rip a hole in the space-time continuum.

"We *are* friends!" I protest.

"You sound like you're telling yourself, not me," she says, laughing. "Maybe if you yell it, it will make it true. Wanna try?"

"You're an asshole," I say, but I can't help but laugh.

"Listen," she says. "My date is back from the bathroom, so I gotta go. But, like, Beau . . . stop being a little punk-ass bitch."

"Excuse me?!"

She laughs, waving at her date. He's a guy from band, Tony.

"Did you come as friends too?" I ask.

"No, he's my boyfriend."

"I thought Tony was gay. And what happened to Jeremy?"

"I broke up with Jeremy before you and me ever hooked up," she says. "Keep up, Bobo. And Tony is bi. Like me."

She sees my surprise and laughs again. "Not everybody is a straight girl, Beau. Get over yourself."

"I just thought—"

"That I was, what, experimenting? Because I used to date Jeremy, you assumed I was straight. You could've asked, bonehead— you were too busy counting yourself out. Too late now, though."

She gives me a very cute wink and then shoves me a little.

"Tell her you love her," she says, giving me a look that implies warning as she walks away. "Like I said, don't be a punk bitch."

"What if I like being a punk bitch?" I call after her.

Wait. Did I just admit that I'm in love with Charm Montgomery?

Trina seems to have realized the same thing—she turns and smiles one more time. "You don't."

38
Charm

Beau said she was going to get drinks. But I can see her blue suit from here. She's dancing. With a girl I bet she's hooked up with before. And it takes everything in me not to walk over and butt in, dance between them like Beau is someone who belongs to me. I have to remind myself that she isn't. That she doesn't. That I'm still waiting for my real date to show up.

But also . . . something seems different about her lately. There's softness where before there was only a wall of flirtation. And I don't know if I'm imagining things, but when Beau calls us friends, there seems to be less and less conviction in her voice. Which scares me shitless. Ezra thinks it's because she likes me. I can't help but be afraid it's because she knows I like *her* and she's trying her best not to hurt me.

Enzo hip-checks me hard enough that my eyes are pulled away from Beau and Trina dancing, and Ezra spins me so fast that my thoughts are pulled away too. I remember where I am—at prom—and who I'm with—my bestie and his dream date (finally!)—and I try to be happy. I try to lean into the moment, dance while the music is good, keep my restless thoughts at bay about all that is uncertain.

And for a while I'm doing it. A new song starts and I close my eyes and raise my arms above my head and let myself get lost in it—the wall of sound, the closeness of Enzo's and Ezra's bodies.

How little I care if after everything, we don't get our revenge, and Maia stands me up.

When I open my eyes, I see bubbles floating through the air, and I vaguely remember voting on the prom theme and hearing that Under the Sea won. I look around, realizing that the decorations are pretty understated. No obnoxious mermaid decals or fish murals, just blue fabric draped softly along the walls, lighting that looks like refracted water dancing across the floor and ceiling, and bubbles floating like butterflies overhead. It all makes me think about Beau again in her blue suit, with her blue eyes. She would hate that I think this, but she matches the theme tonight perfectly, because she's such a dark blue girl. Without deciding to, my eyes search the room for her, and when I find that blue suit, she's not dancing with Trina anymore. She's looking back at me and floating across the dance floor toward us like a wave, drink in hand. It seems like the music is playing just for her. I spin around, just to stop myself from staring, and that's when I see someone else walking toward me from the other direction.

She's in a silver silk dress. The fabric is so smooth it looks like it's made out of water. Her nails are painted silver too, and they shimmer as she reaches up to tuck a few wayward curls behind her ear. Her eyes look gunmetal gray instead of like the moon in the room's low light.

I stop dancing.

Enzo shimmies, like he doesn't have a care in the world, before saying, "Hey, Maia!"

Ezra says, "Look who finally decided to show up." But I don't answer because I mostly can't breathe. I wait to see if she'll hug me like a friend, kiss me like a date, or ignore me like I'm nobody. I don't know which I want it to be.

39
Beau

When Trina walks away, the same song is still playing and Charm is still dancing with Ezra and Enzo. I could stand and watch just that piece of her shoulder all night. But I'm so tired of watching the girl I love from a distance. I think of her in the water at the pool. Touching her and trying not to. Staring at her and trying not to. Kissing her at my desk and stopping. Jesus, kissing her at my desk. The way she leaned into me. The way her eyes changed when I pulled away, went inside a shell.

People talk about lightbulb moments. A click. For me, standing here on the dance floor, it's more like those lamps that have a dial. A gradually brightening glow, and suddenly my head is filled with a realization. Trina was right. About a lot of things. But there's one thing she didn't say outright that locks in with what Celine (and Charm too) have been telling me: I've been getting in my own goddamn way. Turtle shell. Major one. I've been falling for Charm, it's true, and drumming to the beat of *but what if she doesn't feel the same way?* Now, with the dial turning the light up, I think . . . *but what if she does?*

The words "put yourself out there" are made for turtles, in a way. I went to the cat café to do it and couched it in friend-speak, still within the shell. I won't make that mistake again. It's time. Actually.

But I can't go back empty-handed. I said I'd get her a drink, so I go to the tables and my fingers shake as I get a cup of ice. I glance over my shoulder, looking for that flash of pink fabric over her glowing brown skin. I need to go now. It suddenly feels so fucking urgent, like I will combust if I don't lift her chin up to my face. I feel like I'm only half breathing. Fuck dancing. I need to be kissing Charm Montgomery.

I slide through the crowd, barely paying attention to whose dances I'm interrupting. I don't even notice that I never actually poured a drink into the cup of ice until I'm almost to Charm. I glance down at it. I'm so bad at this. I turn to go back, then stop and turn back toward Charm again. Does love turn everyone into a short-circuiting robot? I stop, take a deep breath, and tell myself to get it the fuck together. *Who cares about the drink?*

The cup of ice burns cold against my palm, but I barely feel it. I slip through a group of guys dancing (terribly), and finally there's the pink of Charm's prom dress.

She looks like magic. Literally like someone opened a secret wonder of the world, uncorked the bottle . . . and out poured Charm.

"Charm," I say delusionally. I'm not close enough at all, not for her to hear me. Or even see me.

Especially not when she's looking at someone else.

A flash of silver.

My steps slow, but too late. Now I'm close enough to touch her. But I don't, because someone else is.

Maia Moon is already reaching for the girl that I'm in love with.

40
Charm

"I thought you weren't gonna show" is the first thing I say, and the words feel like vomit as they're coming out of my mouth—too hot and fast, and completely out of my control. I sound more angry than I thought I was, more bothered than I'd ever want Maia to know I am. I look around and beyond Maia, like Tate could be hiding his tree-trunk limbs behind her delicate ones. Like I'm expecting him to jump out from somewhere hidden and say, douchey and horrible: *I can't believe you thought she liked you enough to come out,* maybe, or *She only said yes so we could laugh in your face.*

Maia smiles. "Sorry I'm late," she says, and it feels like a trick.

On either side of me stand Ezra and Enzo. They're looking back and forth between Maia and me like they're watching a tennis match.

"So you do want to be here," I say, "with me."

"I'm here, aren't I?"

Maia Moon reaches out and takes my hand. Maia Moon, with her shimmering, light brown skin and night-black curls that fluff around her face, big as all her secrets, says, "Charm, the reason I'm late is because I dumped Tate. For real this time. And the reason I dumped Tate is because I'm pretty sure I'm not straight." She scrunches her nose. "I didn't mean for all of that to rhyme."

It's so absurd that I want to laugh, but that's when I feel bits of cold hit the back of my leg. I turn to see Beau standing just behind us, and when I look down, the cup she was holding is on the floor, ice spread around our feet like broken glass.

I'm trying to figure out why there's no punch pooling too, though I'm grateful my dress hasn't been ruined, when I look back up to see Beau's face. She looks shattered in every sense of the word, her blue eyes shining, her heavy brows sinking.

I don't know what's happening. Everything is moving too quickly for me to process, but I know this is a moment. I know this is the Moment, the one we've been working toward all these weeks. Even though we called it off, here it is anyway—the moment when I could humiliate Maia Moon the way she humiliated us.

Because ever since she walked in, people have been watching her. Which means that now, people are watching us.

Voices float up and around us like the prom committee's bubbles, and I can only make out a few words here and there—"Tate," "Maia," "prom," "gay"—but instead of thinking about people talking about us, I'm focused on how Beau is turning away now, pushing past everyone. Ezra touches my elbow, and I realize Maia is still holding my hand.

"Beau!" I call, because fuck the moment, fuck the Plan, fuck anything that makes Beau's beautiful face turn in on itself like that. And I don't know why she's sad, just that she is, and I love her and I need to fix it.

"Beau, wait!" I shout again, and I try to pull away from Maia, but she holds on to my hand even tighter.

"Charm," Maia says, "there's something else I want to tell you. Can you wait for just one second?"

I look toward the door, where Beau has disappeared. Then I

look back at Maia, who has the audacity to ask me to wait.

The weeks and months pile in between us like sand in an hourglass, and then hot words are spilling out of my mouth again, truth-vomit I can't stop.

"You used us," I say quietly, stepping closer to her. She blinks her shiny eyes and lets my hand fall. "You hooked up with Beau, who yeah, I know about. Then you flirted endlessly with me, and look—I know this shit is hard. I remember being eight and being afraid someone would think I was looking at them change after soccer practice, or being eleven at sleepovers and being terrified to play truth or dare in case someone dared me to kiss another girl. It hurts to have to hide when you're still figuring things out, or when you know exactly who you are and you're worried other people will be weird about it. But it hurts more to be hidden like a dirty secret. Used like we're disposable. Your pain and confusion don't mean you get to play around with other people's hearts while you're questioning. They don't mean you get to have a boyfriend in public and kiss me and Beau in the dark so you don't have to process. Your feelings aren't more important than ours, and none of this was *ever* okay."

I don't say any of this loudly. I'm not trying to complete the sixth step, or to make people stare more than they already are. I can feel the tears coming and I need to get to Beau, but by the time I'm done talking, Maia looks stunned. Her hands are shaking.

"And look, I'm sorry that I flirted back. Kissed you. I shouldn't have. I did some things wrong too." I sigh and look toward the door again. "So what is it, Maia?" I ask, eyes boring hard into hers. "What else could you possibly have to say to me?"

41
Beau

As I push through the doors to outside, I'm not thinking about Maia Moon or even Charm Montgomery. I wish I could say I was thinking about Celine and my—our?—gap year.

But I'm thinking about turtles.

I'm wishing I had paid attention in biology freshman year, because maybe Mx. Anderson mentioned how long it takes turtles to transform from regular lizards into reptiles wearing a tooth-proof bomb shelter on their back.

I'm jealous.

I'm jealous of Maia Moon, who always gets everything she wants, no matter what. Who plays with hearts and keeps all the winnings. Who I already know has her arms around the waist of the girl I want more than anyone in the goddamn world, breathing in the smell of her hair. Getting shimmer on her cheek from being pressed against Charm's.

And I'm jealous of Charm. Who had the fucking sense and wherewithal to execute the Plan exactly as we said, and not only that, abide by the constitution and not get her feelings tangled with me along the way. I'm not jealous that she fell in love. I'm jealous that she'll get to walk away from this whole thing without a single scar.

But mostly? I'm jealous of turtles and their bomb shelters.

They may not be bulletproof, but they can hide every part of themselves from the world if they want to. And as I make my way across the parking lot, I know that Trina and Celine and everyone else have been wrong. That's exactly what I'll be going back to doing from now on.

42
Charm

"You're right," Maia says.

My eyes don't move from where they've been staring into Maia's, but I feel myself frown.

"What?" I ask.

"I said, you're right, Charm. That's what I came here to say. When I considered dumping Tate again, I thought it was because I was falling for you. But I realized I'm still unsure about so many things. Who I am and who I want to be, how I want the rest of my life to look. Who and how I want to love. I'm so sorry for stringing you along. And all the fooling around I've done with other girls was pretty fucked-up too. When you asked me to prom, I realized that how scared I felt in that moment is probably how you felt when I would come on to you, then ghost. I wanted to talk to you tonight not because I'm expecting you to forgive me, but because I wanted to say this out loud: I'm still figuring myself out, but I think I'm queer. I'm sorry I hurt you in the process."

I look at Ezra, who has his resting bitch face fully activated. I glance up at Enzo, but unlike his date, he has his hand over his heart and his eyes are a little glassy. "I love being present for the induction of a baby gay into our ranks," he says. He grabs one of Maia's hands and kisses her knuckles. "Welcome to the club, baby girl," he says. She smiles at him before looking back at me.

"I just wanted to tell you I won't be dating anyone for a while."

"What about Beau?" I say. "You used Beau too—have you apologized to her?"

"I've tried," she says, "but I want to try again."

When I say Beau's name, it's like a shock to my system. I instantly remember Beau's broken face. I remember Beau giving me the corsage and taking me to Milk It and helping me with the flowers for Ezra. I remember kissing her, and the way her body felt against mine in the pool, and her mouth when she laughs and her brows when she doesn't.

"I went to her show to try to apologize to her, too. She didn't really listen," Maia continues.

"Beau's good at that."

And it's then that I realize I have to *make* her listen to me. I have to find her and tell her that she's beautiful and perfect and that I want her so badly it hurts.

Faintly I hear someone onstage starting to announce prom court, and I know I have to go. Maia will be queen. Tate will be king. The awkwardness of that will be revenge enough. But Ezra can tell me about it later. I sprint to the door.

Outside, it's pouring rain.

The sky has opened and our prom theme was perfectly selected, because I feel like I'm under the sea as I scan the parking lot for Celine's car. When I spot it, I see Beau struggling with her keys, trying to get inside, dropping them and picking them up only to drop them again. I splash across the parking lot and through puddles, trying in vain to cover my fresh braids and laid edges, and then I'm grabbing Beau's arm, spinning her around, pinning her against the car door so she can't run away from me anymore. I can't tell if her face is wet because of the rain or . . .

"Beau," I say. "Are you crying?"

43
Beau

I still don't know how long it takes for turtles to develop shells.

But I bet they need more than five minutes.

To my complete surprise, after I've dropped my keys for the hundredth time, Charm Montgomery has me pinned against my car, and her face is so close to mine that I could kiss her if I leaned forward just a little. But for once I'm not thinking about kissing her—I'm thinking, *Thank fuck it's raining.*

I'm not a crier, and god forbid a "crier in public." *But*, a little voice says in the back of my head, *this isn't public, this is Charm.* Still, when she mentions my tears, there's no way I can answer her.

"What are you doing here?" I manage to say instead. It's raining so hard, I have to raise my voice over the sound of it hitting the car. "You're going to ruin your dress."

"I'm more worried about my hair," she says.

"You're going to ruin your hair."

She backs up a little, and the expression on her face changes. I can't quite read it.

"Blue is your color," she says, making direct eye contact in a profoundly un-Charmish way. "It really brings out your eyes."

"What?" I can't believe she's talking to me about the color of my suit when Maia Moon just came out for her in front of the whole school. I feel dizzy. I press my palms against my eyes.

Her hands touch mine, slowly at first, and then more firmly, pulling them away from my face.

"Look at me," she says. "Look at me until I say stop."

My heart jolts. Is she doing this on purpose? Doesn't she remember that that's what I said to her at the bowling alley? When I was showing her how to "lure in" Maia Moon? Turns out she didn't need my help at all. Not really. Charm is the charm. Either way I stare at her, dumbfounded, and she stares back, her eyes slightly narrowed. Her hands are still holding my hands, but now one lets go. She presses it against my chest.

"Your heart is beating so fast," she says.

"Charm," I say, but she shakes her head.

"Contact," she says. "Attention. Intention."

As she says *intention*, she steps a little closer, back to where she started. Close enough to kiss. That's when I know for sure what she's doing. Running through game. Everything I've supposedly taught her about how to get a hold on a girl, pull her in.

Except this time the girl is me.

Rain runs down my face. It's just like the pool. Her this close, both of us wet.

Except this time I'm not trying *not* to look at her. We're locked in, like when she's anxious, but her eyebrows are neutral, relaxed. She looks like she's made up her mind about something. This mermaid girl.

"I don't have a typewriter this time," she says.

I don't need one. I can remember exactly how each key sounded in my room, echoing as loud as my heart is now. Her fingers hitting each key deliberately: K-I-S-S M-E.

I reach for her face, and the urge to kiss her is like the rain itself: relentless. She's inches away and I know exactly how her mouth will taste.

But even with all the signals, something stops me. There are things she needs to know. And things I need to know. I could kiss her all night, but if she just wants one last practice session, if she turns back to Maia tomorrow, I don't know how I'd survive it.

I drop my hand, pull back.

"Get in the car, Charm."

44
Charm

Beau is calling me Charm. It's what I hold on to when she doesn't kiss me like I'm expecting, when she breaks the moment. She's calling me Charm as she's telling me to get in, closing the door behind me so that I'm safe from the rain. When she opens her door and ducks inside too, she's running her hands through her messy, wet hair, looking at me so differently than she's ever looked at me before. And when she speaks next, there she goes again calling me . . .

"Charm," Beau says. "You don't need to use any of that bullshit on me."

My heart is pounding. I look down at my hands. "What do you mean?" I say, even though I know what she's talking about. My failed attempts at living up to the name she keeps saying. My fiasco of a performance as her student in the school of How to Get the Girl. Sure, I graduated. But I feel like I chose the wrong major.

"The flirting. The touching. The Lesbian Lessons. It's all bullshit, it always was. And like I said, you don't need to use any of it on me."

I look through the windshield, at the rain beading against the glass and running down it like tears, and this is what my feelings for Beau have been like: a sudden downpour, an unexpected storm.

"Are you about to say you told me so? That you warned me

that girls like you when you're not even trying, and I went and fell for you anyway?"

There's a pause that's the length of three breaths, and then Beau says, "You . . . fell for me?"

I put my face in my hands.

"Jesus, Beau," I say. "Can't you tell? I'm so . . . I'm so painfully into you and I've been trying to hide it for weeks but . . ."

"But?" she says quietly.

"But I can't."

For a moment, there's just the sound of the rain.

"What about Maia?" she asks.

"Fuck Maia," I say—a reflex. I slap my hand over my mouth. Beau snorts.

"What I mean is . . ." I search for the right way to say it. "Maia is . . . Maia's not . . ."

God, where are the words? My brain is spinning out, so my mouth keeps moving too.

"I get it. I don't need to use the lessons on you because you can spot your own moves from a mile away and they don't work if you can see them coming, right? I know you're not gonna tell me I'm an idiot because you're too good of a friend. But, god, I'm such an idiot, I—"

"What?" Her voice is so low and breathy as she interrupts me that for the first time since I got in the car, I look at her face. She's frowning. And then she's smiling. And then she's shaking her head and saying my name again.

"Charm," she says. She takes my hand and intertwines our fingers, and in all the weeks we've hung out, and all the times we've touched, Beau Carl has never touched me like this. "You know that movie that girls like? *The Notebook*?"

"That white girls like," I clarify.

She laughs. "Yes, that one. You know that line? 'If you're a bird, I'm a bird'?"

"Beau!" I cry. "I said white girls! I have not seen that movie!"

She rubs her face with the hand not holding mine. There's a tension in the one that is, like she can't let go of me.

"If you're an idiot, I'm an idiot, is what I'm trying to say."

"Beau, *what*?"

In this light, her eyes are the color of where the sky meets the sea. And understanding what she means is like a boat appearing slowly on the horizon.

"Tell me," I say quickly. "Say it."

She swallows hard and holds my hand tighter.

"I want you," she says, very deliberately. "Do you understand? I want you to come to every Favorite Daughter show and to wait for me backstage. I want to take you on dates and eat with you at the diner and for you to come hang out with me at the bowling alley. I want to bring you flowers. I want to sit and watch you braid hair—and yes, I know how long it takes, and that's why. I want to kiss you at school and pretty much everywhere, but I also want to hold your hand on the sidewalk and talk to you every day about everything. And I mean, if you *want* to use some of my own moves on me, I won't stop you, but you don't *need* to. I'm already yours."

"Beau," I whisper.

Beau pauses and smile-sighs and uses the pads of her thumbs to wipe away my tears, because I'm crying, of course I'm crying.

"God, you're so pretty when you cry. And you're always crying and I fucking love that you don't hold anything in, that you're brave enough to feel all the feelings. I'm in love with you, Charm

Montgomery," she says. "And I want to be with you. If you want that too."

I know there are words for this moment. Endless poetic statements I could make to try and show Beau just how much I feel what she feels. But instead of talking, I let go of her hand.

I told Beau once that it wasn't the things she said, but how she said them. That her words were like sex on toast. But everything she just told me was a peach cobbler shake. Waffles with the works. Jam and honey, marmalade and cinnamon sugar—all the best things, on toast. So I feel like this time it's my turn to bring the sex part to the table.

Right there in the school parking lot, with the rain pounding against the car like it wants to get in, on the night when we were supposed to be exacting our revenge, I hike up my dress. I climb over the center console, straddle the girl I love, and cup her face in my hands. I kiss Beau Carl hard and long, with my eyes just a little bit open. Her lips are sweeter than revenge could ever hope to be.

ACKNOWLEDGMENTS

To our agents and agency teams, thank you for seeing the magic right away and turning "like" into "love." Thank you to our editor, Alexa, for your enthusiasm as you cheered on Beau and Charm to the finish line. What luck to have found a partner who loves Love the way you do, and whose regard for queer youth is rooted in love as well. Thank you!

We feel such joy in putting this book out into the world. We have many battles to fight. But damn, it feels good to walk in the sun and to know that this book will sit on shelves next to other titles that imagine lives full of love and affirmation for young queer people. The sun is ours. Let's tell a million love stories.

Finally, shout-out to Ayo Edebiri. Thank you for *Bottoms*. And also, we have a crush on you.